WARRIOR'S HEART

A Dark Ages Scottish Romance

The Pict Wars
Book One

JAYNE CASTEL

WINTER MIST
PRESS

Historical Romance by Jayne Castel

DARK AGES BRITAIN
The Kingdom of the East Angles series
Dark Under the Cover of Night (Book One)
Nightfall till Daybreak (Book Two)
The Deepening Night (Book Three)
The Kingdom of the East Angles: The Complete Series

The Kingdom of Mercia series
The Breaking Dawn (Book One)
Darkest before Dawn (Book Two)
Dawn of Wolves (Book Three)

The Kingdom of Northumbria series
The Whispering Wind (Book One)
Wind Song (Book Two)
Lord of the North Wind (Book Three)
The Kingdom of Northumbria: The Complete Series

DARK AGES SCOTLAND

The Warrior Brothers of Skye series
Blood Feud (Book One)
Barbarian Slave (Book Two)
Battle Eagle (Book Three)
The Warrior Brothers of Skye: The Complete Series

The Pict Wars series
Warrior's Heart (Book One)

Novellas
Winter's Promise

Epic Fantasy Romance by Jayne Castel

The Light and Darkness series
Ruled by Shadows (Book One)
The Lost Swallow (Book Two)

Published by Winter Mist Press.

Edited by Tim Burton

Cover photography courtesy of www.shutterstock.com

Eagle image courtesy of www.pixabay.com

Map of 'The Winged Isle' by Jayne Castel

Visit Jayne's website: www.jaynecastel.com

Follow Jayne on Twitter: @JayneCastel

***

For Tim, who has always believed.

***

Contents

Maps of Scotland and The Winged Isle

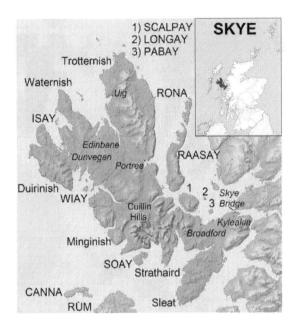

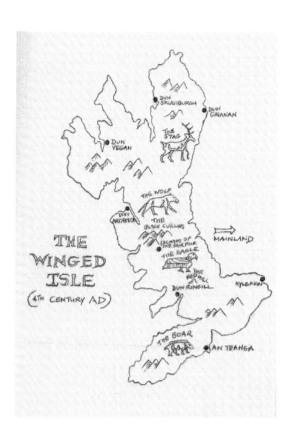

THE
WINGED
ISLE
(4TH CENTURY AD)

DUN SKUGIBURGH

DUN GRIANAN

THE STAG

DUN VEGAN

THE WOLF

DUN ARDIFECA

THE BLACK CUARINS

CERCANNS OF THE FAIR FOLK

THE EAGLE

THE RED HILL

DUN RINGILL

MAINLAND

KYLEAKIN

THE BOAR

AN TEANGA

"From the deepest desires often come the deadliest hate."

Socrates

Prologue

Show Me Your Claws

Summer, 383 AD—The Winged Isle (Isle of Skye)

An Teanga, territory of The Boar

FINA'S BARE FEET whispered over the trampled grass.

She cut through the clusters of hide tents that stretched down toward the lake's edge. The sultry air caressed her naked arms and legs, for she was dressed lightly in a sleeveless leather vest and short plaid skirt.

It was a mild night, perfect for Mid-Summer Fire. Behind her the sky glowed gold. Bonfire flames leaped high into the night, sending out plumes of sparks. She could hear the laughter of the men and women who danced around it.

Fina was not interested in revelry. Instead, her gaze lay to the south. It traced the squat, bulky outline of the great stacked-stone tower. Shaped like a beehive, the fort was a dark silhouette against the waters of the loch behind it that now glittered in the moonlight.

Fina's step slowed. An Teanga was beautiful.

She had never been this far from home before. They were deep in the territory of The Boar—one of the four tribes that inhabited The Winged Isle. This was the Gathering of the Tribes, which took place every five summers. The Boar and The Eagle had once been enemies, but things had settled down over the past decade. Urcal, The Boar chieftain—a huge bear of a man with wild dark hair—had even clasped her uncle Galan in a hug upon their arrival at the Gathering.

As she approached the water's edge, Fina spied the glow of torchlight up ahead. Intrigued, she slowed her pace. It seemed she was not the only one who had grown bored with the music and dancing.

A group of figures clustered around the pebbly shore. They were watching two warriors fight.

Fina crept closer. It had been a day of games, but something told her this fight was not part of them. The watching crowd was young. There did not appear to be anyone over sixteen winters. Fina spied her cousins in the crowd: Muin and Talor. Both a few years older than her, they were cheering on the two lads who fought with their fists a few yards away.

Irritated that they had left her out of this, Fina strode into the midst of the throng and dug her elbow into Muin's ribs. "What's this?"

He grunted, before turning his gaze to her. At sixteen winters Muin—the chieftain's son—was taller and broader than many other lads his age. "What are you still doing up?"

Fina scowled at him. He spoke to her as if she was a bairn. At thirteen she was virtually a woman. Her moon flow would start soon, and when it did, she would be allowed to train with the other warriors.

"We're just having some fun," Talor answered before Muin could. "The Boar and The Wolf are settling old scores." His chin inclined toward where two brawny young men pummeled at each other.

Fina's attention shifted to the fighters. She recognized both of them. The bigger of the two was Varar, The Boar chieftain's son. He fought Calum, the eldest son of The Wolf chief.

As she watched, Varar felled Calum with a vicious right hook, sending him sprawling. Then Varar spat out a gob of blood and waited for his opponent to rise.

Calum did not. Instead, the lad groaned, rolled over onto his side, and cast Varar a baleful look. "You win, Boar ... this time."

Varar grinned. He was attractive, Fina noted. She had just reached the age where she noticed such things. Tall and well-muscled with short, tousled black hair and dark-blue eyes, he was only just growing into his strength.

Varar wiped blood off his mouth with his forearm, his gaze sweeping the amassed crowd. "Who's next?" he challenged. His gaze swept past Fina, as if she was invisible, and alighted upon Talor. "What about you, 'Battle Eaglet'? Are you as fierce as your father?"

"Fiercer," Talor countered.

"Want to try your luck then?"

Fina elbowed her way forward, before Talor had the chance to answer. Head held high, she stepped into Varar's line of sight. "I'll fight you."

Varar's gaze narrowed for a heartbeat, and a grin spread across his face. "And who are you?"

"My name is Fina, daughter of Tarl mac Muin."

His grin turned into a smirk. "Step back, girl ... you're too young to fight me."

Fina drew herself up, hands clenching by her sides. She'd had enough of being treated like a child. Her father had not let her compete in any of the games; Muin and Talor got picked while she was ignored. She itched to show off her skills and wipe that grin from Varar's face. "Worried I'll beat you?"

"Fina." Behind her Muin's voice held a warning edge. "Enough."

She ignored him, instead pushing her way through to the front of the crowd. Young men and women stepped aside to let her pass. Fina noted that a few of them were grinning.

Let them.

Fina walked across to Varar and stopped before him. "Ready?"

The Boar arched a dark eyebrow.

"Scared?" she challenged.

He answered with a derisive snort.

Behind them Calum had picked himself up off the pebbly shore and limped back to the crowd. "Good luck," he muttered.

Fina did not acknowledge the comment. She did not need fortune to shine on her. In the crowd, Muin had not protested again, and Talor was watching her with interest; they both knew she could fight.

Fina attacked Varar without warning, jabbing him hard under the ribs. Her fist hit a solid wall of muscle, but she heard his sharp intake of breath as she danced away.

They circled each other.

"Small but fierce," Varar drawled, deliberately goading her. "Like a wolf pup. Show me your claws, girl."

His comment brought forth a chatter of laughter from the watching crowd. Fina clenched her jaw, swallowing the insults that boiled up within her. He wanted her to curse him. She would not give him the satisfaction.

Fists raised, Fina studied him. Like her, Varar had his guard up, although his body looked relaxed. Rounding her shoulders, Fina brought her elbows down closer to her torso—the stance protected her ribs from blows but also readied her to easily deliver her next strike.

Varar attacked then, a large fist arrowing toward her head. Not bothering to try and block the blow—never a wise idea with a bigger and stronger opponent—Fina dodged his punch instead.

She then danced back from striking range, forcing Varar to follow her. He threw another punch, and Fina slid her head to one side, feeling the air feather against the side of her face. He had barely missed her that time. She rushed in and landed another strike to his ribs.

The blow barely glanced off him—and that maddening grin still had not slipped.

"Surely you can do better than that?" he mocked. "Look at you … you're not even tall enough to hit me in the face."

His fist collided with her shoulder and sent her spinning away from him.

The blow might have knocked another opponent off their feet but not Fina. She swung round and dived for him, slamming her fist up into Varar's jaw.

His head snapped back, and he staggered.

"I'm tall enough to hit you where it counts," she snarled before driving an elbow into his guts.

Varar spat out a curse and made a grab for her shoulder. He missed—but his hand closed around the long braid that she wore down her back.

Fina let out a squeal of outrage as he yanked her toward him. He was not grinning now, and she braced herself for the impact of his fists. Instead, he got her in a head-lock, his arm pinning her hard against him.

Fina struggled, kicking and clawing at him, but to no avail. The lad had a grip of iron; she could not break it.

"I think we're done now," Varar drawled, "don't you?"

"Stinking Boar bastard!"

"Poor loser."

"Let me go!"

"As you wish."

He tossed her away from him. Fina staggered and pitched into the crowd. Muin and Talor caught her, gripping her tightly by the arms when she tried to lunge back toward Varar.

"That's enough, Fina," Muin ordered between gritted teeth. His fingers dug into her biceps as he struggled to keep hold of her. "This is only going to end badly for you if you continue."

"My turn now." Talor let go of Fina, leaving her writhing in Muin's arms like an eel. He favored Varar with a smile, his gaze glinting.

Varar grinned back. "Aye, let's see if you can handle yourself better than your wee cousin."

Fury swamped Fina, pulsing like an ember. *Patronizing, sneering goat.* She would have her vengeance upon him for humiliating her. Next time they fought, she would leave him bleeding in the dirt.

Talor stepped forward, away from the edge of the crowd. "Time someone taught you some manners, Boar," he said, flexing his hands at his sides. "I'm going to enjoy this."

Six years later ...

Chapter One

Meeting The Reaper

Summer, 389 AD

The Valley of the Tors—border of The Eagle and The Boar territories.

FINA LEANED BACK against the sun-warmed rock, heart hammering. Around her the shouts and screams of battle echoed down the valley.

The meaty sound of an iron blade slamming into flesh just a couple of yards away spurred Fina into action as she recovered her breath. She raised a blood-stained hand and plucked the last arrow from the quiver on her back. Then she slotted it into her bow and edged round the side of the boulder.

The valley below was carnage.

Bloodied, twisted bodies lay on the green sides of the vale, while those still alive fought with pikes, axes, knives, and swords. Men and women, some bearing the mark of The Boar on their right bicep, others the mark of

The Eagle, struggled to the death. From this vantage point, it looked like The Boar were winning.

A snarl curved Fina's mouth.

Treacherous bastards. Ever since Urcal, the old Boar chief, had died, relations between the two tribes had grown strained. However, no one—Fina included—believed The Boar would have resorted to this: an unprovoked attack.

Fina brought up her bow and sighted a female Boar warrior who was hacking at her opponent with an axe.

The arrow loosed, thudding into the base of the woman's neck. The warrior reeled back, dropping the axe as she clutched at the fletched arrow.

Fina was on her in moments, drawing her knife as she went. She finished the woman off with a slash across the throat and turned to help the fallen Eagle warrior. He was a young man she knew by sight, not by name, who lived in one of the villages near Dun Ringill. The warrior stared up at the heavens, his sea-blue eyes sightless—it was too late to save him.

Fina cursed, grabbed his shield, and hurtled down the hillside to where a male Boar warrior now charged her. Thin and wiry, his half-naked body painted in swirls of blue woad, the man carried an iron-tipped pike. He bore down on her, his gaunt face a rictus of fury.

Fina was not afraid—she never felt fear in battle. However, a fatalistic sense of doom had settled upon her.

There were few Eagles left alive in this valley. She had led them all to their deaths. Muin warned her to look out for an ambush. How she wished she had heeded him. She had awoken that morning thinking she was leading a patrol—and now she was staring death in the face.

Fina dodged the pike and slashed her attacker across the ribs with her blade. He let out a grunt and rolled. Then he grabbed a hand-axe from his belt and struggled to his feet.

The wound across his abdomen was deep, and blood flowed over his grasping hand as he tried to stop it.

"Eagle bitch," he gasped. "You're coming to meet The Reaper with me."

He lunged for her with his axe—faster than she had anticipated. Fina dodged the blade only barely, yet he came again. The knowledge that she had inflicted a mortal wound upon him had turned the warrior fearless, vicious.

Even injured, he moved with lizard-like speed.

A line of fire burned down Fina's left arm as she dodged another strike of his axe. The blade had caught her, but she didn't glance down to see what the damage was.

She needed to concentrate or she was dead.

The warrior attacked relentlessly, pushing her down the slope toward where a tor loomed overhead, thrusting skyward.

Fina edged around it, her leather foot-wrappings skidding on loose gravel. She tried to get within her attacker's guard, but it was nearly impossible. He came at her, teeth bared, eyes wild.

"Die!" he snarled, throwing himself at her, his axe blade slicing toward Fina's face.

Fina raised her shield, her arm juddering as the blade dug into wood and leather, and took the only chance she would have to bring down her attacker. She slammed her blade upward, under the warrior's ribcage, and twisted.

But still he fought her, with a terrible godlike strength.

Grimly, Fina clung onto that blade, twisting it deeper. His sinewy, blood-soaked body crushed her against the stone. And then, just as she was beginning to think she was getting the upper hand, for she could feel the strength draining from him, the warrior head-butted her.

Fina's head slammed back against the boulder, and the world went dark.

Varar mac Urcal dug his heels into the pony's sides, urging the stallion into a flat gallop. They raced over the rolling green hills of the northern reaches of The Boar lands. His warriors rode hard behind him, the sound of their ponies' hooves shaking the earth.

Great stacks of grey stone rose against the pale blue sky to the north. Varar's gaze narrowed. The Valley of the Tors—their destination—was now in sight.

He crested the brow of the hill and reined in his stallion, Guail. Black like his name—Coal—the stallion's neck was slick with sweat after their race here.

Staring down at The Valley of the Tors, Varar cursed.

He had ridden as if pursued by demons, but they were too late.

The battle was over.

Varar drew the iron sword that hung at his hip. His gaze swept the scattering of broken bodies strewn across the valley.

Who had been the victors here—The Boar or The Eagle?

He spied figures then, moving amongst the dead— picking over the corpses and taking trophies. Without a word to his warriors, Varar urged Guail down the slope and headed straight toward the survivors.

If they were Eagles, he would slay them where they stood.

The man nearest saw him approach and straightened up. An older warrior with a bald head, he held a bronze arm bracer, his expression suddenly taut with alarm.

However, as Varar drew nearer—both men recognized each other.

Varar lowered his blade, and the warrior let out a long exhale.

"Bothan," Varar barked, pulling up his pony. "What happened here?"

"It was as Gurth warned," the warrior replied, dropping his gaze. "The Eagle sent a war band to attack us."

Varar frowned, his attention shifting once more to the surrounding battlefield. The air stank of death: blood, offal, and the lingering taint of fear. Crows would swoop in soon to feast upon the corpses of the slain.

"Cruim sent me word that he was riding out to meet a war party," Varar replied after a moment. "We came as soon as we heard."

Bothan nodded. "The battle ended just a short while ago ... they nearly bested us, but our numbers were greater."

"Where's Cruim?"

The warrior's mouth thinned. "He fell."

Varar's breath gusted out of him. Cruim was a friend. They had grown up together, trained together, drunk together, and fought together. They had even clashed once over the same woman.

"Where?" Varar's question came out in a low growl.

"Over there." Bothan nodded to the right—toward the heart of the valley where corpses were piled the thickest.

Varar swung down from his stallion and moved away. Guail snorted, uneasy amidst the reek of death. Yet the pony did not wander off. Guail would wait until his master returned to him.

Stepping over bodies and skirting around puddles of blood and gore, Varar searched the dead.

Some of the faces he recognized—many he did not. Cruim had been off leading a band in this area. Varar had seen little of him in the past moons as his friend had been busy training warriors to deal with the rising threat from their neighbors.

The Eagle.

Many of the dead he had encountered bore the mark of The Eagle upon their right bicep.

Some of The Eagle bore terrible wounds—their opponents had hacked at them, even after they were dead. Yet the sight of the carnage left Varar unmoved. Instead, anger kindled in the pit of his belly, a slow-burning fury.

Gurth, his father's cousin, had been right: their neighbors were planning to extend their territory south.

Gurth was not here. Varar had sent him out on a patrol to the south west of their lands the morning before. The older warrior was convinced The Eagle had been planning an ambush for moons. Gurth's scouts had seen Eagle patrols near the border on several occasions recently, and Varar had sent out Cruim to provide further protection.

Varar found his friend's body under the corpse of a huge Eagle warrior, an older man with scarred cheeks. He was relieved to see Cruim's end had been swift—a dagger blade to the throat. He had not suffered.

Straightening up, Varar cast a look over his shoulder at where his warriors were picking over the battlefield.

"Leave The Eagles to the crows," he barked, his voice echoing off the sides of the watching tors. "Gather our dead. We will bury them back at An Teanga."

He did not want to linger in this place.

"Chief!" one of his warriors called out, a woman named Gara. Short and broad with wiry black hair, she wore a grim look upon her face as she waved to him. "I've found a live one—an Eagle."

Varar left Cruim's side and strode across to where Gara waited under the shadow of a great stone tor.

A woman lay crumpled against the tor, next to the body of a wiry Boar warrior.

She was small, yet her bare arms and legs were strong and well-muscled. A strip of leather bound ample breasts, and around her loins she wore a flared leather skirt.

"Looks like she fought Iver," Gara commented, her tone dry, "and managed to best him." There was a grudging respect in the woman's voice, for Iver had been a terrifying warrior—one neither Varar nor Gara would have wanted to meet in battle. "Shall I finish her?"

Varar did not reply. Instead, he stepped closer and knelt down next to the unconscious woman.

She bore a wound to her left arm but seemed otherwise unhurt. He reached out and felt around the back of her skull; his fingers came away bloody.

"Varar," Gara prompted him. "I'll slit her throat if you want?"

"I know her," Varar answered. He sat back on his heels and studied the unconscious woman. She had different looks to most folk. Her skin was golden rather than milk-white, and she had aquiline features. Her hair was a deep honey-brown, where it was not soaked with blood, and plaited in a long braid down her back.

"You do?" Gara's voice turned incredulous.

"We met at a Gathering years ago," he replied, his gaze never leaving the woman's face. "She challenged me to a fight. Fina ... that's her name ... she's Tarl mac Muin's daughter."

Gara let out a hiss. The mac Muin brothers were hated among The Boar. "Then she must die, chief. Shall I do it or will you?"

Varar glanced up, meeting Gara's eye. "No one's to touch her," he said coolly. "The woman's my captive. She's coming back with us to An Teanga."

Chapter Two

A Stranger's Domain

WHEN FINA AWOKE it felt as if a tribe of brownies had taken up residence inside her skull and were attacking her with hammers.

Groaning, she opened her eyes, and winced as the light assaulted them. She was indoors, she realized as her vision cleared. The muted light, from the flickering cressets upon the stone wall beside Fina, made her eyes smart and water.

For a few moments Fina found herself utterly disoriented. She did not recognize the chamber she lay in or have any idea how she had come to be there.

Why did her left arm ache dully? Why did her head hurt so? The brownies in there were relentless.

Fina shifted, realizing as she did so that she lay upon a bed of soft furs. She glanced down and saw that she wore a clean leather vest and a long plaid skirt. Fina frowned, moaning softly as the expression hurt her. These were not her usual clothes.

She never dressed in such cumbersome clothing.

Even more worrying, she had no weapons. The knife she always carried was gone, and as her gaze slid around the space in which she lay, she could see no sign of her quiver of arrows either. A rare burst of panic caused her bowels to cramp.

Why can't I remember anything? Where am I?

Reaching out her hand, Fina's fingers probed her aching scalp. She found a lump on her forehead and an even bigger lump, this one encrusted with a newly formed scab, on the back of her head. Fina groaned once more as pain thudded through her skull.

A battle ... I must have been fighting.

That was all it took. It was the key to the lock that held the memories from her. With that one thought, everything came rushing back.

The attack. The fighting. The death.

Bile rose in Fina's throat. She swallowed, panic resurfacing. She looked around the alcove once more, her gaze sharp now.

The last thing she remembered was grappling with a Boar warrior who had proved very hard to kill. Before that she had been one of the few Eagle warriors still alive.

She was still breathing—but she lay in a stranger's domain.

Something was constricting her neck; she felt it with each inhale. Fina's hands came up around her throat, her fingers closing over leather.

A collar.

Her gaze shifted behind her then, to where a length of chain was tied to a beam. She reached up, her fingers tracing the rows of tight knots that held the collar in place; how would she ever manage to untie them?

Muttering a curse, Fina pushed herself up into a sitting position. The furs she lay upon were fine and exquisitely soft. *The furs of someone of note.* This was the biggest sleeping alcove she had ever seen, bigger even than Galan's, the chieftain of The Eagles.

Heart thumping, Fina tried to control her spiraling dread.

Where am I?

In an attempt to calm her breathing, which was now coming in panicked gasps, she forced herself to study her surroundings.

There were two other, smaller, alcoves adjoining this one, but they appeared empty. The cressets that lined the room had been wrought from iron and had bronze decorations. However, when her gaze alighted upon the wall hanging that hung opposite her, Fina grew still.

It was beautiful and edged with golden tassels. The hanging showed an exotic scene: men and woman in flowing white robes, eating what looked like fruit under a bright sun. Fina studied the scene. Her fright eased, her skin prickling, as realization settled over her.

These are ma's people ... the Caesars.

Her parents had told Fina of the campaign to the south many years earlier, of the attack on the Great Wall. That was where they had met, for her mother, Lucrezia, had once lived there and been wed to someone else. Tarl had told Fina that many riches were brought back to The Winged Isle from the fort they had looted. However, he had returned home with the greatest prize of all: her mother. Fina imagined that this tapestry had once hung in a Caesar hall.

"You're awake."

Fina had been gazing so intently at the hanging that she had not noticed the tall, broad-shouldered figure that had emerged to her right, at the corner of the alcove. She jerked her chin toward him, immediately regretting the action as agony exploded in the back of her skull.

She choked back a cry and squeezed her eyes shut.

"You took some vicious blows." The stranger spoke again, his low-pitched voice expressionless. "I was starting to think you'd never wake up."

Fina breathed slowly, riding the waves of pain until they subsided enough for her to gather her wits.

When she eventually reopened her eyes, the man was still there. Muscular with short dark hair and a jaw shadowed in stubble, he watched her with a shuttered expression. An earring, a tiny hoop, hung from one ear, glinting in the light from the cresset next to him. The warrior—for there was no doubt he was anything else—wore tight plaid breeches and a leather vest that exposed brawny arms covered in blue tattoos. He leaned casually against the wall, arms folded across his broad chest, legs crossed at the ankle.

Fina's gaze narrowed. *I know him.* She was struggling to place his face when she focused on the mark of The Boar upon his right bicep.

Her blood chilled.

The man smiled, although to Fina it was more of an arrogant smirk. "*Fina*, isn't it?"

Fina's heart started to race, slamming against her ribs like a battle drum. She felt sick, and the throbbing in her skull worsened once more.

"And you're Varar mac Urcal," she rasped. The words tasted bitter as she spoke. She wished she had died there in that valley. Better that than be taken captive by this man. She had not seen him since the day of the Gathering at An Teanga; even years later the humiliation of that encounter still stung.

As if guessing her thoughts, his smile widened. "Nice to be recognized." His gaze shifted down from her face, sliding boldly over her body. "Although you've changed since our last meeting."

Fina's mouth curled into a snarl. She did not dignify his comment with an answer of her own. Still, the wolfish look in his eyes made her hackles rise.

"Where are the others?" she asked coldly.

He raised a dark eyebrow. "The others?"

"The other Eagle captives," she replied, enunciating each word clearly as if speaking to a half-wit. "From the battle."

Varar mac Urcal held her gaze steadily. "There were none ... save you."

Fina's heart started to pound. Her head ached so badly she could hardly bear it, yet her heart hurt more. Thirty warriors had ridden out with her on the morning of the attack—thirty men and women who would never return to their families.

I should have died with them.

Aware that The Boar chieftain was watching her intently, Fina drew up a mental shield, forcing her face to remain impassive. This man would not see her grief. "Your warriors attacked us," she said after a long pause. "Why?"

Varar huffed out a breath, scorn in his eyes. "You expect me to believe that? The account I have says that you charged onto our lands intent on attacking a patrol. We chased you back, just over the border to the bottom of The Valley of the Tors. There, you turned like cornered wolves and fought."

"Liar!" Fina launched herself off the furs toward him. Her head still felt as if it was about to explode, but rage overcame pain. She did not care if she had no weapons; she was going to rip this insolent dog's head off with her bare hands.

But she had barely traveled two feet when something grabbed her around the throat and jerked her backward. Fina collapsed on the furs, choking.

She had forgotten about the collar.

Fina raised her head and glowered at her captor. "Filthy maggot-spawn," she choked out the words in enraged gasps. "Free me!"

Varar mac Urcal let out a soft laugh. "After that display ... I don't think so. I remember you well, Fina. Why do you think I've got you chained up in here?"

"When I get free, I'm going to slit your throat," she rasped.

Varar merely raised an infuriating eyebrow in response.

Fina sank down onto her haunches, swallowing to ease her aching throat. "We never crossed into your land, Boar." She forced the words out. "We were patrolling *our* border?"

"Aye ... and then you attacked us," he drawled. "I should have seen it coming. Ever since my father died The Eagle have sought to break the peace between our tribes."

"Lies! You have no proof—"

"I've had reports of numerous night raids on our villages close to the border, and livestock has been stolen," he cut in. "At Bealtunn, one of your patrols threatened a Boar hunting party ... and of late you've stopped trading with us."

"More lies," she countered. "All along it's been The Boar agitating, provoking. That's why we've started protecting our border more closely."

Varar's gaze narrowed as he studied her. "Were you *leading* that patrol?"

Fina stared back, refusing to answer.

Varar favored her with a thin smile. "I thought so ... you rage at me when you're really just angry with yourself. Defeat tastes bitter, doesn't it?"

Silence stretched between them. The air was charged.

Fina drew in a deep, shuddering breath. Hate pulsed through her, making her feel sick. Eventually, when she had choked back the venom she wished to spit at him, Fina spoke. "So what is to be my end?" Her voice was cold, controlled. "Will you slay me before your people to make an example out of me?"

A hard knot of dread tightened in the pit of Fina's belly. She was not afraid of death in battle—that was an honorable way to die, a warrior's death—but being put to death in a public spectacle was another matter.

She had never thought that would be her end.

"I considered it," he replied. "You certainly deserve it." He paused then and pushed himself away from the wall, taking a step toward her. He was a big man, taller than she remembered him, and he towered over her now. "No ... you're more useful to me alive."

Fina stared at him, the knot in her belly tightening further. She did not like the smirk on his face or the ruthless glint in those dark-blue eyes.

Tarl mac Muin walked through the battleground, his belly roiling. Dry eyed, his heart thumping painfully against his ribs, he forced himself to keep his gaze down at the ground, searching each face for the one that was as dear to him as his wife's.

His only daughter, Fina.

What had they been doing so close to the border? Fina and her warriors were only supposed to be patrolling the edge of their territory from the hillsides above, not fighting The Boar where the two lands met. The bottom of The Valley of the Tors was 'no-man's land'—Fina should not have led her patrol down there. It did not make sense. His daughter could be reckless, yet she was no fool.

Boar treachery. This slaughter stank of it.

Yet the stench of death was even more overpowering. A shadow fell over him. Tarl glanced up to see buzzards circling. His lip curled. *Carrion feeders ... come for the dead.* He wanted to roar curses at them, but his throat felt dry and raw. He could not swallow, could barely breathe.

Muin, grim-faced and hollow-eyed, met Tarl in the center of the valley. "There's no sign of her, uncle."

Tarl clenched his jaw so tightly that pain knifed through his left ear. When he spoke, his voice did not sound like his own. It belonged to a broken man. "I've checked the western edge ... she's not there either."

"They must have taken her." Talor cut in, striding toward them. Like Muin, his expression was bleak, although his blue eyes glittered with the same rage that boiled in Tarl's veins.

"I'll butcher them," Tarl rasped, his voice catching. "I'll—"

"Look!" A warrior behind them cut in. "A rider approaches from the south."

Tarl turned, his gaze snapping right to where a lone figure upon a grey pony picked its way down the southern slope toward them. Tarl watched the newcomer, a stocky woman with frizzy dark hair. She had a hard face, and the tension in her broad shoulders warned that she did not ride into this valley happily.

As the warrior drew closer, Tarl spotted the mark of The Boar on her right bicep. Beside him Talor muttered a curse. Tarl glanced his way to see his nephew had unslung his bow and was reaching for an arrow from the quiver on his back. Wordlessly, Muin reached out and stilled Talor with a hand on the wrist, only to receive a baleful look in return.

Tarl said nothing. Instead, he turned to watch the approaching Boar warrior. She drew up her pony a handful of yards away, her gaze sweeping over the party of Eagle warriors. "I've a message for Tarl mac Muin."

Tarl flexed his hands at his sides. "Tell him in person ... you're speaking to him."

The woman focused on Tarl; her eyes were cold, assessing. "I'm Gara of The Boar."

"I don't care who you are," Tarl growled. "Where's my daughter?"

"I come with a message from our chieftain, Varar mac Urcal," Gara replied, ignoring his question.

Tarl spat on the ground between them. "The Reaper take your chief. Tell me of my daughter!"

Gara inclined her head, her face like hewn granite. This was not a woman who smiled easily. "She's alive."

Tarl loosed the breath he had not even realized he was holding.

"For the moment," Gara added.

A rustle of movement behind Tarl made him glance over his shoulder. Talor had shaken off Muin's restraining hand and raised his bow, the arrow sighted at the woman's neck. "Shall I kill her now?"

Silence fell. Tension rippled across the valley, broken only by the moan of the wind.

"You could," Gara answered finally. Her gaze met Talor's without a trace of fear. "But if I don't return to An Teanga, Varar will kill Fina."

Tarl turned to Talor and motioned for him to lower his bow.

His nephew glared at him, fury burning bright. But, after a long pause, he did as bid.

Tarl then stepped closer to The Boar warrior. He understood his nephew's anger, for he was barely able to keep a leash on his own rage.

"What do you want?" he choked out.

Gara stared back at him, her face unyielding. "We won this fight ... yet it was your people who attacked ours," she replied.

"Lies," Talor spat.

Tarl's pulse started to race, a red haze descending over his vision. "Say that again, Boar bitch," he growled back, "and you die."

Gara snorted. "The truce between our tribes balances upon a knife-edge, Eagle," she replied. "Be careful."

The warrior backed her pony up, her gaze remaining upon them. Danger crackled in the air. Talor raised his bow once more, and iron scraped against leather as Muin drew his sword.

"There is no truce," Tarl snarled back. "Not after this."

Gara reined her pony around and cast a glance over her shoulder. "And that's why we have Fina. If just one more Eagle warrior crosses into our territory, your daughter dies." She paused, her mouth twisting. "And Varar will send her headless corpse back to you."

Chapter Three

Saved

VARAR DESCENDED THE steps into the feasting hall
on the ground level of the broch. The inhabitants of the
round tower were amassing for the noon meal.

A clamor of voices greeted him, thundering against
the stacked stone walls. He inhaled the rich aroma of
roasting mutton and the scent of freshly baked bread,
and his belly growled.

Varar reached the bottom of the steps and made his
way to the chieftain's table at the far end of the hall,
nodding to folk as he went. They answered with smiles
and calls of greeting. Despite the violence of the skirmish
against The Eagle, the folk here were in high spirits
today. For although the battle had been bloody, The Boar
had been the victors.

None wore a broader smile, however, than Gurth mac
Bolc.

The warrior had not seen Varar approach. He sat, in
his usual position to the right of the chieftain's carven

chair, drinking horn in hand. His shrewd gaze surveyed the hall before him.

Varar took note of Gurth's dominant position. He was his father's cousin, and if Varar had not been born, he would have become chief after Urcal's death. Varar sometimes wondered if the man resented him. When Varar had first become chief, relations between them had been frosty. However, of late Gurth had thawed toward him. Watching the man now, Varar noted that he surveyed the hall as if it was he who commanded here.

Gurth spied Varar's approach then. His manner softened, and he held up his drinking horn to hail his chief. He was a big, broad warrior, with a heavy featured face that bore deep grooves, and a bald pate that gleamed in the light of the cressets burning behind him. Varar considered Gurth an old man these days; he had just entered his fifth decade, yet the years had not seemed to weaken him as they did most men.

"Is she awake yet?" Gurth greeted him.

Varar nodded and sank into his chair. "Aye ... although I think I preferred her unconscious."

Gurth barked a laugh. "That doesn't surprise me. She's a mac Muin."

Varar cast the warrior a sidelong glance. He knew of the bad blood between Gurth and the three mac Muin brothers. His hatred for them ran deep, a rancor that had festered with time.

It all stemmed from the death of Varar's uncles, Wurgest and Loxa, many years earlier. Urcal—Varar's father—had let go of the past, but Gurth could not.

He nursed those grievances like deep bruises that never healed. No wonder he looked so happy today. His reckoning against The Eagle had been a long time coming, and Gurth was savoring it.

"Aye," Varar replied, reaching for a cup of ale. "She's got fire in her belly, just as she did years ago."

Gurth raised his eyebrows. "You've met?"

Varar nodded. "At the last Gathering. Fina challenged me to a fight. She got a few good strikes in too, before I bested her."

Gurth snorted. "So when are you going to take that bitch's head?"

Varar favored him with a level look. "She's more use to us alive."

"And why's that?" The challenge in Gurth's voice made warriors seated farther down the table swivel their heads.

Varar ignored them. "I don't want open war with The Eagle right now. We lost a good number of warriors in that fight, even though we were the victors. We need to get our numbers back up, and strengthen our defenses, before we face them again."

That was partially the truth. The rest of it, although Varar would never have admitted it to Gurth, was that Fina fascinated him. It pleased him to keep her alive. She was as feral as a wolf and just as dangerous, but something about her wildness appealed to Varar. He was at the age now where he was expected to take a wife, only, he had been resisting it. The women that Gurth had paraded before him over the last year seemed insipid and plain compared to the wild beauty he had chained up in his alcove.

Fina could never be his wife, and would likely try to geld him if he touched her, yet he found her compelling nonetheless. She was worth keeping alive for a while longer.

Varar's response had not pleased Gurth. His heavy-featured face tensed; his eyes narrowed into thin slits. When he spoke, his voice was low and threatening. "I thought you had balls, Varar." He paused here, letting his words sink in. "Your father's bollocks shriveled with age. He lost his stomach for battle. He weakened us. Will you do the same?"

Varar ripped off a piece of bread and leaned back in his chair. He was not easily offended, and Gurth was of use to him—otherwise he would have broken his jaw for that comment. The older warrior was a veteran of many battles and had trained numerous Boar warriors, Varar included. It was only his standing here that protected him. Even so, Varar had tolerated enough of his insolence for one day.

"Fina will remain alive," he replied.

Gurth remained silent. Varar noted the muscle working on his heavy jaw. He could be a mouthy brute, but he was not a fool. He knew when it was time to still his tongue.

Fina lay curled up on the furs. The agony in her skull had receded, but she now felt worse than when she had woken up earlier that day. Then, she had not realized she was a captive and that her entire patrol was dead.

Rage seethed within her, like storm-driven waves crashing against the rocks. It longed for an outlet. There had been no raids on Boar villages or threats on hunting parties. Instead it had been The Boar who had turned hostile: border villages refusing to trade, Eagle hunters and farmers being threatened if they ventured into Boar lands.

Varar was a lying dog.

The border attack had been utterly unprovoked. Fina had led out her patrol that morning along the southern fringe of their territory. She loved patrols: the wind in her face, the sense of freedom and joy at being able to ride all day. Perhaps she had made a mistake by riding along the edge of that vale—but it had still been on their land. In truth she had enjoyed the thrill of riding close to the border. It had been a bright, breezy day and The Valley of the Tors had beckoned them all.

Her company had been halfway along the northern edge of the valley, weaving in and out of those giant stone pillars, when a cry to the south had drawn their attention. Fina had craned her neck, reining in her dancing pony, only to see a wave of mounted warriors galloping down the southern slope of the valley toward them.

An ambush had lain in wait.

And now all those who had ridden with Fina that morning were dead.

Fina closed her eyes and drew her knees up against her chest. *This is my fault.*

Her cousin Muin's words came back to her then.

Don't ride too close to the southern border, Fina. The Boar have been restless of late. Urcal's son rules now, and he doesn't trust us like his father did. Stay alert during your patrol today.

Fina inwardly cringed as she remembered how she had cast her cousin's warning aside with a snort. Muin could be an old woman at times. He was even more of a worrier than his father, Galan.

How she wished she had heeded him.

The sound of approaching feet on the stone steps leading up to the alcove roused her. Raising herself up on one elbow, Fina scowled at the narrow curtained doorway. Someone was coming.

She rose to a crouch upon the furs, ready to pounce. She did not want to see that smirking Boar chieftain again.

However, it was not Varar who appeared at the top of the stairs and pushed the curtain aside, but a slight man of middling years. The newcomer had curly, light brown hair that receded at the temples. He wore a plain linen tunic, girded at the waist with a length of string, and loose plaid breeches.

Fina relaxed slightly, relief flooding through her as she eyed him. "Who are you?"

"My name's Eachann," the man replied with a smile that made the corners of his eyes crinkle. "I'm the healer of An Teanga. I tended your wounds while you slept. I'm glad to see you're awake now."

Fina sank down onto the furs, tucking her legs under her. Her voluminous skirt billowed out around her. She could not get used to it.

"Is it true?" she asked, her gaze dropping. "Am I the only survivor?"

Eachann's smile faded. "Aye, lass," he replied gently.

Fina swallowed, guilt choking her. She imagined the horror on the faces of those who would come looking for her patrol, Muin and Talor's grief as they searched the dead. She thought of her parents' desperation when they learned she had been taken—their only surviving child gone.

For the first time in her life, it hit her that there were consequences. She had never really thought about how those left behind would feel if she fell in battle.

"Can I take a look at your wounds?" Eachann asked, moving toward her. "Don't worry ... I won't hurt you."

Fina gave him an incredulous look. He was the one who should be afraid. If he touched her, she could break his arm, force him to free her, or worse. She was tempted but dismissed the idea a moment later.

This man was a preserver of life. She could not hurt him.

Slowly, Fina nodded.

Eachann moved closer, and she spied wariness in his eyes. Wisely, he did not quite trust her. He set down his basket and knelt upon the furs. "Hold out your left arm, lass."

Fina did as bid, watching Eachann examine the crusted scab that had formed over the wound she had taken in battle. "This is healing well," he murmured, "but it was the blow to your skull that worried me more." He moved round and reached out, his fingers gently probing the back of Fina's head. "Sorry if this hurts you."

Fina gritted her teeth and gave a soft grunt. Despite that his touch was light, darts of pain arrowed through the back of her skull. "Will I live then, healer?" she asked finally.

"Aye." Eachann reached for his basket and extracted a clay bottle. "I'll apply some more ointment though."

"I don't know why you're bothering," Fina replied, unable to keep the bitterness out of her voice. "They're going to kill me anyway."

The healer stilled, concern clouding his gaze. "Varar has spared you."

Fina favored him with a jaundiced look. "Really? You know that for certain, do you?"

Eachann's jaw tightened before he looked away, focusing on the bottle he held clasped in his hands. He looked so distressed that Fina felt a pang of pity for him. "No," he replied softly. "I don't."

Chapter Four

Brutish Men

FINA SHIFTED ON the furs, easing her stiff legs. Since the visit from the healer, she had seen no one. The day had stretched on. She had no idea what time it actually was, for this alcove had no windows. There was only a slit in the roof, to let out smoke when the hearth was lit.

The days were long this time of year, and Fina guessed that supper must be approaching.

Heaving an irritated sigh, Fina raised her hands—yet again—to the heavy leather collar around her neck. Her fingers fumbled around the back, struggling to loosen the knots that held it together and fastened it to the chain.

And yet again she failed to loosen it in the slightest.

Fina breathed a curse and dropped her hands. She cast the chain behind her a dark look. She could not stand this, hated being kept prisoner here. Her gaze shifted to the wooden partition next to the furs. A chamber pot, a pail of water for washing, and drying cloths lay behind it. Fina had relieved herself earlier in the day. However, since she had not eaten anything since awaking there had been no need to use it again. The chief had left her a jug of wine to quench her thirst, but her belly now ached with hunger.

Maybe they plan to starve me to death?

Fina rose to her feet and paced in a tight circle upon the furs. She could not stand to sit still any longer. She was used to moving, to being active from dawn to dusk. She hated being locked out of sight.

Her skull no longer throbbed quite so badly. The ointment the healer had administered to her scalp had soothed it, and the wound on her arm was starting to itch as the healing began.

Fina continued to circle the furs.

I have to get out of here.

She needed to flee, to return home to her people and plan her revenge on Varar and his warriors. Her jaw clenched as she imagined taking a knife to that smirking face. She would make sure she repaid his treachery in full.

These thoughts made her already aching belly hurt even more. They also reminded her of all those men and women who had died in The Valley of the Tors. Many of those warriors she had not known that well, yet there were a handful of them she had considered friends: Fingal, Lachlan, Greer, and Thorin. They had all been young, near to her in age, and as such she had grown up with them, trained with them. Greer—a quiet woman with long, curly dark hair and eyes the color of moss— had been about to wed Thorin. They had been in love for years, although Thorin had only recently made the depths of his feelings for Greer clear. They were to be handfasted at Harvest Fire.

But they had died fighting together in that lonely, windswept valley. There would be no handfasting now.

Fina's throat constricted, her gaze misting. She closed her eyes, squeezing them tightly. *Aye, I'll make them all pay.*

"You're hungry I take it?"

A female voice interrupted her violent thoughts. Fina's eyes snapped open, and her gaze settled upon a heavy-set woman with dark hair and midnight-blue eyes. She carried a tray of food.

Fina scrutinized her. One glance told her this woman was kin to Varar. She had the same shaped face and color eyes—the same strong jaw. Varar was handsome, even Fina could not fail to notice that, yet those features on this woman made her look pugnacious.

The newcomer's gaze was hard, assessing.

"Aye," Fina replied, forcing the words out from between gritted teeth. "Did you make sure to poison it?"

The woman's full-lips curved into a chill smile. "I suggested so to my brother ... but he wouldn't allow it."

She approached the furs, just out of reach of the chain, and set down the tray. A clay bowl of thick meat stew sat upon it, accompanied by half a loaf of crusty bread. Fina's mouth watered at the sight of the food, and her belly growled, betraying her hunger.

The woman raised an eyebrow. The expression made her look very much like her brother. "I didn't spit in it either if you're worried." She stepped back from the tray and pushed it toward Fina with her foot. Watching her, Fina wagered that Varar had warned his sister to stay well clear of his captive.

Frankly, she was so hungry she did not care if someone had spat in her supper. Fina approached the edge of the furs, reached down, and took the tray. She set it down before her and picked up the bread, tearing off a chunk. She then stuffed it in her mouth and chewed vigorously.

When she took a mouthful of stew, she nearly groaned. Perhaps it was hunger, but venison stew had never tasted so good. As she ate, she did not shift her gaze from the woman who had brought the meal. She wished the bitch would leave. Yet she did not. She just stood there, arms folded across her heavy breasts.

"My brother has taken a liking to you, Fina," the woman said after a long pause. Her mouth puckered as she spoke her name.

Fina, who was in the process of swallowing a large mouthful of stew, nearly choked. She recovered, wiped her mouth with the back of her forearm, and glowered at the woman. "What do you mean?"

"You're still alive, aren't you?"

"Aye … to deter my people from attacking yours."

Varar's sister shrugged. "So that's why a man chains a woman up in his alcove, is it?"

A chill went through Fina at these words. She suddenly lost her appetite. The mood shifted in the alcove. The woman's gaze glinted as she watched her brother's captive.

Eventually, Fina cleared her throat. "What's your name?"

Varar's sister scowled, hesitating as if she would have preferred to remain anonymous. "Morag," she replied finally.

Fina inhaled deeply. If she wanted to get free she was going to have to be clever. She needed an ally here. "Morag … is Varar going to rape me?"

Morag watched her, gaze shuttered. "I don't know … some of the men of my family have been … brutish. My brother might be too."

That was not comforting to hear.

Fina studied Morag with fresh eyes. She was a plump woman, but there was a noticeable swell to her belly. She was with child. Watching her, Fina wondered if Varar's sister spoke from experience.

Fina swallowed, schooling her features into what she hoped was a cowed look. "I'm afraid," she whispered, feigning timidity. The whining sound of her voice galled her; she hated pretending to be weak. However, Morag would not trust her if she raged. She needed to make herself sound vulnerable to those who might help her.

Morag watched her a moment, her face expressionless, before her mouth twisted. "That was a poor effort," she drawled. "If my brother's fool enough to try and stick his rod in you then he deserves it chopping off."

Fina was waiting for Varar when he mounted the steps to his alcove that night. It was late, and he had expected to find her asleep.

Instead, she sat there, cross-legged upon the furs, glaring at him as he entered. The sight of her angry face caused him to cast her a taunting smile. This woman brought out something vindictive in him. He found himself wanting to enrage her.

Fina was beautiful when angry. Her grey eyes, fringed with dark lashes, were luminous in the light of the cressets, and the lines of her face queenly. Her hair was a mess, for most of it had come out of its braid, yet it just made her appear wild, dangerous.

Varar had not realized till that moment how much he liked such women.

"Good eve, Fina," he greeted her, striding across to where a clay bowl sat upon a narrow table. "Have you had a good day?"

"What do you think?" Her voice was clipped, yet the fury in each word shimmered between them.

Varar splashed water on his face and dried it off with a square of linen. "Eachann tells me you're on the mend?"

She did not reply.

He stifled a yawn and started to unlace his vest. It had been a long day, and as much as he loved to taunt his lovely captive, his furs beckoned. Gurth had not been the only one of his warriors to question his decision not to kill Fina. Many of them clamored to see her dead.

Varar finished unlacing his vest and shrugged it off. He then glanced up to find Fina watching him. It was a speculative gaze. "So ... you've sent word to my father?"

He nodded. "One of my warriors met him in The Valley of the Tors this afternoon. He knows now what another attack on us will mean."

"We didn't attack you," she bit out the words.

Varar snorted. "Aye, whatever you say."

He finished unfastening his belt and started to unlace his breeches.

Fina's eyes grew wide. "What are you doing?"

"Undressing. I sleep naked."

Her jaw firmed, and her skin pulled tight across her cheekbones. "Touch me and you die, Boar."

Varar laughed at that, a deep rumble that rose unbidden from his chest. He raised an eyebrow, still grinning. "I prefer my women willing."

The look of relief on her face was so evident that he almost took offense. Varar mac Urcal was not used to women reviling him. Even so, he could hardly blame her.

"You can look away at any time, you know?" he teased. With a grin, he pushed down his breeches and kicked them off. Fina hastily averted her gaze, yet he saw a slight blush stain her high cheekbones, visible even through her tanned skin.

"And don't worry … we won't be sleeping together either," he added, walking over to one of the other alcoves and retrieving an armful of furs. "I'd risk you strangling me in the night."

"I'd do worse than that," she growled in response.

Varar ignored her threat. Instead, he arranged the furs and climbed into them. Propping himself up on an elbow, he regarded Fina a moment. She was staring down at her hands, a nerve flickering in her cheek.

"What is it, woman?" he drawled. "Spit it out."

Fina's gaze snapped up, snaring his. "You do realize you're only going to stir up hate between our people?"

Stifling another yawn, Varar ran a hand over his tired face. "Aye, but then relations couldn't get much worse than they are now."

"Your father wanted peace."

Varar went still. "Aye, so what?"

She watched him, her gaze burning. "I know all about your family, Varar mac Urcal. I know that your uncles deserved the ends they got. I know that my aunt saved your wretched life."

Varar stared back at her. He rarely thought of his uncles—Wurgest and Loxa—these days. He had been young when they had died.

"And how is Eithni?" he asked casually.

Fina did not reply.

Varar smiled. "When I awoke from that fever, she was standing over me. I thought she was a fairy maid, come to carry me off."

Fina's lip curled. "Eithni is soft-hearted."

Varar sighed, rolling over onto his back. "And lucky for me she is." He glanced back over at Fina. "I've heard the story about how your mother and father met," he said with a smile. "It's quite a tale. If Wurgest had won your mother instead of Tarl, we'd be cousins."

Fina gave him a disgusted look in response that made Varar's smile widen to a grin. "I had barely three winters when Wurgest died," he told her, "but my earliest memory is of him. I can still remember his rage when he returned home from that campaign to the Great Wall. In the end, it wasn't your mother he wanted. It was revenge. It drove him mad."

"Madness must run in your family," she replied. "Loxa wasn't any better."

Varar shrugged. He was not about to make excuses for two men that were long dead and gone. "It's just as well he abducted your aunt." He flashed her another grin. "Or fate wouldn't have brought her to An Teanga, and to my sickbed."

Fina glared back. "She should have let you die."

Chapter Five

Taking a Walk

"IT'S TIME YOU saw a little of the world beyond this alcove."

Varar's announcement, spoken while Fina broke her fast with oatcakes smeared with butter and honey, made her stop chewing and glance up. The chief stood, leaning against the stone lintel, observing her.

"What?"

"Want to take a walk in the fresh air?"

Fina watched him a moment before swallowing her mouthful of oatcake. She then reached for a cup of milk and took a gulp. "Aye."

He pushed himself off the wall and moved toward her. "I'm going to untie the chain but keep the collar on. Stand up and hold out your hands in front of you."

Fina frowned, although she obeyed him, rising to her feet. After days of being cooped up inside this alcove, she longed to see the friendly face of the sun again, to feel the wind on her skin, and to breathe fresh air. She would even suffer having her wrists bound for it.

Varar stepped closer, and she noticed he carried a length of string in his left hand. "Can I trust you to behave yourself?" he asked.

"No," she replied coldly.

He grinned, and Fina resisted the urge to lunge for him and smash her fist into that arrogant mouth. "I'll just have to keep a close eye on you then," he replied.

Fina looked away, breathing deeply as she allowed her temper to cool. Raging at him was not going to help her. Yet after her conversation with Morag, an idea had taken form in her mind. Fina was now acutely aware that the The Boar chieftain wanted her. He did not need to say anything; she saw it in his eyes. She had just then.

Maybe she could use it to her advantage.

A short while later, Fina descended the narrow stone steps to the lower level of the broch. She walked carefully, as her bound hands unbalanced her, and her limbs were stiff and clumsy after days of inactivity. Her head felt much better this morning though, with only a very slight ache to remind her of the injury she had taken. Varar followed behind her, carrying the chain that still kept her prisoner. She could feel his presence, the weight of his gaze upon her.

"So you're going to parade me before your people?" she growled, forgetting her plan to sweeten him up.

"Aye," he drawled. "That's the idea."

Anger flooded hotly through Fina, making her stomach cramp. Of course, this outing was not for her benefit, but for his. The chieftain wished to show off his spoil of war. Gods, how she hated him. How could she encourage this man's attraction toward her when she itched to break his jaw?

Fina descended the last step and walked onto a narrow platform that circuited the edge of a wide space. A glowing hearth in its center and burning cressets along the walls illuminated the feasting hall. She was loath to admit it, but the interior of An Teanga was impressive, even grander than Dun Ringill. Heavy beams, blackened by age and countless winters of wood and peat-smoke, stretched overhead.

It was still morning, though now that most folk had broken their fast, the hall was empty save for a handful of women. They were clearing up and beginning preparations for the noon meal. Fina looked around, and the women stared back, their gazes hard and unfriendly.

An unexpected sensation hit Fina then—a hollowness that lodged in the pit of her belly. She was unused to having such hate directed at her. Fina fisted her hands, nails biting into her palms. She would need to keep her wits about her to survive.

One of the women cursed Fina as she moved around the edge of the hall toward the open doorway. "Haughty Eagle bitch! I hope he cuts your head off!"

More curses followed as she left the hall.

Outside, Fina stepped into a bright summer's morning. Blinking in the blinding sun, she inhaled the scent of brine, the pungent smell of burning peat from the smoldering cook fires, and the odor of livestock. They were the smells of life, and after days of imprisonment, Fina sucked them into her lungs as if she were breathing in the scent of honey-suckle and heather.

She and the chieftain did not speak as she picked her way down the steps to the wide grassy space before the broch. Above her rose a great roundtower, its broad bulk dark against the blue sky. Smoke rose vertically from its roof, for there was not a whisper of wind this morning. The waters of the surrounding loch were still, gleaming like a polished shield boss.

Fina looked about her with interest. She remembered An Teanga well from her visit here six years earlier. The broch sat at the end of a spit that jutted out into the loch. Its position afforded the stronghold a clear view in every direction. If anyone attacked, they would be spotted many furlongs distant.

Walking away from the broch, the grass soft underfoot, Fina noted that a wall separated the fortress from the village beyond. She took in her surroundings with a keen eye—on the lookout for anything that might aid her escape.

Fina's gaze swung left. North, and home, lay in that direction. *I will get free of this place,* she promised herself.

They reached the wall and passed under a wide archway guarded by warriors, who watched Fina with a predatory intensity. She ignored them.

Beyond the wall they entered a wide dirt square flanked on one side by stables, and on the other by a long, low-slung building that was likely an armory. In front of the building was a cordoned-off area where two bare-chested male warriors hammered at each other with wooden practice swords.

Fina continued to observe her surroundings. To the south of this area, there was a wooden perimeter, and beyond that rose the turf roofs of the village, where the laughter and shrieks of children rose into the gentle morning air. A patchwork of tilled fields climbed up the foothills surrounding the village, giving the fort a prosperous and long-settled look. It was a nice spot, Fina was forced to admit, although she preferred Dun Ringill's dramatic position. Her home perched on a headland looking out over a wide expanse of water.

Fina's appearance in the yard had not gone unnoticed. The men and women stopped what they were doing and stared. They were hard-faced warriors dressed in leather and plaid—and they displayed the mark of The Boar as proudly on their right biceps as she did the mark of The Eagle on hers.

A low male voice thundered across the yard. "At last ... you bring her out to meet us?"

The crowd parted to allow a man through. He was an older warrior, yet age had not weakened his appearance. Heavy-set and barrel-chested, the man had a leathery, scowling face and a bald head. His gaze raked over Fina as he approached.

"Aye, I have." Varar stepped up to Fina's shoulder. "Fina meet Gurth, my father's cousin. He carries a deep dislike for your uncle, the infamous Battle Eagle."

At the mention of Donnel, the older warrior's heavy-featured face twisted. He spat on the ground between them, making his opinion of her uncle clear.

Not remotely intimidated, Fina favored the warrior with an icy smile. "Gurth." She spoke his name slowly, savoring it. "I've heard of you. My uncle told me about how he nearly crushed your windpipe. He'd have killed you if it wasn't for Urcal's mercy."

Gurth watched her, malice glinting in his dark eyes. "Maybe I'll crush yours to even the score."

Fina's smile widened. She stepped forward and raised her bound wrists defensively. "Go on then."

Gurth tore his attention from Fina and cast Varar a dark look. "I thought you might have broken her," he challenged. "A mouth like that needs to be kept busy."

The comment drew snorts and sniggers from the surrounding warriors.

Varar's mouth quirked. "And you'd let her mouth near your rod? She'd bite it off."

His comment drew a rumble of laughter from the crowd. Fina cast Varar a cool look. However, she was not about to contradict him. It was the first thing he had said that she agreed with.

"I'll bet she's a fiery pony to ride," one of the other warriors called out.

"Aye," Varar replied. His tone was nonchalant, almost bored. "Fights me the whole way ... but I like my women wild."

This comment brought forth jeers. Fina flushed hot as some of the men leered at her. They thought their chief rutted her every night.

Why would he let them think that?

Then she remembered the naked interest she had glimpsed in his eyes earlier. It appeared that her captor was spinning an illusion. He wanted to keep her for himself.

Fina dropped her gaze, so no one would see the truth in her eyes. Varar had his own reasons for lying, but it was also better for her if the folk of An Teanga believed she was their chief's concubine.

Be clever, she counseled herself. *Use this to your advantage.*

They were less likely to bay for her blood if they thought Varar had claimed her—and she had just moved closer to gaining her freedom.

Varar stepped back then and jerked his head right, in the direction of the village. "I'm taking her to meet the folk of An Teanga," he said smoothly. Something in his voice made Fina glance up. His grin made her go cold. "Follow us, if you want some fun."

The comment made cheers ring out across the yard; even Gurth, who had been glowering at the chief, managed a tight smile. Fina tensed at the news. She cast Varar a venomous look, but he merely gave her a push between the shoulder blades that propelled her toward the wooden perimeter.

"Bastard," she hissed at him.

In response, he merely laughed.

The walk that followed made Fina hate Varar mac Urcal with a vehemence that twisted her gut till it hurt. He paraded her before him, a leashed beast, through the village, his warriors following close behind, while the villagers unleashed their fury upon her.

They spat and threw rotten eggs, handfuls of goat turds, and worse, at her. She bore it all stoically, even when a loaf of stale bread smacked her across the forehead and nearly knocked her over. Yet all the while she nursed her hatred for these people, letting it burn through her veins.

One woman picked up a stone to throw at her, yet a sharp word from the chieftain, who followed a few feet behind, made her drop it. Likewise, when a man brandishing a hand-axe pushed his way to the front of the baying crowd, Varar warned him off.

He let them curse her and pelt her with turds and rotting food, but he would not let any of them draw blood.

It seemed to take an age to complete a circuit of the village and return to the yard between the armory and the stables. Here, Varar had his warriors go fetch pails of water from the loch and douse her with it.

"Maggot," she cursed him between clenched teeth as yet another bucket of cold water hit her.

Varar smiled. "I don't want you carting filth back into my alcove, do I?"

Dripping wet, her skirts clinging to her legs and her hair plastered against her scalp, Fina led the way back into the broch. The women inside hooted and pointed at the sight of her, soaked and bedraggled.

Fina stared directly ahead, ignoring them. She was saving her anger for one man.

Varar followed her upstairs to his alcove. They had just entered it, walking out onto the fur that spread across the stone floor, when Fina rounded on him.

"Stinking piece of dung," she snarled, shoving him hard in the chest with her bound hands. However, he did not even budge. "Did you enjoy that?"

"Not really," he replied with that same bored tone that he had used with his warriors earlier. "But it was necessary."

"Liar!" she choked, shoving him again. It was like hitting a stone wall. "You loved every moment of it, especially letting them think you've been humping me."

He arched an eyebrow, grabbed hold of her bound wrists, and pushed her away from him. Fina resisted the push, yet she found herself propelled back so she was standing on the edge of her furs. "That was for your benefit," he replied. He let go of her and crossed to the beam behind them, where he refastened the chain. "Better for you if they think I'm using you ... better for you too if I let the folk here vent their rage. It was humiliating for you, but you weren't harmed. They'll stop baying for your blood now."

Fina's lip curled. "You must think me a dull-wit," she growled. "You didn't do it for me, but for yourself. You're hoping I'll be so grateful to you for 'saving' me that I'll spread my legs."

She had meant to keep that knowledge to herself, to use as a tool to gain her freedom in the coming days. But now the red haze of fury had descended upon her, she forgot her resolve. She wanted to lash out, to wound.

"You have a high opinion of yourself, Fina." He returned to her and began unfastening her wrists. His voice was still an arrogant drawl, yet his face had changed, his gaze had hooded. "If I wanted you, I wouldn't go to so much trouble."

"Pig!"

The instant Fina's hands were free, she lashed out. She struck Varar hard in the solar plexus with one fist, while she slammed the other into his jaw.

He grunted, reeling back from the force of her blows. But he recovered with alarming speed. Fina was not close enough to knee him in the groin. She was delivering another strike, this one at his neck, when he caught her fist and shoved her backwards.

Two strides brought the pair of them back against the wall.

Fina found herself pinned there by the hard, heavy length of Varar's body. He grabbed hold of her wrists and yanked them above her head, slamming them against the pitted stone.

Panting from rage, Fina bared her teeth at him. "This is what you wanted all along, wasn't it, Boar?"

They were pressed close. Too close. She could feel the hard, muscular length of his body through her wet clothes. Their position was far too intimate. Her breasts pressed against the wall of his chest, and he had pushed a leg between her thighs to stop her from bringing her knee up and injuring his cods.

He stared down at her. His dark-blue eyes narrow, his face hard. He looked angry, dangerous. Varar was so close she could see the texture of his skin, the length of his dark eyelashes. And she could smell him: a spicy blend of leather and maleness. A tendril of fear curled in the base of Fina's belly, penetrating her outrage. Had she pushed him too far?

The moment drew out. Then, Varar's mouth twisted. "I'll take this as my thanks, Fina," he murmured. "And worry not ... you're *very* welcome."

Chapter Six

Return to Me

"THAT WAS CLEVER of you today, brother."

Varar glanced up from his brooding to find Morag standing next to him, a ewer in hand. Their gazes met, and he forced a smile, holding his cup up for her to fill. "How so?"

"You couldn't give your people that Eagle woman's blood—so you let them humiliate her instead. Well done."

Varar favored his sister with a curt nod, resisting the urge to frown. He was not in the mood to talk about Fina. His altercation with her upstairs had left a sour taste in his mouth. His jaw still ached from the punch she had delivered, but it was her words that had struck deep. The woman had a tongue like a boning knife.

He did not like being made a fool of. He did not like how easily she had seen through him.

But despite his anger, Varar still wanted her. She had known it too, mocked him for it. The feel of her body—

lush, firm, strong—crushed against his had inflamed him. His groin tightened now at the memory.

Varar took a gulp of bramble wine. The heat of it slid down his throat and pooled in his belly. It was a pity she detested him, for he would have enjoyed plowing Fina.

See it as a challenge ... she might thaw with time.

Varar suppressed a snort. The sun would set in the east and the sea would boil before that would ever happen.

Beside Varar, Gurth let out a growl. "I'd have preferred her blood."

"Aye," the warrior seated next to him agreed. His name was Frang, a short, squat man with a luxurious mane of dark hair brushed back from his face and ruddy cheeks. "The bitch needed more than a bit of muck thrown at her—she needed stoning."

Morag huffed a breath. "A few days ago I'd have agreed with you ... but now I understand Varar's reasoning. She's kin to Galan mac Muin, he'll not dare attack while he thinks she's still alive."

"No one asked your opinion, wife," Frang snarled. "Now still that flapping tongue and fill my cup."

Morag's gaze narrowed, an expression Varar knew all too well. His sister was as stubborn as him and had never taken kindly to being silenced. It made her choice of husband surprising, for Frang was a dominant, intolerant man, who had been in a permanent ill-temper since wedding Morag. She was not meek enough for him.

Minding her husband's reprimand this time, Morag continued down the table, pouring wine into cups. However, Varar noted she saved Frang's till last.

The warrior's cheeks had turned an alarming shade of purple by the time she sat down next to him. Morag shifted uncomfortably on the bench. Her belly had grown large over the past moon; the babe was due at Gateway.

A young woman carried a heavy tureen to the chieftain's table and set it down before Varar, drawing him out of his thoughts. "Boar stew?" she asked him with a smile.

Varar nodded, holding out a bowl for her to fill. He then ripped off a chunk of coarse bread and dipped it into the stew. Swallowing his first mouthful, he turned his attention to where Gurth sat brooding beside him.

"Of course," Varar said softly, breaking the silence, "Tarl mac Muin might still do something rash in his desperation to get his daughter back."

Gurth raised a grizzled eyebrow and met his eye. "Aye ... he might."

"Take a patrol north tomorrow and check on the border, just in case. Then lead your warriors east, up to the coast. I don't want any rescue parties slipping into our territory."

Gurth nodded, adopting a determined expression that Varar knew well. There were times when Varar did not like Gurth much, times when he wished The Reaper would come for him. Yet at moments like this, Gurth was a valuable ally to have at his side.

"Tarl mac Muin wouldn't have the balls to ride into this fort and take his daughter back," Frang spoke up. His cheeks had now dimmed to their usually ruddy red, although his pale blue eyes were glassy with drink.

"I'd not underestimate the mac Muin brothers," Varar replied. "From the tales my father told me, Tarl is easiest the most reckless of the three."

Frang snorted. "They're just tales. He won't come here."

"So, you'd leave your daughter captive with the enemy would you?" Varar asked.

"Aye," Frang replied without hesitation. "Daughters and wives are expendable."

Varar did not miss the look of scorn that Morag favored her husband with. However, Frang, as usual, seemed oblivious to it.

Dun Ringill—Territory of The Eagle

"I'm going after her—alone if I have to."

Tarl stood before his brothers, arms folded across his chest, gaze narrowed.

Galan heaved in a deep breath at these words and ran a hand over his face. Watching his elder brother, Tarl noted that the years weighed heavily upon Galan this evening. Deep grooves had formed either side of his mouth and between his brows. His dark hair, which he wore long, was laced with grey. The role of chieftain had come at a cost to him. For over twenty years he had led the Eagle tribe, taking over after their father fell in battle. During that time Galan had striven for peace—yet ultimately in vain.

Never had relations between The Eagle and The Boar been worse. While Urcal mac Wrad had been alive the peace had held, but since his death three years earlier, tension had risen between the two tribes. It had started with minor disputes: arguments over livestock grazing and trade. Then The Boar had started actively patrolling their border, questioning any who dared cross it. Yet no one, Tarl included, had thought Varar mac Urcal would engage in cold-blooded slaughter.

Galan met Tarl's eye, and for a long moment the two brothers merely looked at each other. It had gone quiet in the hall, all gazes riveted upon the chief and his brother.

"I'm not going to stop you," Galan said finally, his voice weary, "even though I think it's unwise to go."

Tarl scowled. "Are you calling me a fool?"

Galan held his gaze, his expression hardening. He never liked it when Tarl tried to draw him into an argument. "I question the wisdom of offering yourself up to Varar mac Urcal," he replied. "The Boar will expect you to come for Fina ... it's a trap."

Tarl shook his head. "Then I'll be ready for it. I'll circle in from the north—take a boat from Kyleakin and approach An Teanga from the water at night."

"Alone?" Donnel asked, speaking up for the first time. His younger brother stood a few feet away next to his wife, Eithni.

Tarl glared at Donnel, angry that both his brothers were questioning him at a time like this. He could barely suffer standing here in the hall. His belly clenched in a hard ball, his head pounded, and he felt sick. "Aye," Tarl growled, "if I must."

"I'll go with you," Donnel countered.

"No!" Eithni gasped, gripping Donnel's arm, her hazel eyes wide with fright. "You can't go!"

"Eithni's right," Galan interjected sharply. "Why don't I join you too? That way we can offer The Boar up a real prize: all three of the Mac Muin brothers at once. Varar would love that."

It was rare to hear Galan use sarcasm and so a hush fell upon the hall. Galan's wife, Tea, sat at the table behind him. Her strong face was taut with worry as she watched their conversation.

"Galan's point is valid." A tall warrior of a similar age to Tarl, stepped forward from the watching crowd inside the feasting hall. The man's face was scarred from a lifetime of fighting. "I'll go in Donnel's place."

Tarl met his eye and favored him with a grim smile. "Thank you, Lutrin."

"And I'll come too." Another warrior, whom Tarl had grown up with stepped forward. Solidly built with short greying hair, Namet stopped at Lutrin's side. "Three is as many as you need if you want to arrive in An Teanga unseen."

Tarl nodded, relief flooding through him that no one had tried to stop him. He had been expecting things to get heated with Galan. Over the years, his brother had gone to great lengths to keep the peace, even risking the goodwill of his own people to do so. This evening though, the fight had gone out of him. His usual stubborn insistence that they do their best not to anger their neighbors had gone.

Dun Ringill was still mourning for the deaths of many of their warriors in the rock-strewn valley. Such slaughter would not be readily forgiven.

It would never be forgotten.

"I want to come with you."

Tarl looked up from where he was undressing, his gaze meeting that of his wife.

Lucrezia sat in their furs, her shapely naked form glowing golden in the light of the single cresset that burned on the wall. Tarl stilled at the sight of her. Even after all this time together, he never tired of gazing at his wife. The years had deepened her exotic beauty. Her thick black hair still did not even have a thread of grey through it, although her face had grown leaner with the years, her high cheekbones more pronounced.

Tarl loosed the breath he had been holding. "It's better if you don't, love," he replied gently. He finished unlacing his breeches and pushed them down, kicking them off. "Galan was right. If things go ill on this mission, I don't want Fina to lose more kin than she has to."

Lucrezia's jaw firmed, and she raised her chin. "But what about *your* life? Or doesn't that matter?"

"I'm her father." Tarl crossed to the furs and knelt before his wife. Despite the warm day, her fingers were ice-cold when his hands reached for hers. "I must go."

Ever since receiving the news that her daughter had been taken by The Boar, Lucrezia had withdrawn into herself. She had not wept, nor raged. Tarl wished she would, for her silent, brittle despair worried him.

"I don't want to be left behind ... waiting." Lucrezia replied, her voice barely louder than a whisper. "I swear my heart will break if I lose either of you."

Staring into her dark eyes, Tarl saw tears well for the first time. He swallowed the lump that had suddenly blocked his throat, and squeezed her hands. "Then I'll do my best to ensure we both come home safe."

Her mouth twisted into a rueful smile. "I remember us having a similar conversation many years ago ... before you went off to fight Wurgest. The years haven't made you any less rash, Tarl mac Muin."

He forced a smile. "Admit it ... that's one of the things you love about me."

Her mouth trembled, and Tarl's chest constricted at the sight of Lucrezia struggling to contain her grief and fear. He gathered his wife in his arms and felt her sag against him. Her arms wrapped around his torso and squeezed tight.

"Return to me." Her broken whisper made Tarl's vision blur. He could not bear to cause her pain, but Fina's life was in danger, and he had to save her. "Promise me you will."

Chapter Seven

A Coming Storm

SLATE-GREY CLOUDS TINGED with ominous shades of purple hung in the western sky. They grew darker and heavier with each passing moment.

"Let's hope we hit land before that storm catches us."

Cathal mac Calum snorted at his brother's remark. He cast a wry look to where Artair rowed, his face red and sweaty, his dark auburn hair frizzy with humidity and the salty air. "You whine like a lass," he replied. "Afraid of a little summer rain?"

Artair scowled back at him. "Afraid of being hit by lightning. That's not a light rain shower approaching."

Cathal rolled his eyes and looked away from his brother, his gaze fixing upon their destination once more. Ahead, a green headland inched closer—a land of swiftly sloping mountains that appeared to erupt from the sea. They stretched across the horizon in a sculpted, majestic outline.

An t-Eilean Sgitheanach—The Winged Isle—approached.

A smile crept across Cathal's broad face, the first in many moons. This isle, protected from the Land of the Cruthini by a body of water, was a symbol of hope to Cathal and his people—a new land, a new start.

Tearing his gaze from his destination, Cathal glanced right at the boats that traveled level with his.

Mor, his daughter, sat at the bow of the nearest boat. The Boar warrior, Tormud, who had come to live among their people many years earlier, perched behind her, oars gripped in his meaty hands. Sweat beaded upon Tormod's brow as he rowed, his dark eyes fixed upon green bulk of the mainland to the east.

Cathal paid The Boar warrior little attention. Instead, he studied his daughter's profile, noting her proud stance and fierce expression as she stared at their destination. Tall and strong with dark red hair tumbling down her back, she was the equal of her brothers and a constant reminder of Lena, her mother.

The thought of his wife, who had died the previous winter, made the smile fade from Cathal's face. He twisted then, his gaze traveling to the swarm of small wooden boats that crossed the strait between the mainland and The Winged Isle.

Hundreds of men, women, and children—all his responsibility. Cathal clenched his jaw and faced forward once more. Conflict had pushed them out of their home, lands his folk had farmed and inhabited for generations. Yet more conflict lay ahead, for the inhabitants of this lonely isle would not take kindly to their presence.

A new life came at a price. Blood would have to flow in order for them to put down roots here. Cathal mac Calum was ready for it though—he had been preparing for this moment for years.

The storm hit as they brought their boats aground upon a shingly shore.

Artair's prediction had been right: it was vicious. Sharp needles of ice pelted them, the rain driving in heavy sheets across the exposed hills.

Cathal raised an arm, shielding his face from the weather as he staggered up the shore.

Soon after, a deep boom exploded overhead and the sky to the west lit up, exposing the carven edge of far off mountains.

Excitement rose in Cathal's chest while he stood there, the rain sluicing down his back. He lowered his arm and let the rain wash over him, ignoring the clamor of voices as the rest of his people landed their boats and climbed up onto the shore.

The Gods were with them this afternoon. The Warrior loomed above, banging his sword upon his shield, calling for the battle to begin. Cathal grimaced into the rain, raising his face to the sky. And begin they soon would.

"Father." Mor appeared at his shoulder, her moss-green eyes bright with the same excitement that coursed through his veins. "Tormud says that Kyleakin lies to the south. Do we camp here or keep moving?"

He met her eye. "How far is the village?"

Mor inclined her head to the heavy-set warrior who had halted beside her. The tattoo of a boar's head, faded with the years, still marked his right bicep. It had been a long while since Tormud mac Alec had set foot upon The Winged Isle. The Boar had fallen in love with a Cruthini woman during the campaign to the Great Wall years earlier and had made a new life afterward with her people. Cathal wondered how it felt to return to his homeland.

"We'll reach Kyleakin by nightfall," Tormud told them with a grin. "If we march now."

Cathal nodded briskly, his thoughts racing ahead to the first settlement that would fall to his people. He turned his attention back to Mor. "Tell your brothers to get everyone out of the boats," he barked. "We keep moving."

"That was the mother of storms last night," Namet grumbled as he saddled his pony ready to ride out. "All our supplies are soaked through."

Tarl did not answer as he stretched his back, stiff from a night sleeping rough. *I'm getting old*, he thought with a wince as an ache stabbed him through the shoulder. Time was he could have slept on the hard ground for a moon without struggling in the morning. Yet these days, one day out from home and he missed his soft bed of furs and the warmth of his wife's body.

The three of them had made camp on the sheltered side of a steep, stony valley. A few hawthorn bushes dotted the slope above them, but there had been little else to provide shelter from the storm that had come on suddenly, shrieking across the hills like a wrathful demon.

Digging into one of his saddle bags, Tarl extracted a tightly wrapped package of oatcakes Lucrezia had prepared for them. He opened the parcel, relieved to see the rain had not managed to seep in. "Here." He passed one to Namet. "Some food in your belly will improve your mood."

Namet snorted, but he took a big bite of oatcake and ceased his grumbling.

"I think we traveled farther yesterday then we thought," Lutrin announced. The warrior strode up the incline toward them. He carried their water bladders, now filled from the burn that ran through the bottom of the valley. "I recognize that mountain to the east of us—it looks over Kyleakin."

Tarl glanced east, a grim smile spreading across his face when he realized Lutrin was right. They had left just before dawn the day before and ridden hard before the storm caught them.

"Come on then." He picked up his saddle and strode over to his waiting pony. "Let's not waste time now ... if we find a boat at Kyleakin we could reach An Teanga tonight."

A short while later all three warriors were riding south, cantering down the valley toward the curving green mountain that heralded their destination.

Tarl led the party, his gaze fixed ahead. After the violent storm the night before, the morning was clear and bright, the air rich with the scent of damp earth and vegetation. The morning literally sparkled around them as if blessed by the Fair Folk. If his thoughts had not been elsewhere, Tarl might have enjoyed it. As it was, he could think about nothing but his missing daughter.

Fina was brave and resilient, but she would make a poor captive. It would be like trying to take a storm prisoner. She would likely goad her captors into taking her head.

Tarl's mouth thinned as he dwelt on the possibility. He had to reach An Teanga before The Boar lost patience with his fiery daughter.

They approached the coastal settlement of Kyleakin as the sun lifted high into the heavens. A breeze blew in from the mainland, bringing with it the smell of brine and the woody perfume of heather.

Tarl caught sight of the knot of stone dwellings that crested a low hill overlooking the water. He had not visited Kyleakin in years, yet the village looked as it always had: an isolated collection of thatch-roofed huts surrounded by a high wooden palisade overlooking the gateway to the mainland.

Urging his pony on, Tarl drew closer to the settlement. However, a few moments later, as his gaze roved over the wooden palisade and the tilled fields below, his warning instincts flared.

The hair on the back of his neck prickled as if The Reaper had just breathed down his spine.

Tarl reined in his pony. The stallion tossed his head in protest, but complied, dancing on the spot.

"What is it?" Lutrin pulled up alongside, his brow furrowed.

"Something's wrong. Where is everyone?"

Namet drew his pony up to Tarl's left, his keen gaze sweeping the surroundings. "Look closer," he said, his face growing taut. "The fields ..."

Tarl did, and his belly contracted. The vegetable plots—rows of kale, onions, and carrots—had been trampled. And as Tarl surveyed the wooden perimeter fence, he saw a gaping hole.

"We'll find a boat somewhere else," he muttered. "We need to leave ... fast."

Neither of his companions argued with him. Despite the bright, breezy morning and the friendly face of the sun, a shadow had fallen over Kyleakin.

Danger, the wind whispered. *Run.*

All three men turned their ponies south, away from the eerily silent village. But a heartbeat later they abruptly drew them up once more.

The hillside, which had been empty as they had ridden across it moments earlier, was now thronged by a line of warriors.

On foot, spears bristling against the sky, the column snaked like an eel south and then west, cutting off their escape.

Tarl stared at them, taking in the newcomers' fur, leather, and plaid clothing—their large, loose-limbed bodies, and aggressive stance. Many of the warriors had brown or red-hued hair, worn long with braids.

These were not folk from this isle. Tarl had fought alongside men and women with these looks at the Great Wall to the south as a young man.

They were Cruthini—from the mainland.

Beside Tarl, Lutrin muttered a curse. "One of us should make a run for it," he growled. "Someone has to warn Galan."

Tarl shook his head, his gaze still upon the wall of bodies surrounding them. "They've got archers," he replied. "Best we stay where we are."

As he finished speaking, a big man of around Tarl's age with wild auburn hair stepped out from the ranks and walked toward them.

Clean shaven, with a heavy brow and a lantern jaw, the warrior strode with a self-confident tread. A rectangular shield, its iron boss gleaming in the morning sun, hung over one arm, while in the other hand he carried a massive iron sword.

His arms, bare and heavily muscled, were covered with battle scars, and as he drew closer, Tarl noted a long silver scar slashed the man's left cheek.

Tarl needed no introduction to know that this was their leader.

The warrior halted around three yards back from the riders, his gaze assessing them. He had moss-green eyes and a stare that made Tarl's hand itch to draw his own blade.

"Those are fine ponies," the warrior drawled before his gaze alighted on Tarl. "I think I'll take your stallion for my own."

Tarl's mouth twisted into a snarl in response.

Watching him, the stranger grinned. His gaze then dropped to the tattoo that Tarl bore upon his right bicep.

"Eagles ... I fought with your warriors at the wall."

"Aye," Tarl answered between gritted teeth. "I was there."

The warrior met his eye. The grin faded, replaced by a speculative look that Tarl did not like at all. The wall of bodies closed in, iron and wood rattling as they formed a circle around the three riders.

Tarl inhaled slowly. He did not need to look at Lutrin and Namet's grim faces to know they were in trouble.

A noose had just been cast about their necks, and now it was tightening.

Chapter Eight

Gurth Returns

HE TREATS ME like his hound.

Fina shifted position on the wooden platform and resisted the urge to tug at the leather collar around her neck.

She also forced herself not to glance up at the long table above her where her captor reclined with his kin.

Serpent, she thought, flexing her fingers against the worn wood beneath her. How she longed to clamber up and grab one of those knives they were using to slice a haunch of venison into chunks. Vicious satisfaction flowed through her as she imagined the shock on his face when she slit his throat.

She actually considered the act for a moment. Only the fact that Varar held her leashed on a short chain— and that she wanted to live long enough to escape— prevented her.

Laughter rumbled across the hall in response to a tale one of the men had just told. It was a boastful story about how many Eagles he had slain during the battle in The Valley of the Tors.

Fina had no doubt the tale had been told for her benefit.

She did glance up then, her attention snapping to where Varar sat upon a carven chair at the center of the chieftain's table. The chair had armrests carved into the likeness of two boar heads—ferocious looking beasts with huge tusks and mean eyes.

Drinking horn in hand, the chief looked bored this evening. He barely seemed to notice the merriment of those surrounding him. Instead, he wore an aloof expression.

Watching him, Fina's throat constricted with loathing. Her hatred of him burned like a Gateway bonfire within her—and the fact that she had never laid eyes upon a man more attractive just made her detest him even further.

Fina had seen the hungry looks on women's faces in the hall when they gazed upon him. Varar mac Urcal oozed sensuality. Even now, leaning back in his chair, his long muscular limbs relaxed in repose, the man's presence overshadowed everyone at his table.

Feeling the weight of Fina's stare, Varar blinked, his gaze dropping to meet hers.

Fina held his eye, unflinching. She hated this new habit he had taken to over the past two days, dragging her out here like his tamed hawk to sit at his feet while the rest of the hall stared at her.

"Are you hungry, Fina?" he asked. The smoothness of his voice made her hackles rise, but she nodded. "Here." He picked up a wooden platter that had some bread and slices of venison on it and leaned forward. "Take this."

She did, ungraciously, aware of the smirks and whispers around them.

"Venison's too good for that bitch." One of the warriors at the chieftain's table, a florid-faced man with slicked-back hair called out. He sat next to Varar's sister, Morag. Fina assumed he was her husband. "Give her the dog scraps."

Fina ignored him, ripping off a piece of bread and taking a bite. If she was free of this chain with a knife in her hand, his would be the second throat she would slit. She would be doing Morag a favor. No woman should have to endure the company of that man. He had heckled and insulted Fina at each meal while the rest of them cheered him on.

Fina's gaze flicked back to Varar. He was not even paying attention. Instead, he was cutting himself some more meat, his expression shuttered.

"Better still," the warrior continued, encouraged by the mirth around him. "Put her in with the pigs and let her fight for food with them."

The comment drew loud guffaws, but Fina noted that Morag did not smile. She ate her supper slowly, her expression as bland as her brother's.

The warrior's florid cheeks reddened further as he leaned across the table, leering at Fina. "Aye ... I'd strip you naked and watch you cavort in the mud with the other sows."

Fina swallowed the mouthful of bread she had been chewing and met his eye. "And I'd stick a pike through your gut so I wouldn't have to listen to your yipping."

Laughter erupted in the hall. Beside the warrior, Morag smirked. However, her husband did not find Fina's comment humorous at all.

He leaned forward. "Mouthy wee bitch ... I'll—"

"Enough, Frang," Varar drawled, cutting the warrior off. "You keep heckling her ... you get what you deserve."

The man's ruddy cheeks deepened to purple. His throat bobbed as he swallowed.

Fina watched him, a smile curving her lips. She hoped he would lose his temper, or even better, try and attack her. She would wrap her chain around his neck and throttle him.

But any reaction from Frang was forestalled by the rumble of male voices approaching beyond the open door to the broch. A moment later a broad figure stormed into the hall.

Gurth wore a ferocious scowl, his powerful shoulders rounded. A group of warriors followed him into the broch. Their faces were flushed, their brows sweaty from travel.

Frang forgotten, Varar rose to his feet. In an instant Fina saw the chieftain's demeanor change, from bored and distant, to predator-sharp. His dark-blue gaze tracked Gurth across the floor. "What is it?"

Gurth stopped a few yards back from the chieftain's table, his gaze riveted upon Varar's face. He had not even noticed Fina sitting there.

"Invaders," he barked.

A deathly hush followed his words. Fina's breathing stilled, her body going cold.

"I led a patrol along the coast and then up toward Kyleakin … that's when one of our scouts spotted them … Cruthini," he rasped. "A horde of the bastards. They've taken Kyleakin and are traveling into our territory … towards An Teanga."

The announcement sent a ripple of alarm through the broch. Fina stared at Gurth. She did not want to believe him, yet the grim look on his face, the haunted expression in his eyes, warned her that he spoke the truth.

"How long have we got?" Varar barked out the question.

Gurth's expression grew even grimmer. "A day, no more. They're traveling on foot … we spotted only a couple of ponies. They're well-armed though." His mouth twisted. "It looks as if they landed upon this isle for one purpose—to conquer."

Fina's belly cramped, and she clenched her fingers around the edge of the ledge where she sat.

I have to escape. Her mind whirled, frantic now. *I need to warn my people.*

"How many warriors do we have?" Varar asked. The man's calmness in the face of such calamitous news was impressive. Instead of panicking, he was thinking ahead, planning.

"Seventy to hand," Gurth replied. "With some time, I can gather more."

Varar's face tightened, and he grew still. "We don't have time."

"I can gather one-hundred by dawn," Gurth assured him.

Fina frowned. One-hundred against a horde—the odds were definitely against The Boar.

"You can't defend An Teanga alone," Fina spoke up, her voice echoing across the now silent hall. "Let me ride to Dun Ringill. If we band together, The Eagle and The Boar might be able to repel them."

Lies. She would never help The Boar. Her suggestion was just a means of escape. She could not care less if the invaders destroyed this fort, tore it down stone by stone.

But if lies would buy her freedom, she would happily weave them.

Gazes swiveled to her, including those of the chieftain and Gurth. Their looks were not friendly or grateful. Fina was not surprised. She had not expected gratitude.

"I think not," Varar replied. For the first time since their capture, he watched her with hostility. He looked what he was: a ruthless leader. Her enemy. "We'll handle this ourselves."

She held his eye, undaunted. "But we could—"

"Shut your mouth, woman!" Gurth's roar shook the walls of the broch.

Fina jerked her gaze from Varar, just in time to see Gurth lunge for her, his meaty right fist flying. She raised an arm to block the blow, too late.

Gurth's fist connected with her jaw.

The strength behind that punch was formidable. It slammed her back as if hit by a battering ram. Fina collided with the table behind her, the sharp edge biting into her temple.

Pain exploded in her skull, razor sharp darts radiating out from the point of impact. She heard a cry of pain. It must have been her, yet the hoarse, agonized edge to it sounded like the cry belonged to someone else.

Fina collapsed upon the floor at the foot of the table, darkness clouding her vision. A high pitched squeal filled her ears. Through it she heard commotion echo through the broch.

Men's shouts shook the walls, before she heard Varar's voice slice through the din. "Touch her again, Gurth, and I'll kill you."

Chapter Nine

With the Dawn

FINA AWOKE TO the feel of something wet and cool upon her brow.

Eyelids flickering, she let out a low groan.

"You're awake ... good." She recognized the voice, the gentle lilt of Eachann the healer.

Fina's vision cleared, and she stared up at his lean face, witnessing the concern in his blue eyes. The healer held a wet cloth in hand as he knelt at her side.

"You've had too many knocks to the head of late, lass," Eachann continued. "You took a while to wake from this one."

Fina wet her lips. Her throat was dry, and her mouth felt like a strip of cracked leather. "I'm thirsty."

"Here." Eachann knelt beside her, lifted her head, and raised a cup of water to her lips. "Sip slowly."

"How long ..." she croaked when she had wetted her mouth and throat, "... have I been asleep?"

"All night. It's just after dawn." Eachann's features tensed, his brow furrowing. "The warriors are about to ride out."

Fina let out a long breath. Her temple ached, and her head felt as if it was twice its normal size. It was difficult to think straight.

"I need to warn my people," she said, reaching up to touch her throbbing temple. It was bandaged. "They have to know."

Eachann's expression turned pained. "I—"

"So she's awake, is she?"

A low male voice interrupted them. The healer's gaze widened, and he drew back as Varar stepped into the chamber. Dressed head to toe in dark leather, twin swords strapped across his back, he was an intimidating sight. Eachann turned to the chieftain. "Aye, but she's still—"

"Thank you, Eachann ... you can go now."

The healer hesitated. "But I should—"

"You can check on her later. Leave us."

With a glance in Fina's direction, Eachann dipped his head and obeyed. He scooped up his basket of healing herbs and powders, and exited the chamber, the curtain swishing shut behind him.

Lying upon the furs, her limbs heavy, her head pounding, Fina looked up at Varar as he approached her. "What do you want?"

He hunkered down next to her. "To say goodbye. We're going now."

Fina snarled at him before wincing as pain shot across her forehead. "I hope they gut you. I hope they stick your head on a pike and leave it for the crows."

He watched her, his face dispassionate. "You may get your wish."

Silence stretched between them then. She stared into the loch-blue depths of his eyes and felt a strange pull. She resisted it.

"Won't you send someone to Dun Ringill?" she asked finally, tempering the rage that simmered in her breast. "The Eagles need to know."

His face hardened. "They'll find out soon enough."

Fina pulled herself upright, clenching her teeth at the pain in her head. "Whatever you believe ... it wasn't us that started the massacre in that valley," she countered. "You'd doom my people out of petty vengeance?"

His gaze narrowed. "I don't have time for this."

"None of us do," she shot back. "The Eagle must be told."

Varar rose to his feet and stepped back from her. "I'll see you once the battle's done." His voice was as hard and flat as his gaze.

"If you aren't slaughtered," she replied, injecting as much malice as she could muster into her voice.

He walked away before pausing in the doorway and glancing back at her. "For your own sake you'd better hope I survive," he said quietly. "I don't like your chances if the invaders take this broch."

And with that he left the alcove, his footsteps scuffing on the stone steps until they faded into the rumble of activity in the broch below.

Fina sank back onto the furs. Bile rose in her throat, and she swallowed, glaring up at the rafters.

Gods, she hated feeling this helpless. She was to be chained here like a sacrificial beast while these Cruthini sacked the isle. For the first time since being taken captive despair swamped her. It dawned on her then that she would likely never see her kin again.

Fina was sitting propped up against the wall, staring sightlessly into the distance, when Morag brought her up a tray of food: bread, cheese, and boiled eggs. The woman's expression was stony, her gaze veiled, as she lowered the tray onto the edge of the furs and took a step back.

Fina did not thank her; there was nothing in Morag's expression that invited gratitude. Instead, she shuffled forward and grabbed a slice of bread and cheese. Her belly was growling with hunger. Gurth's arrival the night before had interrupted her sparse supper, and she had eaten nothing since.

Swallowing her first mouthful, she glanced up and saw that Morag had not moved. She usually just dumped the tray and stalked off. Not so this morning. Instead, she watched Fina with a narrow-eyed intensity that made Fina's hackles rise.

"What?"

Morag inclined her head. "The warriors are gone ... ridden east to face the Cruthini. You're one of the few left at An Teanga."

Fina snorted. "A warrior in chains ... not much use to you."

Morag's lip curled. "You'd not help us anyway."

Fina shrugged and took another bite of food, chewing vigorously. She swallowed and reached for the mug of milk on the tray. "That husband of yours is a brute ... surely you don't want him to return home?"

Morag's laugh was a surprising, musical sound. "You didn't warm to Frang then? Few do."

"I've met turds with more charm." Fina's gaze settled upon Morag. "Why did you wed him?"

Morag's mirth faded, her expression turning guarded. "I'm no beauty ... men weren't fighting over me. And when Frang showed an interest, I was flattered." She paused here, her mouth tightening. "My father was happy with the match. I wanted to please him so I accepted Frang's attentions."

Fina huffed a breath. "My father thinks I'll never wed. No man would put up with me."

Morag's dark brows arched. "Frang says a few good beatings would see you right ... but then that's his answer to any dispute with a woman."

The dark undertone in Morag's voice was impossible to mistake.

Fina did not reply. She had met a few men like Frang and enjoyed putting them in their place. Unfortunately, it had been impossible to do so when chained up.

Morag moved back from the furs, indicating that their brief conversation had ended. Fina said nothing more as the chieftain's sister turned and walked back to the curtain that concealed the stairs. Instead, she reached for another piece of bread and a hard-boiled egg.

When Morag reached the doorway, she turned, her gaze fixing upon Fina once more. "The answer to your question is 'no'," she said quietly. Seeing Fina's frown of puzzlement, Morag favored her with a wary smile. "No ... I don't want my husband to return home."

The healer did not visit again until late in the day. The pale sliver of light that filtered in through the slit in the roof, warned Fina that the day was drawing out. The twilights seemed to go on forever this time of year.

Sitting in her usual position, back braced against the wall, she wondered if Varar and his warriors had met the invaders yet—and if they had, how the battle had gone. Restlessness churned within her at the thought.

So grossly outnumbered, there was only one way that confrontation could go.

"You're looking much better, lass," Eachann greeted her as he entered the alcove. "I'm heartened to see color in your cheeks."

"For all the good it'll do me," Fina replied tersely. She had warmed to the healer during her time here, yet his attentiveness toward her seemed futile.

Eachann set down his basket and lowered himself onto the furs so that he sat next to Fina. He met her gaze steadily. "I once spent a summer at Dun Ringill," he said after a pause. "The best summer of my life."

Fina's gaze widened. "Really?" She did not know of any of The Boar having spent time at her fort.

He smiled. "I trained with Eithni. When she saved Varar's life, she learned that this fort had recently lost its healer. She invited the chief to send someone to train with her. Urcal sent me." Eachann's smile turned wistful. "She was a great teacher ... and I think I fell in love with her during my stay in Dun Ringill. Not that there was any hope in Eithni returning my feelings … she only had eyes for her husband."

Fina nodded in understanding. Her uncle and aunt had a union much like her parents'—solid even after many years. Eithni had given her heart completely to Donnel. There was no room in it for another man. Even so, Fina felt a little sorry for the healer. "I can understand why you'd love her," she said quietly. "Eithni is a special woman."

Eachann met her gaze squarely. "I always told myself that if there was a way to repay her kindness to me I'd do it. I never went back to Dun Ringill, and then with relations souring between our people over the last few years … I never got the chance." He paused here, his lean features tightening. "But now Eithni's niece sits before me … and she needs my help."

Fina's breathing hitched, and she grew still. "What do you mean to do?"

A smile spread across Eachann's face, making him appear years younger. He reached over to his basket and retrieved a knife with a long thin blade. "I mean to set you free."

Chapter Ten

Into The Night

"VARAR WILL KILL you," Fina pointed out. As delighted as Eachann's declaration made her, she felt compelled to point out the consequences of his actions. "Healer or not, he'll gut you for freeing me."

Eachann's smile turned wicked. "Not if he thinks you somehow got hold of a blade, attacked me, and forced me to free you."

Fina gave him a long look. "You've thought this through?"

He nodded. "I've no quarrel with Varar, but he should have let you return home to warn your family." Eachann held up the blade, its slender length glinting in the light of the cressets. He handed it to her with a smile. "This now belongs to you ... turn round and let's get started on that collar."

It took the healer a while to untie the knots and peel back the layers of leather that bound Fina's neck. He worked silently while Fina kept her gaze upon the curtained doorway, ears straining for the sound of anyone approaching. Eachann was taking a huge risk in helping her; she had to ensure no one found him out.

Eventually, the collar fell away, landing heavily next to her on the furs.

"Can you swim?" Eachann asked.

Fina nodded.

"Good. The best way out of this fort is across the loch. Most of the warriors are gone, but Varar has left some guarding the village gateways. I don't want you having to kill anyone in order to get out of here."

Fina huffed. Once she was unshackled, she would slay anyone who got in her way. However, she understood Eachann's concern; he sought to save lives at all costs.

"So I'll climb down from the base of the broch and swim out from there?" she asked.

"Aye, turn left at the bottom of the steps outside the broch to get to the water. Then swim north-west." Eachann glanced up at where the daylight had now stopped filtering in through the smoke hole. "It's almost dark enough."

He reached back into his basket and withdrew a small leather garment, handing it to Fina. "This belongs to you ..."

A smile stretched across Fina's face. "My skirt."

"Aye, you can't swim in that heavy thing you're wearing. Put it on underneath and then cast the plaid skirt away when you reach the water's edge. It's best the folk of this broch don't see you wearing that or they'll know I've helped you. We will have to walk past everyone on the way out."

Fina inclined her head. "*We* will?"

"Aye ... the only way you'll be able to leave this broch, without fighting your way out, is if you take me prisoner. Hold that blade to my throat until we're outside the broch. Once you let me go, I'll alert the guards."

Fina's mouth quirked. "Make sure you take your time ... give me a head-start."

Eachann smiled back, although she could see a muscle flickering in his cheek. Despite his apparent confidence, he was nervous. "Worry not ... I will."

A short while later, the pair of them descended the stone steps to the feasting hall. Eachann walked in front of Fina. She held an arm twisted behind his back with one hand, and with the other she pressed the blade to his throat. They moved slowly, carefully, for a misstep would bode ill for Eachann.

The inhabitants moving about the hall did not spot the pair at first. It was only when Fina and the healer reached the bottom of the steps that a cry of alarm went up. A woman who had just emerged from an alcove let out a shriek, before she jerked her head toward the back of the hall. "Morag!"

Varar's sister, who had been left in charge of the fort in her brother's absence, looked up from where she was mending clothing before the hearth. Her expression, which had been introspective as she worked, froze. Her gaze swept to Fina. She then cast aside her mending and rose to her feet. "What are you doing?"

Fina smirked. "What does it look like?"

The hall went silent around them. Some folk, who had already bedded down for the night, pushed themselves up from the floor. There were only a handful of males remaining: the elderly and the young. One of the old men reached for a knife and rose to his feet.

"I'll cut you up, girl," he growled, taking a threatening step toward her.

"Stop, Seumas." Morag's command lashed across the hall.

The old man turned his head toward the chieftain's sister. "We can't let her escape."

"She has our healer." Morag's voice hardened, the edge to it reminding Fina of Varar. "I'll not risk Eachann coming to harm."

The elderly warrior's face twisted, but he did not argue with Morag. Instead, he turned back to Fina and spat on the rushes before him. "You'll not get far. We'll hunt you ... and this time no one's going to spare your life."

Fina did not reply. She had no interest in arguing with any of them. Her mind was already flying, planning the next step of her escape. She ignored Seumas, instead locking gazes with Morag one last time.

The woman stared back at her, stone-faced, one hand resting upon her swollen belly. A look of understanding passed between them.

Fina nudged Eachann forward. "Come on. Careful now ... or my knife might slip."

A hiss of outrage reverberated around the hall at these words. Fina heard a few muttered curses and smiled. Good. They needed to believe she'd do the healer harm.

Outdoors, a cool night breeze whispered against their faces. A waxing moon was rising, a silver disc in the fathomless darkness. The sight pleased Fina; she needed the moonlight to find her way.

As Eachann had said, there were no guards here. The nearest sentries were at the gate leading to the stables, around ten yards distant.

Fina removed the knife from Eachann's throat, and they hurried down the steps. Peat-filled braziers burned around the base of the broch, gold and red flames licking the darkness.

Eachann's lean face was all shadows and angles as he turned to her. "Go," he whispered. "May The Mother protect you."

Fina gave him a fierce smile. "And you, Eachann. Thank you—I will not forget this."

She turned, pivoting on her heel, and fled. Skirting the base of the broch, she then clambered over the rocks that led down to the water on the north-western edge. Moonlight had given the loch's surface an oily look, and as her eyes adjusted to the darkness, Fina could make out the darker bulk of the headland beyond.

Behind her, angry shouts split the night. Eachann had alerted the guards. Fina had little time left; she had to go now. Shedding her heavy plaid skirt, Fina kicked it aside and stepped into the loch.

The chill of the water against her bare thighs made her stifle a gasp; even in the height of summer, the loch's waters were never warm.

The shouting grew louder behind her, but Fina ignored it. They would not catch her now. No one would. Clamping the blade between her teeth, she took a deep breath and dove into the water.

A while later Fina emerged on the northern shore of the loch and crept up the heather-strewn bank. Pausing to catch her breath at the top, she glanced back at the fort. The squat tower sat like a beacon in the distance, silhouetted against the dark sky, illuminated by its fires.

She could hear voices, although they were distant. They would have sent out a group to hunt her by now.

A slow smile spread across Fina's face. Let them—they would not find her easy prey.

She had swum like an otter across the loch, and now she sprinted—knife in hand—light-footed and keen-eyed, over the hills that stretched north-west of An Teanga. Eachann had told her that a small village lay in this direction. Fina needed to reach it before her hunters caught up with her.

The breeze cooled her wet skin as she ran. Her gaze scanned the moonlit landscape around her. She set a fast, yet steady pace for herself, but after a short spell, her limbs and lungs protested. The forced inactivity of the past few days had already started taking its toll on her physical condition. She could usually run for a long while without any strain.

Her lungs were starting to burn when she crested a hill and spied a huddle of huts in the valley below her. Firelight seeped out from the shutters and doors, and the scent of peat laced the night air.

Fina skirted the edge of the village and crept into a byre. She was hoping to find a pony, but instead she discovered a pair of oxen dozing in a stall. Such beasts could not be ridden so she left the building. She found a pony shortly after, snatching hay from a manger in its stall.

The animal snorted at her sudden arrival, but Fina soothed it with soft words as she ran her hands over its back and legs. The pony was old and fat, with a sway back, and a bowed tendon on one of its forelegs, yet it would have to do.

Locating a halter, Fina slipped it onto the pony's head and led it out of the stall. Once they were well away from the edge of the village, she swung up onto the pony's bare back and turned it for home. Together, they crested the northern side of the valley, and at the top Fina drew her mount to a halt so she could cast her gaze back the way she had come.

The red-gold halo of torches cast a faint glow on the southern horizon. The party sent to catch her were nearer than she had thought. There would not be many of them, for An Teanga could not risk leaving itself undefended. Even so, Fina was keen to keep ahead of her pursuers. She should now be able to outrun them, provided she and the pony kept moving.

With one last glance to the south, Fina reined her mount north-west and dug her heels into its furry flanks. The pony lurched into a jolting trot and then a bumpy canter. Fina clung on, clenching her thighs against the beast's barrel-like sides, her hands tangling in its mane. Around her the rolling hills of The Winged Isle appeared frosted in the hoary light of the moon.

The Fair Folk were said to come out to play on nights such as these, and Fina was glad that there were no fairy mounds, that she knew of, nearby. The thought of being abducted by the Aos Sí and dragged down into the underworld did not appeal. She had a life to return to, her people to warn.

Vengeance to seek.

Chapter Eleven

Blood Dawn

VARAR GRITTED HIS teeth as he wrapped a strip of
leather around a wound to his right bicep. The slash he
had sustained during the fighting the day before was
merely an annoyance. But it was a distraction that could
easily slow him down and spell his end next time he
faced the Cruthini.

He could not risk that.

Finishing the bandage, Varar turned back to his pony.
He had been trying to saddle Guail when the wound had
reopened and started bleeding. Around him his warriors
readied themselves to ride out to meet the invaders once
more. There was little conversation this morning, and
the faces of the men and women surrounding him were
harsh.

Yesterday had gone badly for The Boar. After clashing
with the enemy a few furlongs north of here, they had
lost nearly twenty warriors before Varar had yelled for
them to fall back.

The loss galled him.

Pushing aside his brooding, Varar finished saddling Guail and glanced up at the lightening sky. A red blush stained the eastern horizon. The sight made him frown. A weight settled in his gut, a sickly feeling. His father had told him once that to see a Blood Dawn before battle was an ill omen. A sign of looming defeat.

Varar shook his head in an attempt to dislodge the thought and reminded himself that the enemy would be viewing the same sky. He would not let superstition weaken his resolve. They had no choice but to face the Cruthini again this morning. They were all that stood between the invaders and An Teanga.

He swung onto Guail's back and urged the stallion forward to where Gurth sat waiting upon his pony. The older warrior was scowling, his gaze fixed upon the red-hued dawn. Beneath Gurth's swarthy complexion, Varar saw that he was pale. Gurth was a formidable warrior, yet he fervently believed in omens, as Varar's father, Urcal, had.

Spying the chief's approach, Gurth tore his gaze from the sky and met his eye. "Ready to face those Cruthini hounds?"

Varar grinned, showing his teeth. "Aye."

Neither man mentioned the Blood Dawn, although behind him, Varar heard Gara mutter an oath, calling upon The Warrior to aid them in the coming battle.

A bitter smile tugged at Varar's mouth. He was not a defeatist, but all the same, he knew it would take more than that to save them. The Cruthini army was too large, and despite that his warriors had fought like wolves the day before, they could not hold back the tide.

Turning in the saddle, Varar fixed his attention upon Gara. The warrior was adjusting her stirrups but, upon feeling the weight of her chieftain's stare, she glanced up.

"I want you and Bothan to take ten warriors and return to the fort," he said.

Gara drew herself up, anger flaring in her eyes. "What?"

"An Teanga needs to be emptied."

"We can't spare ten warriors, Varar," Gurth growled next to him. "We need every sword, axe, and spear for this battle."

Varar cast Gurth a cool look. "You saw their army. We need to prepare for the worst ... I don't want my people enslaved should the enemy take An Teanga."

Gurth's heavy jaw clenched, his eyes smoldered, yet he did not argue. He did not like it, but he knew Varar was right.

Turning his attention back to Gara, Varar saw that she was frowning.

"I've always fought at your side," she growled. "I don't want to abandon you right before battle."

The warrior's loyalty made Varar smile. "Worry not. I'll make sure I live through this so you'll get a chance to fight alongside me again." His attention flicked to where Bothan had just mounted his pony behind him. "Go now ... and ride fast. We don't have much time left."

Gara and Bothan's party departed, galloping south, while Varar led the rest of their war band north-east. The company of riders and warriors on foot fanned out behind him in a crescent. They had camped on the edge of a hazel and hawthorn thicket, around ten furlongs south of where they had faced the invaders the day before.

As he rode, Varar breathed in the damp air and readied himself for what was to come. The Cruthini had gained ground, and he knew that once they reached the top of the hill before them, the enemy would be waiting beyond. As such, he and the other mounted warriors slowed their pace and let the warriors who would fight on foot take their place in the front ranks.

The Boar war band crested the hill and halted.

There on the opposite hillside, a bristling carpet of spears and shields, waited the enemy. The sight of them made Varar's breathing still. There seemed even more of the bastards than the day before. He had cut down many Cruthini, but it looked as if they had multiplied overnight. It was hard to gain a sense of their numbers, and Varar had the sinking sensation that he was not facing their full strength.

Unlike The Boar, none of the invaders before them rode on ponies. Instead, they would fight on foot. Some of the warriors in the front stood completely naked, their muscular bodies painted in blue swirls and symbols. These were the best fighters, placed at the front so they could cut their way through the enemy ranks.

Gurth had once been one of these fighters, a howling naked beast, carrying nothing more than a wooden shield and a sword as he bore down on his enemies. Varar too had fought in the front while his father was alive. Now, as chief, he took his place in the first row of riders.

As they waited upon the crest of the hill, a big auburn-haired man, naked to the waist and clad in plaid breeches, strode forward. The front ranks parted to let him pass. Face smeared in blue, a heavy iron sword in his right hand, the huge warrior scanned the band before him. A grin split the man's face when he spied their chieftain.

Varar's mouth twisted at the sight of him. Cathal mac Calum. They had already made their introductions the day before. How he longed to ram his sword into this man's guts—and if given the chance, he would do so this morning.

"Varar mac Urcal!" Cathal's voice rang out across the valley. "Back for more, I see."

"Aye," Varar shouted back. "We're not done yet, Cruthini dog!"

Cathal barked out a laugh. "Fighting talk, Boar. I like it!" His gaze remained on Varar as he continued. "Only, it's a sure way to end up dead. Surrender now, and I might spare your lives. Fight us, and I'll butcher every man, woman, and child we find in your fort."

Next to Varar, Gurth let out a low growl, while his chief's response was even stronger. Varar stretched out his neck, spat on the ground, and raised his hand in an obscene gesture. "We will never surrender."

The Cruthini leader snorted, his gaze lingering upon Varar for a moment longer, before he glanced back at the crowd of warriors behind him. "The Boar's keen to die," he called out. "Let's give him what he wants then, shall we?"

A roar went up, the sound so loud that the very air in the valley seemed to tremble.

Varar drew his sword, iron scraping against leather as it slid free of its scabbard. Next to him, Gurth put the hunting horn he carried to his lips and blew hard. Its wail split the air.

A heartbeat later both sides charged. Blood-curdling cries echoed off the hillsides, and a tide of screaming warriors descended into the valley.

Fina reached Dun Ringill as a rain squall blew in from Loch Slapin. Blinking water out of her eyes, she urged the old gelding into a jolting trot and guided him in through the fort's outer wall. The warriors posted there gaped.

"Fina!" One of them cried out. "You got free!"

"Aye," Fina replied, favoring the man with a tired smile. After riding all night and this morning, she felt ready to fall off the pony's back. "And just as well too—invaders from the mainland have landed on the isle. Spread the word in the village while I tell the chief."

The joy on the warrior's face froze. "Invaders ... Caesars?"

"No, Cruthini ... they're dealing with The Boar first, but as soon as An Teanga falls, they'll ride north. We don't have much time."

The news delivered, Fina kicked the pony into a loping canter and made her way up the path toward the inner perimeter and the high stone arch that led to the broch. The squat stone round-tower of Dun Ringill rose before her, against a mottled sky.

"Fina!"

A familiar voice hailed her as she headed toward the broch. Twisting her head, she spied a shapely young woman with long, wavy dark hair and pert features. The woman waved frantically to her from outside a squat hut near the outer perimeter. She had been braving the rain to pick herbs in the rambling garden when she had spied Fina.

Joy blossomed in Fina's breast at the sight of Ailene, the young bandruí of Dun Ringill. She had taken the seer, Ruith's, place after her death two winters earlier.

Fina waved back but did not draw up her pony to greet her friend. "I must speak to Galan," she called. "I'll find you later!"

A bemused expression settled upon Ailene's face as she lowered her hand and watched Fina thunder past.

Reaching the inner wall of the fort, Fina drew her gelding to a trot. It was then that she saw a man walking toward the gate, hauling a cart of vegetables after him. She recognized him. She had not seen Ethan in a long while; she had avoided him after his handfasting.

The man, broad-shouldered, brown-haired, and tanned, stopped short, surprise spreading over his face. "Gods ... you're alive!"

Fina grinned. "I'm not so easy to kill, Ethan mac Brennan."

His smile widened. "I'm pleased to see that."

The moment drew out as their gazes held. Ethan's smile grew uneasy then, and he looked away. The welcome grew awkward, and Fina knew why.

They had once been lovers.

Ethan, who worked a large plot of land north of the fort, had wanted them to wed, but Fina had shied away from agreeing. She had been too young to be tied to a husband and bairns. She was a warrior; her first loyalty was to her chief. After last summer, when things had cooled between them, Ethan announced that he was handfasting someone else.

They had barely spoken since. Fina had been angry at first—and then after a few moons passed, she had been surprised by how little she cared.

Seeing him now though, she felt a pang of regret.

"I'd better go," she murmured. "I've much to tell Galan ... none of it good."

He nodded, his smile fading. "It's good to see you," he said, meeting her eye once more.

A heartbeat passed, and Fina found herself wondering if he was happy. If his choice in wife had been a good one. "Aye ... and you."

The feasting hall went silent upon Fina's entrance. Galan was standing near the hearth, speaking to his brother Donnel. The Eagle chieftain glanced up, a smile erupting when he spied Fina striding toward him.

"Here's a sight," he greeted her. Tarl actually managed it!" Galan stepped around the hearth and went to meet her, arms opening as he prepared to embrace his niece.

Fina slowed her step, a frown creasing her brow. "Managed what?"

Galan's smile faltered, and his slate-grey gaze shifted past her toward the entrance of the broch. "Tarl isn't with you?"

Fina halted. "No. I escaped An Teanga last night and came straight here." Her own gaze swept around the interior of the broch. Her mother, Lucrezia, stood before her alcove, her usually golden complexion suddenly pale. Their gazes met, and Fina's belly clenched.

She swallowed, turning her attention back to Galan. "Where's my father?"

Chapter Twelve

He Lives

GURTH WAS DYING. He'd taken a pike to the guts and now lay in agony, slowly bleeding out upon the damp ground. A misty rain fell in the gloaming. It settled over them in a fine veil, soft and cool.

Varar knelt next to Gurth, his gaze upon the warrior's haggard face. Around them sat the remnants of The Boar war band. One-hundred warriors had departed An Teanga two days earlier, but now there were barely thirty of them left.

"End it," Gurth muttered between clenched teeth. "I don't want to start screaming like a bairn. Finish me now."

Varar nodded. It was the least he could do. He reached down and unsheathed the knife he carried on his thigh. Around them the other warriors, many of them injured, went silent. Their chief was about to show Gurth a great mercy, an honor.

The chief and warrior's gazes met and held. There was no fear in Gurth's eyes. The pair had clashed more often than they had agreed, but Varar respected the man. He had fought bravely today. In fact, it was only when Gurth fell that Varar had emerged from the haze of battle fury. He had looked around him and realized that his remaining warriors were moments away from being encircled completely and butchered where they stood.

It was the hardest decision he had ever made—whether to battle on to the death, or flee and live to fight another day.

He had called his warriors to retreat, but the bitter taste of defeat soured his mouth. He had done it to save their lives, yet he now regretted it.

Better to go down fighting than run like whipped hounds. Only, he would never get his vengeance on these Cruthini if he died on the battlefield today.

"What will you do?" Gurth asked, each word an effort. His hands, slick with blood, clutched his abdomen.

"Gara and Bothan will have emptied the fort by now," Varar replied. His voice reflected his mood: flat, exhausted. "We'll find the others and head north."

"Will you go to The Eagle for help?"

Varar's mouth twisted at the suggestion, especially coming from the likes of Gurth. "With relations as they are ... I don't think so."

Gurth's face twisted, agony causing his big body to convulse. Varar shifted forward, his fingers tightening around the bone hilt of his knife. This was an unpleasant task. It was best not to linger over it.

"Wait!" Gurth gasped. "Before I die ... you need to know something."

Varar paused, lowering his knife.

Gurth drew in a trembling breath. His face was the color of milk, his lips grey. "The attack at The Valley of the Tors ... it didn't happen as you think."

Varar went still.

Gurth continued. "The Eagle ... they didn't attack first. We did. The raids on our villages, the stolen livestock, and the threatened hunting parties ... none of it happened. I invented it all."

Silence drew out, before Varar finally spoke. "Why?"

The warrior's face twisted. Even in agony and facing The Reaper, his loathing of The Eagle consumed him. "I had to have my reckoning on them," he rasped. "I hated Urcal for making peace with those bastards ... for letting Tarl and Donnel mac Muin humiliate us. I had to wait, but eventually I was rewarded ... in that valley."

Varar sat back on his heels. "Do you realize what you've done?"

Gurth grinned, the expression more a grimace than anything else. "Aye ... I've settled an old score. For Wurgest ... for Loxa."

Fool.

Varar's gaze locked with Gurth's. The warrior stared defiantly back up at him. He would never be sorry for what he had done; the hatred went too deep.

Varar's father had worked hard to keep the peace with their neighbors. Yet that alliance had been fragile. Varar should have worked harder to preserve it, instead of believing Gurth's tales. Did he even have the right to be outraged? Was he any different? He had been eager to believe The Eagles capable of treachery. He had not believed Fina when she had insisted they had not attacked.

"That's all I have to say," Gurth concluded. Sweat beaded his brow, and his eyes rolled back as agony seized him once more. "You can finish me now," he panted.

Varar stared down at him. He was tempted to let the man lie, to let him die in slow, excruciating agony. Make him pay for his treachery, for catapulting The Boar and The Eagle into conflict on the eve of a much greater threat.

Perhaps reading the expression on his chieftain's face, fear flickered in Gurth's eyes. He was not afraid of death it seemed, but of the pain that accompanied it. "Please," he croaked. "Don't leave me like this ... I beg you."

Varar hesitated. It was a sorry thing to witness, to see a man like Gurth reduced to begging. As much as his gut churned with rage right now, he could not let him suffer. He would give him a clean death.

Varar leaned over the warrior and raised his knife once more.

"Galan has called a meeting."

Fina glanced up to see her cousin, Talor, leaning against the door to the stall where she was grooming the sway-backed, old pony she had stolen. Her cousin's face was unusually solemn this afternoon, the strain evident. His blue eyes were shadowed, his mouth thinned. It gave a hard edge to his good-looks.

"What ... now?" Fina resumed grooming the pony in long sweeping strokes. The task calmed her. Learning that her father had gone after her, had shattered the joy she had felt at being home. Namet and Lutrin were also with him—and when her mother told her that the party had traveled northeast to Kyleakin, with the intention of arriving at An Teanga by boat, Fina knew what had happened.

Her father would have ridden straight into the path of the invading Cruthini.

Her mother had gone ashen when she too realized why Tarl had never returned. Fina was still struggling with the knowledge. She could not, would not, believe her father was dead.

"Aye, he's summoned us all." Talor replied softly. "Come on."

Fina stepped back from the pony, who was snatching hay from the manger next to him, and tossed aside the hog's bristle brush. She did not want to go back into the hall, did not want to see or talk to anyone. She needed to think, to plan. But if the chieftain had summoned them, she would obey.

The pair of them walked out into the yard. The morning rain squalls had ended; the sky was now colorless, and a wind gusted against the sturdy broch.

"We'll find him," Talor said. Fina glanced her cousin's way to find him watching her, his expression more intense than she had ever seen it. "We'll tear this isle apart until we do," he continued.

Their gazes fused, and Fina found herself blinking rapidly. She had not wept since hearing that her father had gone after her, and would not. Tears would not help Tarl, Namet, and Lutrin. Even so, Talor's words made her throat constrict. He was fiercely loyal; she did not doubt him for a moment. Forcing a smile, she nodded.

They joined the flood of men and women entering the broch and walked into the wide feasting hall which was now crammed full of the residents of Dun Ringill. Fina and Talor pushed their way to the front, taking their place near where Muin and his brother Aaron stood, while Talor's younger sister, Bonnie, pushed up behind them.

Seventeen winters old and clad in a short leather skirt and vest, Bonnie wore a determined look on her heart-shaped face this afternoon. She looked so much like her mother, Eithni, with walnut-colored hair braided into tiny plaits and wide hazel eyes. Yet the young woman had not followed her mother's path as a healer. Instead, she was a warrior, her body sinewy and strong.

Stopping next to Fina, Bonnie cast her a worried look. Yet the girl held her tongue.

Upon the raised platform before them stood Galan and his wife Tea. The chieftain's gaze was hard as it swept across the amassing crowd, his big leather-clad body tense. Donnel and Eithni stood nearby with their youngest daughter Eara, while the fort's seer, Ailene, waited at the bottom of the dais, hands clasped before her.

"Thank you all for coming so quickly." Galan's voice cut through the rumble of voices, hushing them. "Time is short so I will not waste it. I take it you have all heard of the menace that approaches our borders as we speak?"

A murmur of 'ayes', accompanied by grim looks, followed.

"The Boar rode out to face them two days ago," Galan continued. "Fina tells me that the Cruthini horde far outnumber The Boar war band. Varar and his warriors will have slowed their path, but they won't stop them." Galan paused here, his gaze shadowing. "Neither can we."

A stunned silence rippled over the interior of the broch at this announcement. Fina agreed. They had lost a number of warriors at The Valley of the Tors. Even calling in fighters from the surrounding villages, they could not gather a war band of more than one-hundred and fifty.

"The only way we'll survive this is if we unite with The Wolf and The Stag," the chief continued. "We need to face the invaders together, or they'll pick us off, tribe by tribe as they work their way north." Galan's gaze swept over the crowd of people before him. "I've sent out riders to Dun Ardtreck and Dun Grianan with instructions to meet us at the Lochans of the Fair Folk, three days from now."

An excited murmur went through the waiting crowd. Fina drew in a sharp breath. Galan's plan made sense— and yet she felt a stab of betrayal at the same time.

"What about my father," she called out. "And Lutrin and Namet. Are we going to abandon them?"

Galan's gaze swept to his niece. "No," he replied. "Never." A muscle ticked in his jaw. "But the best way to help Tarl and the others is to unite our strength with the folk of this isle. If they live, then they will be captives— spoils of war. We will need to plan a rescue carefully, if we want it to be successful."

"He lives," Lucrezia's voice cut in. Fina glanced right to see her mother standing alone to the right of the platform. Her beautiful face was gaunt, her dark eyes hollowed. "If Tarl was dead, I'd know it."

Galan's mouth thinned, and he nodded. "We'll get them back," he promised, his voice lowering. "Even if it means I have to slaughter my way into the enemy camp to do it."

Beside Galan, Tea nodded in silent agreement. Her face was taut, her eyes shining. "We'll all go," she added.

Fina drew in a shaky breath and looked down at the rushes beneath her feet. The love she felt for these people—her mother, her uncles, aunts, and cousins—rushed through her. She knew Galan had meant every word, and yet she hated having to wait here. She hated feeling so helpless.

"Ailene has cast the bones," Galan said after a pause, causing the murmuring in the hall to cease once more. "She has asked the Gods what lies before us."

Fina glanced up, her attention settling upon Ailene. Her friend had been watching her and gave a nervous smile. She had not long taken on the role of bandruí. This was the first time the chieftain had asked her to speak in front of the inhabitants of the fort.

"I cast the bones three times," she said, a slight shake in her voice betraying her tenseness. "In the first, the signs of The Wolf, The Eagle, and The Stag all fell together under a crescent moon." She glanced over at Galan. "This would mean that your decision to unite the tribes is a wise one."

Galan held her gaze, nodding. "And the second?"

The bandruí swallowed. "This one showed the bones bearing the signs of The Eagle and The Boar, side by side, overlapped by the mark of the selkie."

The hall went still, as did Fina. The selkie was a symbol denoting love and union."

"Does this mean the rift between our tribes will be healed?" Donnel spoke up, frowning. "After everything that's happened?"

Ailene nodded. "Aye … through marriage."

Fina suppressed the urge to laugh. "No one in their right mind would wed a Boar," she muttered.

Agreement rippled through the crowd surrounding her.

"And what of the third casting of the bones?" Galan pressed.

Ailene's pretty face tightened, and she licked her lips, her nervousness getting the better of her. "Perhaps I was mistaken in the reading," she murmured. "I wish Ruith were here ... she'd know better than me."

"Tell me what you saw," Galan pressed. "Ruith believed in your abilities, as do I."

Ailene heaved in a deep breath. "Two bones bearing the mark of The Bent Arrow upon a Crescent Moon, directly above and below the sign of The Eagle," she said. The young woman's voice was soft, yet it carried in the now silent hall.

Fina's belly clenched at this telling. Around her she heard indrawn breaths, while beside her Bonnie whispered an oath under her breath.

"Death and destruction," Ailene said after a pause, confirming Fina's fears. "Dark times are coming for The Eagle."

Chapter Thirteen

Leaving Home

FINA DID NOT want to leave Dun Ringill. It went against all her instincts to pack up her things and ride away from the fort.

She was not alone in her reluctance to abandon the fort. Outside the broch, a woman lifted her struggling child onto a wagon loaded up with sacks of provisions.

"I don't want to go, ma!" the lad wailed.

"Hush, Iain." The woman pushed him back as he tried to launch himself into her arms once more. "This is only a short trip ... we'll be home soon enough."

Her voice was brittle, unconvincing, and the boy was not fooled. He started crying in earnest, his wails echoing off the surrounding stone.

Saddling her pony in the yard before the broch, Fina's loosed a sigh. She did not blame the lad, although his screeching was stretching her already frayed nerves to breaking point.

Fina's gaze shifted over her pony's back to where Galan stood a few feet away. He was speaking with two of his most trusted warriors: Cal and Ru. They were staying behind with a small group of warriors to look after the fort.

"Make sure you keep scouts outside to watch the approach at all times," Galan instructed. "If the enemy nears, do not engage them. Leave and ride north to find us."

"What?" Ru's sharp-featured face tightened. "And leave the fort open to them?"

Galan frowned. "I'd rather that than have you and the others butchered."

"Maybe we should set fire to Dun Ringill?" Cal suggested. "Leave nothing for the enemy."

Galan shook his head. "No ... we'll be back."

A tense silence fell. Fina, who had given up all pretense of saddling her pony, witnessed the struggle on Cal and Ru's faces. She also saw the determined expression her uncle now wore.

Once Galan mac Muin made up his mind, he would not be moved.

Her pony, a grey gelding named Ceò—Smoke— snorted and stamped his foot. Fina hastily shifted back to avoid having her toes crushed. Unlike Fina, her mount was impatient to be off. After returning home from An Teanga, she had been relieved to find her pony safe. He had been with her that day at The Valley of the Tors. She had leaped down from Ceò's back not long after the battle started and had not seen him since. Fortunately, Muin had found the pony grazing on a hillside north of the valley afterward.

"Ready?" Muin appeared at Fina's shoulder, leading his feather-footed bay mare.

Fina cast him a sour look. "No ... don't tell me you're happy to leave?"

Muin shook his head, his face serious in the dawn light. "No one's glad of this, Fina," he reminded her. "But with a Cruthini horde bearing down on us, my father's only trying to save us."

Fina huffed, turning from him. She should have known better than to complain to Muin. He rarely disagreed with his father on anything.

She knew too that the weight of responsibility weighed heavily upon Galan. He would not risk having them massacred inside these walls. Part of her understood that. But the reckless side of her just wanted to face the enemy here.

The sun was rising into the eastern sky, gilding the hills beneath, when the people of The Eagle left Dun Ringill. It was a long, solemn-faced column. Warriors upon ponies led them and brought up the rear-guard, while most folk in the midst of the column traveled on foot. There was little conversation this morning, no laughter or smiles. Sensing the mood of the adults, children whined and bickered, their gazes wide with worry.

The travelers brought what they could with them— wagons laden with sacks and crates of food, and clucking fowl. Many people led their prized livestock, goats and sheep, yet they had been forced to leave much behind. The fields around the fort brimmed with produce, for the summer had been warm so far: kale, cabbages, carrots, and onions planted in long rows. The departing folk had picked as much of it as they could carry, but so much remained behind—fodder for the invaders.

Fina's gaze swept over the fields, before she twisted in the saddle and cast a long look over her shoulder at Dun Ringill. The broch sat outlined against the glittering waters of Loch Slapin. A thin column of smoke rose from the roof, the only remaining sign of life.

Her throat constricting, Fina swallowed. She could not bear the thought of the invaders taking her home.

"We'll return," Muin's voice brought Fina back to the present. She tore her attention from the fort and swiveled back to face him.

"I hope you're right," she muttered. "I hate not knowing exactly how many of those Cruthini are out there. What if more of them cross from the mainland?

Once they get a foothold in our broch, we'll never be able to turf them out."

"It's not like you to concede defeat so easily," Muin replied, his mouth curving.

"I'm not ... I'm just pointing out that it's easier to defend a stronghold than to attack one."

Muin dragged a hand through his long dark hair, his grey eyes turning pained. "I'm sure father took that into consideration before making his decision."

Fina gave her cousin a hard look. "I hope so ... or we're all doomed."

Varar found his people half a day out from An Teanga. They had taken shelter as night fell in The Valley of the Tors.

He reached the southern edge of the rocky vale and reined Guail in. His gaze swept down to the valley floor, where a cluster of hide tents huddled. From this distance it appeared a tiny community.

Varar clenched his jaw. It was. And with many of his folk in the northeast of his territory killed or enslaved by the Cruthini, it was also a precious one.

The Boar were now teetering on the brink. Another attack like the one he had retreated from and they would fall. There were a few remote villages, in the south-west extremities of their territory, which would take the enemy some time to reach. However, An Teanga was lost.

Pain lanced through Varar's ear, and he forced himself to relax his jaw.

He did not want to dwell on that, not tonight. The thought of those Cruthini turds sullying his fort made him want to choke.

Urging his stallion forward, he led the way down the slope toward the camp.

Morag came out to meet him. Her face was pale and strained in the dying light, her eyes haunted as she watched the war band approach. Varar saw the shock in her eyes when her gaze slid behind him, taking in the pitiful numbers that had survived the fighting. They were a bloodied, bedraggled company.

He was grateful that she did not comment on the graveness of the situation. He could count on Morag to know when to speak and when to hold her tongue. She had always been able to read him well.

Bothan and Gara emerged at the edge of the encampment moments later. Varar swung down from Guail and then turned to them. "An Teanga is empty?"

"It was when we left," Gara replied, her expression shadowed. "But the enemy will have the fort now." She paused a moment before continuing. "Is it safe to camp here?"

"For tonight it will be." Varar loosened his stallion's girth and slapped the beast upon his sweat-soaked neck. Guail had done him proud over the past days. The pony had not faltered once. "But we will need to be gone with the dawn ... the hounds are baying at our heels."

Varar turned from Guail and shifted his attention to Bothan. He fixed him with a hard stare.

The warrior's face tensed. "What is it?"

"Gurth fell ... but before he died he told me the truth about the attack against The Eagle."

Bothan paled.

Varar took a menacing step toward him. "You and the others who followed Cruim all knew, but you hid it from me."

"Gurth made us swear to keep it all a secret." To his credit, Bothan did not look away as he replied. However, Varar had never seen a man look so sorry. It mattered not though—Bothan had still deceived him, had betrayed his chief.

"I should kill you ... here and now," Varar growled.

Bothan's throat bobbed. He drew his sword from his hip and held it out to Varar, hilt first. "Aye, Varar ... you should." He then dropped to one knee before him.

Varar took the sword, his fingers flexing around the hilt. Rage thrummed through him, as it had ever since he had learned of Gurth's betrayal. He longed to strike out, to punish those who had done the warrior's bidding so readily.

Gara cleared her throat. "Varar ... we can't afford to lose Bothan. Our numbers are already too few."

Varar's gaze swiveled to Gara. He frowned. "You defend him?"

Gara shook her head. Her jaw set. "I'm thinking of us ... not him. We can't lose any more warriors or soon there will no Boar left."

Silence stretched between them. Varar was aware of his sister watching him, her gaze hooded. However, she still did not speak. Morag would let him make his decision without her counsel.

Varar turned back to Bothan. "I'm taking your sword," he growled. "From now on you'll fight in the back ranks with a pike." He saw Bothan's gaze gutter. He had just stripped the warrior of his honor—a fate worse than death.

"Varar," Bothan rasped, his voice breaking. "I—"

"Enough." Varar turned his back on him. "We're done ... from now on, keep out of my sight."

After seeing to his pony, Varar went in search of his tent. His temples throbbed, his body ached, and his skin—caked in the blood and sweat of battle—itched. His feet felt as if he had rocks strapped to them, and his eyes stung with fatigue. He had to lie down. He had barely slept in two days.

Night had fallen in a cool, misty curtain. It was silent in the valley, save for the occasional snort of a pony or the low timbre of the voices of the sentries standing guard on the edge of the camp. The weight of the tors pressed down upon Varar, pitch-black shapes against the dark sky.

His confrontation with Bothan had soured his mood, but he was also uneasy, making camp here in no-man's-land. Circumstances had given his people little choice. Tomorrow, they would be forced to enter Eagle territory.

His brooding made him think of Fina. She would get her wish to return to her kin after all. However, Galan mac Muin's welcome for The Boar was likely to be a bloody one.

Stuck between two enemies, Varar would have to choose.

He grimaced. The Eagles it would be.

Varar had almost reached his tent, the largest of the conical structures situated in the heart of the camp, when he caught sight of his sister walking toward him. Morag wore a woolen shawl about her shoulders to ward of the night's chill. Her expression was pinched.

"It's late," Varar greeted her. "You should be resting."

"I'll join Frang shortly," she replied with an impatient shake of her head. "But I need to speak to you first."

Varar stopped before his sister. "What is it?"

Morag raised her eyebrows at the shortness of his tone, but continued. "If you're hoping to find that Eagle woman warming your furs, you're going to be disappointed."

Varar tensed. "Where is she?"

"Gone. Somehow she must've got hold of a knife. She threatened Eachann when he went to tend her, and got free."

Varar spat out a curse. "Didn't you send anyone after her?"

"Aye," Morag shot him a quelling look, "but the woman runs swifter than a deer. They never caught her."

Varar took a step back and sought to calm the seething fury within him. His temper was already on a short leash today; hearing about Fina's escape just about untethered it.

He glanced back at Morag and saw she was watching him with a look of thinly veiled disapproval. "What now?" he barked.

Morag folded her arms under her breasts, raised her chin, and looked down her nose at him. As his elder sister she had done that a lot while they were growing up, whenever he did anything that displeased her. Varar did not appreciate the look now, not tonight.

But Morag was not remotely intimidated by the baleful look he gave her. "Are you vexed because you had your own plans for that wench?" she asked coolly. "Or because you no longer have something to hold over The Eagle?"

Varar breathed another curse. "What does it matter?"

He moved, heading toward his tent. The oblivion of sleep beckoned, a void where he would not have to think, rage, or worry about what lay ahead. He had just reached the flap when Morag's voice brought him up short.

"I take it you intend to go before Galan mac Muin tomorrow and ask for his help?"

Varar twisted, glaring back over his shoulder at his sister. "What's wrong with you tonight?" he growled. He had been grateful earlier when she had not questioned him—but it appeared she had merely been saving her interrogation for when they were alone. "You seem determined to enrage me."

Her mouth curved. "I wouldn't if you'd just answer my question," she replied. "I want to know where we're going tomorrow."

Varar met Morag's eye then. "Dun Ringill, of course." The name of The Eagle fort stuck in his craw. "Get ready to watch your brother crawl."

Chapter Fourteen

Bend or Break

THE RAZOR-EDGE BULK of the Black Cuillins loomed overhead as Fina climbed the path to the Lochans of the Fair Folk. Even in the midst of summer, the mountain range was a forbidding sight. It seemed as if those mighty peaks had been carved out of coal, their dark outline etched against a pale blue sky.

Fina heard her destination before she saw it, a distant rumble that grew steadily louder as she climbed. The path had gotten so steep that she had been forced to dismount Ceò and lead him the rest of the way. Muin had done the same, leading his mare behind him. They had set off from Dun Ringill at first light, and the day was now waning as they approached the pools.

"How much farther?" Muin called out.

Fina huffed. He had asked her that three times since they began the climb. "Nearly there."

A few moments after she had spoken, Fina crested the top of the hill and caught sight of the first waterfall. A foamy cascade thundered down a grey cliff-face. The fall created a soft mist that caressed Fina's face, soothing her nerves. Traveling usually calmed her, but with each furlong north, she had worried increasingly about her father's fate. She wanted to believe he was still alive, prayed to The Mother that it was so. And yet part of her feared the Cruthini had butchered him and the others.

"That's more like it." Muin had stopped next to her, his gaze sweeping over the glittering pool. His cheeks were flushed from exertion, sweat beading his brow. Fina was sure she looked just as hot and bothered. It had been a sultry afternoon with not even a light breeze to cool their faces. "I could dive in."

Fina cast him a rueful look. "Wait until we reach camp or you'll hold everyone up." She tugged at Ceò's reins. "Come on, lad."

They skirted the pool, winding their way alongside the babbling River Brittle to where the rest of the lochans—or pools—lay. A magical spot, ringed in grey stone with lush green hillside behind, the Fair Folk were said to bless this place. Blood had never been shed here; it was a safe and sacred location for the tribes to meet. Here, they would plan their campaign against the invaders.

The column of travelers, snaking its way up the hillside, stopped before a large pool filled with limpid blue water. A great stone arch framed one side of The Wishing Pool, as it was known. Fina's chest constricted at the sight of it.

Tonight she would kneel before the pool and make a wish to the Gods on behalf of her father. If there was any place where they would be listening, it would be here.

The Eagles were the first to arrive at the meeting place, and as such, they set about making camp: a sea of hide tents that spread across the hillside behind the pools.

Fina and Muin helped take care of the ponies, watering them at the pools before tethering them nearby. As she rubbed down Ceò, Fina cast a thoughtful glance in her cousin's direction. With each passing year, Muin reminded her more and more of his father. He had the same hawkish features and storm-grey eyes. He had also inherited Galan's steady temperament. Tea had passed her fiery nature on to his younger brother, Aaron.

In fact, a few yards away, Aaron was now bickering with Talor.

"I say we should pitch them here, close to the water," Aaron insisted.

"Higher ground is better," Talor replied with a shake of his head.

"Why?"

"It's safer."

Aaron, who had just started to grow his first beard, snorted and folded his arms over his chest. "From what?"

Talor raised an irritated eyebrow. "You get a view of the pathway from higher up. We need to be able to see who's coming."

"And we need to be able to access the pools."

"For the love of The Mother," Talor growled, his already limited patience giving out. "Don't argue, boy. Just pitch the tents where you're told."

"Don't talk down to me. I'm not a bairn."

Talor snorted. "A bit of fluff on your chin doesn't make you a man."

Muin and Fina shared a look, before Muin's mouth twitched. Then, his gaze shifted toward where Ailene, clad in a plaid skirt and leather vest, walked toward them carrying skins of water. The seer grinned at him, holding up one of the skins. "You look like you could do with this?"

Ailene stopped before them. Holding her gaze, Muin took the skin with a smile. "Thank you."

Ailene dipped her head before holding the other skin out to Fina. "The Wolf is here ... our scouts have just spotted them climbing the hill. They'll be at the pools shortly."

Fina nodded. That was welcome news. The sooner the others got here, the sooner they could focus on rescuing Tarl, Lutrin, and Namet. The Stag had a bit farther to come, but they were likely to reach the pools by the following morning.

"It'll be good to see Wid again," Muin said, his gaze still upon Ailene. "It's been too long."

The smile he had given Ailene had faded, and he now watched her with a serious look that made Fina wonder whether Muin harbored some secret passion for the comely seer. They were not related; Ailene was Talor's cousin, for their mothers had been sisters. There was no barrier to a union between Muin and Ailene—only Ailene's complete lack of interest in the chieftain's hulking son.

Fina frowned. She hoped she was wrong in her suspicions. She did not want Muin pining over a woman he could not have.

A horn blew then, the long wail echoing off the surrounding stone. The Wolf had announced their arrival.

Varar's first view of Dun Ringill surprised him.

He had always thought of his home as having a beautiful setting on the edge of a deep blue loch, yet this fort outshone his. The broch perched on a headland, looking out over a wide stretch of water. Layers of mountains lay to the south, while the mighty shadow of the Black Cuillins rose far to the north.

The second thing that took Varar by surprise was the emptiness.

The fields leading into the fort were vacant, the carefully tended rows of vegetables abandoned.

So this is Fina's home. The thought of his former captive soured his mood. It was probably for the best that she had escaped, for it would make his confrontation with Galan mac Muin easier. Even so, losing her still galled him.

The stone arch on the outer perimeter was unguarded, and as Varar led the way up the path toward the inner perimeter, he saw that the village beyond also lay empty. No smoke rose from the turf roofs, no children played in the dirt. The silence was eerie.

"Where is everyone?" Gara pulled up her pony next to his before the gates leading into the broch. "It's as if a plague visited this place."

Varar opened his mouth to reply when a man's voice, hard and unwelcoming, split the air. "State your business here, Boar."

Varar glanced up to see a warrior, clad in plaid and leather, standing atop the wall. The man held a bow at the ready, the arrow pointing directly at Varar's chest.

Slowly, Varar let go of the reins and raised his hands, a sign that he came in peace. "An Teanga has fallen. I bring all that is left of our people north ... to seek your aid."

The warrior, an older balding man, sneered. "I wish Galan was here to see this: The Boar slaughter our warriors and then come asking for our help."

Varar drew in a deep breath. Every furlong that had brought him closer to Dun Ringill had galled him, and the bowman would know it too. However, with the fate of his people in the balance, he could not let his feelings show. "So Galan isn't here?"

"No."

"Where is he?"

The bowman eyed him coldly, his arrow not shifting an inch. "Why should I tell you?"

"Because hundreds of Cruthini are but a day away. We don't have time to play these games ... and neither do you."

A chill silence stretched out, before the warrior finally spoke. "The tribes are uniting. The Eagle, The Wolf, and The Stag are meeting as we speak."

Varar's pulse quickened at this news. "Where?"

The man stared back at him, his jaw tightening. He was on the cusp of refusing to reply. Then, he loosed a sigh. "The Lochans of the Fair Folk."

"They won't welcome us," Gara pointed out as they rode north a short while later, leaving Dun Ringill behind. "You do realize that?"

Varar swung his gaze toward the warrior. "Aye. That's why I'll leave you and the others at the base of the hills and go up to speak to Galan alone."

"That's madness," Frang interrupted. The two warriors rode either side of him, leading the column of thirty warriors and another thirty or so men, women, and children from An Teanga, many of whom traveled on foot. "They'll kill you for sure."

"Frang's right," Gara said. "Take some of us with you at least."

Varar shook his head. Around them the light was starting to fade. They would have to make camp soon and would not reach the lochans until the following day. "They're more likely to welcome me if I go alone," he said. It was only partly the truth. The real reason he did not want the others there was that going before Galan would be humiliating. He did not want Frang or Gara to witness it.

"I don't like this plan," Gara replied. Her raw-boned face had gone hard, her gaze flinty. "We've never needed the other tribes of this isle, and we shouldn't start now. The Boar deal with their problems alone."

Varar huffed a breath. His father had always said that The Boar were loners. "That was before the Cruthini landed on our shores," he said after a pause. "Things are different now ... so we need to change too. Shunning others won't work for us anymore."

Frang spat on the ground. "You can't trust an Eagle— and The Wolf aren't any better."

"Aye," Gara agreed. "I wouldn't put my life in the hands of The Stag either these days. Fortrenn was a friend of The Boar, but his son has never been."

Varar let out a soft, humorless laugh. "You might both be right, but the fact remains that these people are all we have. We have to bend, or we will break."

Chapter Fifteen

Loss

FINA TURNED THE spit over glowing embers, ensuring that the grouse was evenly cooked on both sides. The gamey aroma of roasting meat wafted up from the fire, one of many that glowed around the camp.

Her gaze shifted over the figures huddled around the surrounding fires. The mood was subdued this eve. There was an air of dread—so different from other gatherings that usually took place here. The Lochans of the Fair Folk was a sacred spot, the location of handfastings and celebrations. No blood had ever been spilled here, and yet the following day it would witness a council of war.

As soon as The Stag arrived, the discussions would begin.

Releasing a sigh, Fina glanced over at her mother. Lucrezia was staring into the fire. For the first time ever, she noticed the signs of age upon her mother's face. Lucrezia had incredible bone structure, but her high cheekbones seemed more pronounced this evening, and there were lines around her eyes and either side of the mouth that Fina had never noticed before.

Wordlessly, Fina reached out her free hand and placed it upon her mother's knee, squeezing gently. Lucrezia looked away from the fire, the distant look in her dark eyes vanishing as she focused on her daughter. When she spoke, her voice was husky, tired. "I hate this waiting ... I want to be ... out there searching."

Fina nodded. "It takes all my will not to ride off to find him," she admitted. "I'm sure Talor and Muin would come with me if I asked."

The two women's gazes locked. "I'd come with you too," Lucrezia replied firmly.

Fina's mouth quirked. She sometimes forgot that her mother was a warrior as well. She had once been the pampered wife of a Roman centurion. Meeting Tarl mac Muin had turned her world upside down. Lucrezia still trained sometimes, although these days she focused more on tasks such as gardening and cooking.

"I know you would," Fina said gently.

Her mother glanced away, her eyes guttering.

Silence fell between them. Fina's throat contracted. Lucrezia had never recovered from the loss of her three sons: Bradhg, Fionn, and Ciaran. All of them had been born after Fina, but none had lived beyond their fifth winter.

The sadness of those losses had a cast deep shadow over the happiness of their family. Fina had worried that her brothers' deaths might cause a rift between her parents. She had thought they would cast blame on each other, even if they both knew that none of the deaths were their fault. However, she had underestimated the depth of her parents love for each other. The union had remained strong, so strong in fact that there had been times when Fina felt excluded.

It was as if they needed no one besides the two of them.

Fina eventually broke the heavy silence. "As soon as the discussions tomorrow are over, I will ask Galan again," she assured her mother. "He promised me that he would go after them. We can't leave it much longer."

Restlessness filled Fina after supper. Lucrezia retired to her tent early, her mood dark. The change in her mother worried Fina; she was strong, and yet Tarl's capture had made her grow distant. She wanted to reassure her, and yet she knew there were no words that would make this right—just action.

She hated feeling so useless.

Agitated, Fina left the fireside and wandered in amongst the sea of tents and glowing hearths. Leaving the edge of the camp, she approached the pools, where the sound of rushing water soothed her. At the edge of The Wishing Pool, she knelt and retrieved a pebble. Clutching it tight, she closed her eyes.

She did not pray to the Gods often, not like some folk did. She was always too busy for such things. She liked to make her own luck. Kneeling to the Gods and asking for their benevolence felt so passive.

It seemed selfish to call upon them now, but such was her need—her welling desperation—that she cast aside her hesitation.

"Great Mother," she whispered. "Keep my father, Namet, and Lutrin safe from harm. Look after them." Fina paused, swallowing the lump in her throat. "Warrior of the Earth and Sky ... guide my blade in the coming days. Give me the strength I'll need to bring them safely home."

Opening her eyes, Fina drew her arm back and threw the pebble far into the pool. It landed with a hollow thunk and sank into the cool depths.

"I made a wish of my own earlier." A female voice roused Fina. She glanced right to find Ailene standing behind her. Her friend's lush figure was outlined by the firelight, the flowing waves of her dark hair cascading over her shoulders.

Fina favored her with a tight smile. "Let's hope the Gods are listening then." With a sigh, she lowered herself onto the ground and crossed her legs. "Sometimes I think they're deaf."

Wordlessly, Ailene lowered herself down next to Fina. "Aye," she replied softly. "So do I."

Fina cast her a sharp look. Of course, Ailene was no stranger to loss. She had been barely four-years old when her father had died suddenly. He had simply collapsed one day and died moments later. Her mother had never recovered from losing him. The Reaper took her four years later too after she developed a wasting sickness that even Eithni's skill could not heal. The seer, Ruith, took Ailene in after that and had raised her as her own.

"Our lives are so hard," Fina said after a long pause, her voice a whisper. "So brutal ... so fragile."

"Aye, and so fleeting," Ailene added.

Fina studied her. It was impossible to make out Ailene's expression, for they were facing away from the fire, and her face was cast in shadow. Yet Fina could hear the edge to her voice. Earlier in the day, Ailene had appeared so confident. Not so now.

"Ailene," Fina began slowly. "Are the telling bones ever wrong?"

Ailene sighed. "Ruith warned me not to believe all they showed me," she admitted. "Sometimes they can mislead you ... or be open to interpretation. Much also depends on the bandruí who casts them." Ailene paused here, and when she spoke once more, her voice was hushed. "I wish she was still with us. She'd be much better at this. I'm out of my depth."

"No, you're not," Fina countered. She had seen Ailene cast the bones a few times and was in awe of her friend's wisdom and intuition. "You did well ... and we're going to need your skill in the days to come."

The Stag party arrived mid-morning. One hundred and twenty warriors, each bearing a tattoo of a stag upon their right bicep, filled the dell around the fairy pools as they unsaddled their horses.

Fina stood amongst the crowd that encircled the clearing on the edge of The Wishing Pool, where the chieftains would meet. Flanked by Talor and Muin, she watched The Stag's chief's arrival. Tadhg mac Fortrenn was a big man of around forty-five winters with greying brown curly hair and a short beard. Leaving his pony to be tended by his warriors, Tadhg strode across to where Galan and Wid mac Manus, Chieftain of The Wolf, awaited him

Tadhg embraced Galan, before Wid crushed him in a bear hug of his own. "I wish we were meeting in happier circumstances." The Stag chieftain drew back, his face grim. "Is it as bad as the messenger told?"

Galan rubbed a hand over his face. "Aye ... I'm afraid so. There are hundreds of them. None of us can face the Cruthini on our own. We must band together or soon we'll be slaves."

"Or dead," Wid muttered. Fina had never seen the dark-haired Wolf chieftain look so tense.

"How many warriors have we got if we unite?" Tadhg asked, his blue eyes narrowing.

"Close to three hundred and fifty," Wid replied, "if we call everyone who can wield a sword, axe, or pike to arms."

Tadhg's frown deepened. "That's not enough. What of The Boar ... why aren't they here?"

A tense silence fell over the clearing.

Fina clenched her jaw at the name of her enemies. She had been distracted since arriving back at Dun Ringill, yet she had not forgotten their treachery.

"They rode out to meet the invaders," Wid said, breaking the hush. "We don't know what became of them."

"Slaughtered, I hope." The words were out of Fina's mouth before she could stop them.

Tadhg mac Fortrenn's gaze snapped up, spearing her.

Galan cleared his throat. "Tad ... this is Fina, She's Tarl's daughter."

"You probably haven't heard," Fina replied, ignoring the warning look that Galan gave her, "but The Boar attacked one of our patrols recently. I was the only survivor, and they took me prisoner. When they marched off to battle, their healer helped me escape."

The Stag chief's eyes widened. "Why would The Boar attack you?"

"Because they're cunning, false bastards."

"Fina," Galan cut her off, a warning note in his voice. He turned his attention back to Tadhg. "We've been having problems with them for over a year. But the situation is worse than my niece describes it. My brother took a party out to rescue Fina but never returned. We believe the Cruthini captured them."

Tadhg's face hardened, before he glanced back at Fina. She saw sympathy shadow those blue depths. His reaction made Fina clench her jaw. "He's not dead," she muttered. "We're going to get him back."

The Stag chief nodded, and then he shifted his attention back to Galan. "It's a pity about The Boar," he murmured. "We could have done with their help."

Galan opened his mouth to reply when a warrior shouldered his way through the crowd. He bore the mark of The Wolf on his right bicep.

"Dom," Wid greeted the newcomer with a frown, irritated at being interrupted. "What is it?"

The warrior's gaze swept over the three chieftains before resting upon Wid. "The Boar ... they've come."

Shock rippled across the crowd. Fina stared at The Wolf warrior, wondering if she had misheard.

Galan was the first to recover. "What?"

"Around sixty of them, warriors and families. They've stopped at the base of the hill. Their chief has gone ahead ... Varar mac Urcal is on his way up here to speak to you now."

Chapter Sixteen

Rage

VARAR MAC URCAL lives.

The knowledge had a strange effect upon Fina. Fury swamped her, turning her hot and then cold, and yet the sensation was edged with a faint relief.

I will get my chance for reckoning after all.

Her heart started to pound, sweat beading upon her skin. She could not believe her luck. That bastard had balls to show his face here—but he certainly made things easier for her. This way she would not need to hunt him down.

The crowd before the three chieftains drew back to reveal a tall, broad-shouldered figure approaching. Varar, clad in plaid leggings and a leather vest, bore no weapons. His hands hung loosely at his sides. As he approached, Fina saw the marks of recent battle upon him. One of his arms was bandaged, and a thin cut snaked down his right cheek.

And yet, the injuries did not detract from his attractiveness.

Damn him to eternal torture, but The Boar's presence seemed to suck the air out of the clearing. He walked slowly, but with supreme confidence, shoulders thrown back as if this place belonged to him.

Fina flexed her hands and wished she carried a weapon on her. She would gut him where he stood.

Varar's penetrating gaze swept the clearing, the tiny hoop earring on his left earlobe glinting in the sun. And for an instant his attention paused upon Fina, before he focused upon the chieftains who stood awaiting him at the edge of The Wishing Pool.

Fina let out a low growl and took a step forward. Beside her, Muin shifted. His hand clasped around her arm. "Not now," he murmured.

Varar walked into the clearing and stopped a few yards before the other chieftains.

"Boar," Galan snarled. "You made a mistake coming here."

And with that the chieftain of The Eagle lunged.

A gasp went up. Tadhg reached out to stop Galan, but he was too quick. He had already reached Varar, crashing into him with such force that both men toppled backward onto the ground.

Fists flew. Snarling and cursing echoed across the glade.

Out of the corner of her eye, Fina saw Tea elbow her way forward. Like the other wives, she had been observing the meeting from the edge of the crowd.

"Galan," Tea called out, but her husband was oblivious now to her.

Fina watched the fight, taken aback. She had never seen her uncle like this—unleashed.

Controlled, calm, and even-tempered Galan fought like an uncaged beast. And Varar matched him punch for punch.

The two men went at each other in a fury that made the surrounding crowd draw back. Muin stepped forward to stop them, but Tea reached out and hauled her son back. "Leave them," she ordered, her voice low and fierce. "You'll get hurt if you intervene."

Over and over the two men rolled, kicking, punching, and gouging. Oblivious to all else, they hurtled down the pebbly bank and fell into The Wishing Pool.

Neither of them seemed to notice their surroundings. It was only when Varar ended up on his back and The Eagle chief pushed him under the water that the fight shifted.

Danger crackled in the air. Fina glanced askance at Tea, before her attention shifted to the two other chiefs looking on. Neither Wid nor Tadhg had moved to intervene. Nonetheless, both men wore tense expressions.

The Wolf and Stag chiefs exchanged looks. Galan and Varar were disrespecting this sacred place by fighting, yet neither of them seemed to care.

A few yards away, Varar kicked up savagely, his knee jamming into Galan's belly. His opponent did not let go, but Galan lessened his grip for an instant.

It was enough for Varar to twist out from under him. The Boar chief rose spluttering from the water and slammed Galan under him.

The floor of the pool fell away sharply just a couple of feet from the edge. Both men disappeared under the surface in a frenzy of violence, turning the once glassy surface into a frothing whirlpool.

Donnel stepped forward, approaching Wid and Tadhg. "One or both of them is going to drown if this continues," he pointed out.

Galan and Varar resurfaced, both gasping for breath, before they started slugging at each other once more. Galan punched Varar in the mouth, sending his opponent's head snapping back.

"Aye," Tadhg replied, never taking his gaze from the pool. "And although I understand your brother's anger ... killing Varar isn't going to help us. We need him alive."

"No we don't," Fina spoke up. "Let someone else lead The Boar. We'll never be able to trust that snake."

Tea gave her a quelling look, odd coming from a woman who had never been timid about speaking her mind. Fina knew her comment was vengeful and bloodthirsty, yet she wished she could take Galan's place.

She wished it was *her* fist that had just smashed into Varar's arrogant mouth.

In the pool, Galan went under as Varar got him in a head lock.

Tea's full lips thinned. She glanced over at where Donnel stood, his storm-grey eyes riveted on her. "Go on then," she muttered. "Haul them out."

Donnel strode forward, motioning to Wid and Tadhg. "Muin, come with us."

"I'll help too." Talor stepped forward and followed Muin toward the pool's edge.

"No," Donnel replied. "Four is enough."

Talor halted, his handsome features tightening. However, he did as bid, stopping at the side of the pool.

What followed next might have been comical if Galan's killing rage had not been so real.

It took all four of them to separate Galan and Varar. Despite that he had not begun the fight, Varar's blood was now up. He snarled and cursed at Galan as Wid and Tadhg yanked him back. Likewise, Galan struggled to free himself from Donnel and Muin's iron grip.

They dragged the two chiefs back to the edge of the pool and dumped them around five yards apart on the pebbly bank. Tadhg and Wid positioned themselves between them, for both Galan and Varar still wore murderous expressions and looked as if they would lunge for each other's throats again if given the chance.

"Enough!" Tadhg panted, pushing his long wet hair off his face. "This isn't helping us."

"He's right." Wid massaged his shoulder, where Galan had accidentally struck him during the scuffle. "This is what the Cruthini want … us fighting amongst ourselves. If we keep this up, they won't have to defeat us in battle. We'll do the work for them."

Wid's comment made the excited crowd settle.

A few feet away Varar spat out a gob of blood. "Aye … that's why I'm here," he rasped. "An Teanga has fallen.

The Cruthini have my people's land. The same will happen to yours if we don't join together."

"You're here not because you want to help us, but because you *need* our help," Galan snarled. The rage still had not left him. "You broke the peace, murdered my people, and took my niece as hostage. Don't talk as if we matter to you."

As Galan spoke, Tea drew near him. She did not reach out to touch her husband to try and pacify him. And yet he noticed her nearness. Galan's gaze shifted from Varar, focusing on her for a moment. His expression changed, a little of the savagery fading. However, his gaze was still hard as it swept back to Varar once more. "No words for that, eh Boar? ... I thought not."

Fina inhaled deeply. Varar sat just a few yards away. She longed to lunge at him and fasten her hands around his throat.

Look at me, you bastard. Let me see the treachery in your eyes.

And yet Varar did not glance her way. Instead, he continued watching Galan. The Boar wore an expression she had never seen on his face. During her time in An Teanga, he had either looked vaguely bored or supremely confident. But there was no arrogant smirk now, no dismissive gaze.

A muscle ticked in his jaw; tension laced every line of his body. His dark-blue eyes were shadowed.

Galan rose to his feet, swaying slightly. Tea was at his side in an instant, supporting him.

"Weasel," Galan snarled at Varar. "Eithni should have slit your throat all those years ago. You shame your father's memory."

Varar had not reacted to Galan till now, yet Fina saw him flinch at these words. He too rose to his feet, as unsteady as Galan. Yet no one moved to assist him. "I'm here to put things right," he said finally. There was a rasp to his voice. Fina could almost believe the bastard was telling the truth, that he was sorry. Almost.

Galan's face was hawkish in his fury. "You can't."

With that, The Eagle chief turned on his heel, pushed away from his wife, and stalked off through the crowd.

Silence followed.

Varar was sitting alone on a boulder by The Wishing Pool when Eithni approached him.

Tadhg mac Fortrenn had sent warriors down to escort The Boar survivors up to the Lochans of the Fair Folk, and the crowd had dispersed. He had seen Fina go too, although not without casting him one last hate-filled glance.

"Hello Varar." The healer stopped before him, her basket under her arm. Varar had not seen her since the last Gathering of the Tribes. Small and fey with thick, walnut-colored hair and hazel eyes, the woman's heart-shaped face appeared ageless. "Can I take a look at you?"

Varar surveyed her. He did not want to be rude to this woman, and yet her presence was like salt in an open wound.

Eithni should have slit your throat all those years ago. You shame your father's memory.

Vicious words, they had struck home in a way Galan's fists never could. The Eagle had known that.

As if reading his thoughts, Eithni's mouth curved. "For all it's worth, I don't regret saving your life."

Varar snorted. "You'd be the only one here who feels that way."

Eithni sighed. "Give them all a bit of time to cool their tempers. Emotions are running high at the moment." She took a step closer. "Your bottom lip needs looking at."

"I've got a healer with my people," Varar replied. "Eachann will be here soon."

Eithni's face lit up. "I look forward to seeing him again." She moved closer still and placed the basket down. "But I can take a look now … since I'm here?"

Varar huffed, wincing as pain lanced through his lower lip. "You don't give up easily, do you?"

Eithni's smile widened. "Donnel says I can be even more bull-headed than him … he's probably right." She busied herself with the contents of her basket, wetting a cloth and dripping a tincture onto it before raising it to his mouth. "This is going to hurt at first."

Varar nodded, and she pressed the cloth to his mouth. He bit down, stifling his reaction as a burning pain lanced across his lip. A dull throb set in; his bottom lip felt three times its normal size. His eyes smarted, and he blinked rapidly.

Seeing his reaction, Eithni favored him with an arch look. "Men," she murmured as she dabbed carefully. "If it's any consolation, Galan's torso is going to be mottled with bruises by tomorrow."

Varar gave a snort in response. It hurt to breathe, and he wondered if he had suffered a cracked rib in the fight. He had never met his match till Galan mac Muin attacked him. Even over twenty years his elder, The Eagle chief was a formidable opponent. "So will mine."

Chapter Seventeen

Restless

FINA COULD NOT sleep.

She was too angry, too restless. How could she rest when Varar mac Urcal and his people were here at the lochans? Despite Galan's reaction, despite the fact her chief had avoided the newcomers for the rest of the day, she knew he would eventually soften. Once his anger had subsided, and Tadhg and Wid counselled him, he would join with The Boar.

The thought made Fina grind her teeth.

She tossed and turned in her furs. It was an airless, humid night, and despite that she slept naked, her skin was damp with sweat.

Finally, after she had changed position for the umpteenth time, Fina cursed and sat up.

It would not do.

She had to deal with this. She had to face him.

Working by feel, for she had no brazier burning in her tent, Fina donned her skirt and vest. She also strapped her hunting knife to her thigh. Then, she slipped out of her tent into the darkness.

It was late. The camp slumbered, the smoke from the dying peat fires drifting up into an overcast sky. There would be almost a full moon out tonight, yet the clouds obscured it. Torches burned around the perimeter of the camp casting a faint gold glow over the huddled outlines of the tents. Warriors were keeping watch beyond, and the chieftains had also put sentries out at intervals down the hill. If anyone crept up on them, they would know it.

Fina padded barefoot through the slumbering encampment toward the eastern perimeter. The Boar had made camp there, in the only remaining space, the farthest spot away from the pools. There were still a few Boar warriors awake, a handful of men sitting near a central fire pit. No doubt, The Boar were on edge tonight, for they did not trust The Eagle. Word of Galan's fury must have worried them. They would fear an ambush in the night.

Slipping around the back of the tents, Fina crouched in the shadows. Her gaze scanned the group by the fire, but she did not spy Varar among them. However, she did spot Frang—the red-faced warrior who had insulted her back in An Teanga.

Unfortunately for Morag, he had survived the battle with the Cruthini.

Fina's gaze narrowed at the sight of him. Once she dealt with the chief, that turd would be next.

Varar was not hard to find; the chieftain's tent sat in the midst of the group, rising high above all the others. It sat only a few yards back from the fire so Fina could not risk slipping in through the entrance. Instead, she crept round to the back.

Drawing her hunting knife, she paused. The night was still. Surely the men sitting nearby would hear her cut a hole in the tent?

A moment later laughter exploded at the fireside in reaction to something Frang had muttered. Seizing her chance, Fina deftly slit the hide.

The sounds of mirth faded and stillness settled once more. Yet it had been sufficient. Fina had cut a hole large enough in the side of the tent for her to wriggle through. Still gripping the knife, she dropped onto all fours and entered the tent, moving with the stealth of a stalking wolf.

Inside, she rose to her feet and looked around.

Unlike her tent, which was tiny, this space indeed belonged to a chieftain. It was bigger than the huts of most folk. A brazier sat in the center of the space, the glowing embers casting a reddish hue over the interior. But despite its grandeur, the tent was unadorned.

A pile of furs lay to Fina's right, and on it sprawled Varar mac Urcal.

Fina's fingers flexed around the hilt of her knife, and she moved forward. But a few paces toward the furs, she abruptly halted.

It was a warm night, and Varar slept naked atop the furs, his chest gently rising and falling. The sight of him made her stop breathing.

The Mother save her, no man had the right to be that beautiful.

She was no maid. He was not the first man she had seen naked, and yet the sight completely threw her; for a few moments she even forgot why she was here. Instead, her gaze drank him in: the long planes of his virile body, the intricate circles and patterns of the tattoos covering the left side of his chest and shoulder, and the ridges of muscle in his belly that led down to the matt of dark hair between his legs where his manhood rested against a thigh.

Fina's mouth went dry, and a strange melting sensation flared in her lower belly.

"Have you looked long enough?" A sleepy male voice drawled. "Or shall I give you more time?"

Fina snapped out of her reverie, her gaze sweeping to where his eyes had opened. Varar was now watching her through half-shut lids. His eyes, partly veiled by long eyelashes, were dark, amused.

"Cur," Fina growled. She could feel a flush creeping up her neck. He had caught her blatantly staring at him. Hot humiliation thrummed through her. "I'm here to cut your throat."

"But you thought you'd admire me first?"

There was no fear in his voice, and he made no attempt to cover himself, or even reach for a weapon. Instead, Varar merely watched her. His lower lip was swollen, a crust forming where Galan's knuckles had split it. His abdomen was mottled with purpling bruises from the fight. But even battered, his sensuality disarmed her as it had back in An Teanga.

Fina swallowed. She hated him for it.

An instant later she was kneeling over him, her knife pressed to his throat. "I was deciding whether to kill you fast or slow," she lied.

Varar's mouth curved. The expression made him wince as his lip pained him. He seemed wholly unconcerned that she was holding a blade to his naked throat and that one sharp movement and his blood would be spilling onto these furs.

"And what did you decide?" he asked.

"Fast ... that way I don't have to listen to you plead."

His eyes glinted. "Very well ... but before you end me, Fina. There's something you must know."

"Get on with it then," she growled, pressing the flat of the knife harder against his windpipe.

Varar swallowed. She could feel the tension in the big body under hers, although he had not reached up to try and stop her. Instead, his hands still lay by his sides. "You were right," he murmured, holding her gaze. "About the attack. The Eagle didn't start it."

Fina arched an eyebrow. "Convenient for you to admit that now."

"I didn't know the truth until recently. Gurth admitted it ... before he died. Apparently he had been causing trouble between our tribes for some time. He nursed his revenge for years against your people. My father let the past go, but Gurth never could."

Fina's lip curled. He must think her dull-witted to believe such a tale. "So you're telling me you had no idea?"

"It's the truth. Gurth didn't tell me because he knew I'd never agree to the attack."

"So noble." The words tasted like ash in her mouth. There was nothing noble about this man. He was as cunning and treacherous as the other Boar, and he deserved to die.

Their gazes locked. "I'm sorry, Fina," he said. This time there was no trace of arrogance in his voice, no humor. "For the loss of all the warriors, your people and mine, in that valley. It was senseless. Gurth was a fool."

"And you were an even greater one for believing him."

"I was."

Fina glared down at him. "Why didn't you speak of this earlier … in front of the other chiefs?"

His mouth quirked. "It wasn't the time. They wouldn't have believed me."

"And I will?"

"Look into my eyes and tell me I'm lying."

Cunning Boar. Of course when she looked into those dark-blue eyes she saw only honesty—but that meant nothing. He was a practiced liar.

"Still your tongue and prepare to die," she growled. "I've heard enough."

Silence stretched out between them, before Varar spoke once more. "You won't kill me."

Anger cramped her belly, and her grip on the bone hilt tightened. "What?"

"You're not a butcher, Fina. You won't kill an unarmed man."

"Conceited stoat … just watch me."

"You know the truth now," he reminded her, his voice low. "You won't do it."

The blade wavered. A fraction to the left and she would pierce his skin.

A heartbeat passed, and then another. Finally, Fina reared back off him with a curse, yanking the hunting knife away from his throat. The Reaper take him, he was right. She could not do it.

As much as she hated him, she could not kill him.

Shame filled her, making her feel sick. What kind of warrior was she if she could not end the life of a man like Varar mac Urcal? He deserved to die. Galan would have finished him if given the chance, why could not she?

Fina scrambled back, edging toward the hole in the tent's side. Varar propped himself up on his elbows and tracked her progress.

"Fina ..."

"Enough ... not another word." She reached the side of the tent. "This changes nothing, Boar." Fina spat out the words with as much venom as she could muster.

The way he raised an eyebrow then, the look of pure masculine arrogance settling upon his face, made her tremble with rage. She despised him, yet she loathed herself even more for her weakness.

Ducking out of the tent, Fina crept away into the shadows, face burning.

Inside the chieftain's tent, Varar let out a long exhale and sank back down onto the furs.

His heart was pounding like a Bealtunn drum. He wiped his damp palms on the fur and ran a hand over his face. That had been a risk, one he never wished to take again. The rage in Fina's eyes had been a thing to behold as she loomed over him and held a knife to his throat. For a few instants he had believed she would actually do it, that he had miscalculated.

And then she had pulled back.

Fina had looked at him with loathing then, her eyes glittering with the force of it.

Varar closed his eyes and heaved another deep breath.

Gods, she was magnificent. He had never seen such a beautiful woman. Fina had intrigued him at An Teanga, but now she was free, she mesmerized him. She was as dangerous as a kelpie—a creature who could take human form before dragging their victims down into lochs to their death.

But as dangerous as she was, he wanted her.

Chapter Eighteen

Time Is Against Us

"THEY ARE ORGANIZED, highly-trained, and desperate. We should avoid facing them in open combat."

Varar's words caused a stir amongst the gathered crowd. Folk muttered, some exchanging dark looks.

"Coward," a man growled.

"What can you expect from a Boar?" another warrior grumbled.

Looking on, Fina checked Varar's face for a reaction. Nothing.

The four chiefs had gathered in the clearing by The Wishing Pool. Galan sat crosslegged on the ground, flanked by Tea and Donnel, while Muin, Talor, and Fina stood behind them. Likewise, the other chieftains sat with their kin. Wid sat to The Eagle chief's right— accompanied by his wife, Alana, and their two strapping sons. To Galan's left sat Tadhg and his wife, Erea. Their two daughters stood behind them.

The Boar sat opposite The Eagle. Morag knelt next to her brother. Behind her stood Frang and a heavy-set female warrior.

The rest of the gathering stood back, leaving a respectful distance for the council to discuss matters.

"What would you have us do then?" Wid asked, his tone challenging. "Would you have us tuck our tail between our legs and run?"

This drew snorts of derision from onlookers, but none of the other chiefs reacted. Fina was standing behind Galan, so she could not see his face. But Tadhg mac Fortrenn did not look amused.

Varar gave Wid a long, cool look. "At best, we have no more than four hundred warriors—they have many more than that. They are mobilized, driven, and united in their purpose. We are not."

Silence fell after these words. The Boar chief let them lie for a few moments before he continued. "I've faced the enemy. They like to fight on open ground, to use their great number to their advantage. We need to push our own strengths."

"And what's that?" Tadhg asked.

Varar shifted his attention to The Stag chief. "They don't know this land like we do. Our people have farmed and hunted upon this isle for centuries. We know every valley, every hillock. These landmarks need to become our allies."

"You want to draw them into a trap?" Galan spoke up for the first time. His voice was low, with a harsh edge to it, yet civil.

Varar met his eye. "Aye. We meet them in the open, feign a retreat, and push back to an area where we can trap them and lay an ambush."

The crowd around them stirred, this time in excitement.

Fina drew in a deep breath. She was loath to admit it, but Varar's idea had merit.

"Go on then," Tadhg replied. "Tell us more."

Varar heaved himself up off the ground, stifling a wince as he did so, and moved to the center of the clearing. There, he retrieved a stick, knelt down, and drew a picture in the dirt. He traced the outline of the lobster-shaped isle, before making a cross upon its southern edge.

"After they have secured An Teanga, they will march north-west to take Dun Ringill."

Varar drew a line from An Teanga up to the west coast and marked another cross. He then glanced up at Galan. "How many warriors did you leave there?"

Galan's broad shoulders tensed. "Twenty. Two of my best, Ru and Cal, lead them."

Varar's mouth thinned. "Then you've left them to die."

"They have orders to leave the fort if the Cruthini approach," Galan growled back.

The Boar chieftain's mouth curved into a bitter smile. "Then they should be on their way here now ... the enemy was no more than half a day behind us."

A tense hush followed this proclamation. Fina's skin prickled. She hoped Ru and Cal had obeyed Galan.

Varar turned his attention back to the map he had drawn in the dirt. Fina's gaze tracked him as he drew a line northeast toward the Black Cuillins. "They will know we have all fled north, and they will track us. They may have already started."

Fina's belly clenched. He was right. They would have to move out soon. The Lochans of the Fair Folk was not the place for combat.

"I suggest that we ride out to meet them," Varar continued, drawing the stick south and then east. "But we take them inland before we do so. After the first encounter, we fall back, drawing them into the interior. Unbeknown to them, we will have already sent a portion of our army ahead." Varar drew a cross at the heart of the isle. "We lead them into Bodach's Throat ... where we close the trap."

Fina swallowed. She glanced over at Talor, briefly meeting his eye. Her cousin's face had tensed, while next to him Muin was scowling. That valley was a cursed place. An evil old man who was said to lure travelers to their death had once lived there. These days not even hunters would enter the valley.

"Couldn't we try somewhere else?" Wid asked, scratching his stubbled jaw, his gaze wary. "Surely there are other valleys?"

"Not any so perfectly positioned," Galan replied, speaking up once more. "Bodach's Throat has high rocky sides, with boulders our warriors can hide behind. It's perfect."

Varar glanced up, his eyes glinting. "Aye, it is."

"I'd rather not lead my warriors into that dark place," Wid replied, his tone sharpening. He was observing Varar, his gaze narrowed. "Why don't we draw them north? The Kraikish Gorge is a better place for an ambush."

Wid's words made Fina tense. That gorge had been the sight of the last bloody battle between The Wolf and The Eagle over two decades earlier. Both Galan and Wid had fought there. The Eagle won that day, but both chieftains had fallen. The battle had been a turning point for relations between the two tribes, the start of a long road to peace.

"The Kraikish Gorge is too distant," Varar countered. "The Cruthini won't follow us that far north."

"He's right," Galan admitted reluctantly. "They'll know it's a trap."

Another hush settled, before Tadhg spoke. His gaze was shuttered, although he wore an expression of grim resignation. "Does anyone have any other suggestions?"

Galan and Wid exchanged glances, while around them a low mutter rose from the crowd. "In other circumstances we'd discuss tactics for days," The Stag chief continued, cutting through the chatter and causing it to die away. "But time has run out. I say this is the best plan we've got. I vote for it."

"As do I," Varar replied, casting aside his stick and rising to his feet.

A few feet away, Wid screwed his face up. "It seems I'm outnumbered," he grumbled. "I'd better not live to regret this."

All gazes shifted to Galan then, and a watchful, expectant silence settled. Galan turned his head, his gaze meeting his wife's. Tea stared back, her chin rising as she gave him a slight nod.

"Bodach's Throat it is," Galan said, his expression turning hawkish. "We pack up camp now and ride south."

A gold-hued dusk settled over craggy hills, bringing another warm day to a close.

Tarl barely noticed the sunset. He stumbled, his feet dragging with exhaustion, as he followed the tide of Cruthini north. Around him rose the gilded outlines of great mountains. Bruach na Frithe and Sgurr nan Gillean to the east, and Sgurr Dearg to the west. The rough terrain had slowed their path north.

Hands bound before him, naked to the waist, and stripped of his boots and weapons, Tarl stopped at the brow of a hill. He drew in gulps of air. The army had pushed hard since leaving An Teanga, driving north while a large band of warriors had split off and ridden west toward Dun Ringill.

Tarl's blood had chilled as he watched them depart. He had been unable to think about anything else as the day dragged.

His bare shoulders had burned in the sun, and his feet were now bleeding. His back throbbed from where one of the Cruthini warriors had taken a whip to him at An Teanga.

He had initially expected the invaders to torture him, Lutrin, and Namet for information. But they had not. They seemed to already possess a reasonable knowledge of the isle, including the location of An Teanga and Dun Ringill.

Frustration pulsed within Tarl. He had to get free. He had to warn Galan and the others.

Lutrin and Namet staggered to a halt next to him. Lutrin was sporting a black eye, and Namet was limping. Both of their rugged faces were stone-hewn.

"Looks like we're stopping for the day," Namet panted.

"Aye," Tarl replied. "The Cruthini are mortal like the rest of us it seems … even they have to rest."

"They're mortal alright," Lutrin snorted. "And once I get free and slit a few throats I'll prove it."

A vicious smile twisted Tarl's face. Like Lutrin, it was the same thought that kept him going.

Below them the Cruthini army started to make camp. He watched the hide tents push up like mushrooms from the valley floor, and a short while later the scent of peat smoke wafted up into the humid air.

Cathal mac Calum's people appeared to be used to living this way, to changing location every night.

"Move on, lads." A big man with bushy red eyebrows and short hair strode up to the three Eagles. He carried a heavy braided leather whip in one hand. "Cathal wants a chat with you tonight."

Tarl scowled at the warrior and spat on the ground before forcing his tired limbs to move on.

The three of them picked their way down the slope, leaving the other captives behind. There were around a dozen of them now; the others were men and women of The Boar who had been taken from outlying villages as the invaders passed through. Those who had survived the attacks, who had not had time to flee.

Tarl wove his way into the center of the camp, in-between tightly-packed tents. On the way, he studied his captors: their lean faces, high cheekbones, and tall, muscular frames. They were well-armed, many carrying enough iron to take down a charging boar: knives, axes, pikes, and heavy swords.

What was their story? Had they come to The Winged Isle looking for more territory or had they been driven out of their own?

Tarl wanted to know more about these people—it was hard to fight a mysterious enemy.

A large hearth burned in the center of the encampment, at the lowest point of the shallow valley. The chieftain's tent sat around five yards back from it, a massive conical structure.

Cathal mac Calum stood before it, awaiting them. A dark-haired, stocky warrior of middle years stood next to the Cruthini leader; the man watched Tarl with fierce eyes. Something about the warrior seemed familiar to Tarl. Had he seen him somewhere before?

"It's a fair isle your people have," Cathal greeted them with a wide smile, drawing Tarl's attention back to him. "We shall enjoy living here."

Beside Tarl, Lutrin gave a low growl. Namet said nothing, while Tarl cast a withering look at the Cruthini leader. "What is the name of your tribe?" he asked.

"We are the people of The Serpent," Cathal rumbled. He was still smiling, yet his green eyes were not friendly. He motioned to the tattoo that curled its way down his right arm, from shoulder to elbow. "Beware our venomous bite."

This comment drew laughter from the surrounding warriors.

Tarl ignored them all, his gaze still riveted upon Cathal. "Aye, serpents indeed ... slithering across our land, defiling it."

The Cruthini chief's smile faded. "Your land no longer, Eagle." Cathal's gaze snapped up then as he spied movement farther down the valley. Warriors were approaching. Tarl's breathing stilled when he realized it was the war band that had gone off to Dun Ringill that morning.

"What news?" Cathal greeted his warriors. He ignored his captives for the moment, his attention wholly focused on the man and woman who stopped before him and swung down from their ponies—Lutrin and Namet's ponies. Tarl recognized the auburn-haired woman. She was Cathal's daughter.

"The Eagles have moved on," the woman announced, "The fort is now ours. We've left a company of warriors behind to defend it."

Cathal's gaze narrowed. "That's not enough ... send another two companies to help guard it. I'll not risk losing Dun Ringill should the Eagles decide to fly home."

His daughter nodded, her expression shuttered. "Aye, father."

Tarl swallowed. A pressure built in his chest. *Galan has abandoned the fort.* He knew his brother would not have taken the decision lightly, but now their home was in the hands of the enemy. At least the tribe was safe for the time being.

"You can take what doesn't belong to you, but it will never be yours," he growled at Cathal.

The Cruthini leader smirked. "High ideals won't save your people, Eagle. Dun Ringill belongs to whoever has the balls to defend it. Your brother is clearly a eunuch."

Tarl lunged forward. His wrists were bound, but he could still inflict harm. He would wipe that grin off Cathal's face.

He never reached him.

The heavy-set, swarthy warrior left Cathal's side and smashed into Tarl, driving his shoulder into his chest. Tarl toppled backward and landed hard on the rocky ground.

Pain lanced across his sunburned and whipped back. Tarl rolled to his feet, only to find the warrior before him, dagger drawn.

"Calm down," he warned. "Or you'll find this in your belly."

Tarl grew still. The man spoke their tongue with a local accent. He noted then, the faded tattoo upon the warrior's bicep. *A Boar.* Tarl's blood chilled as he realized how Cathal had known the location of the isle's strongholds. "Traitor," he growled.

A tense heartbeat passed, before Cathal's voice cut in. "Aye ... Tormud's one of us now."

The Boar smiled—a feral expression. Casting Tarl a lingering, hungry look the warrior stepped aside so that Cathal could face his captive once more.

There was no humor on the Cruthini leader's face now, just anger. He took the whip from the red-haired warrior and unfurled it. Blood stained the plaited hide dark.

Cathal advanced on Tarl. "Tormud's been of great use, but there are some things he doesn't know." He raised the whip high. "Tell me ... how many does your tribe number these days?"

Chapter Nineteen

The Rescue Party

FINA STRODE THROUGH the camp and approached the clearing where the chieftains stood, deep in conversation. Around them the united army of the tribes settled down for the night. To the west the sky blazed gold.

As she neared, Fina recognized the faces of two men talking to the chiefs. Her step faltered as her pulse accelerated. Cal and Ru. Both their faces were haggard, and Galan's expression was thunderous.

Dun Ringill has fallen.

A sickly sensation crept over Fina. She paused, drew in a steadying breath, and focused her attention on her uncle. This was not the right moment to interrupt him— but she was sick of waiting.

Galan was not looking at her. He was listening to Wid.

Fina strode up to her uncle and halted before him. "You promised me we'd go after him," she said, cutting

The Wolf chief off mid-sentence. "It has to be tonight, or it'll be too late."

Galan scowled. "Fina ... now isn't—"

"We've waited long enough," she countered.

Fina was acutely aware that Varar was watching her. His gaze pulled at her; it took all her effort not to look his way. Instead, she clenched her jaw and kept her attention focused upon her uncle.

Galan was now scowling. "I haven't forgotten about Tarl, Lutrin, and Namet," he replied. His voice was low, a definite sign his patience was being tested. "However, we've got to plan for tomorrow's battle."

Fina crossed her arms over her chest and lifted her chin. "We need to get them out before then. Before it's too late."

"What's this?" Varar spoke up. Of course—he did not know of her father's capture.

She ignored him.

Much to Fina's irritation, her uncle dragged his gaze from hers and glanced over at The Boar chief. "After you took Fina captive, her father went after her," he said coldly. "The Cruthini have Tarl and two others ... if they are still alive."

"He *is* alive," Fina insisted, panic rising in her chest as she said the words. She did not like the despair she saw in Galan's eyes.

The Eagle chief muttered an oath, before dragging a hand through his hair. "I shall go tonight," he announced. "I'll take Donnel, Muin, and Talor with me."

Fina stepped closer, her anger flaring. "I'm going after him too."

"We can't spare you, Galan," Tadhg interrupted. "The Eagles can't lose their chieftain on the eve of battle."

"Let Fina go," Wid agreed. "She's got as good a chance as any of rescuing them."

"Talor and Muin have already agreed to come with me," Fina added.

Galan's gaze narrowed. "Gods," he rasped. "You're even more stubborn than your father."

Fina huffed. "It's one of his finest qualities."

Galan's eyes glistened. "Aye ... sometimes."

"I'll join your rescue party." Varar spoke up, interrupting them.

Fina started, before she turned, looking at The Boar chieftain for the first time. His expression was inscrutable, yet his gaze was determined.

"No, you won't," she snapped. "We don't need your help."

"Keep out of this, Boar," Galan added. His voice had dropped to a low, threatening growl.

Varar ignored the Eagle chief. Instead, he kept his gaze upon Fina. "Your father is captive because of me," he reminded her. "If relations are to improve between our people, you need to let me help you."

Fina's lip curled. "I don't *need* to let you do anything."

"We can't afford to lose you either, Varar," Tadhg pointed out. "The chieftains need to be united tomorrow."

"And we will be." Varar cast him a cocky smile. "I intend to be alive to see the sunrise." His gaze shifted back to Fina. "And so will your father."

Fina hugged her mother tight. Likewise, Lucrezia clung to her. When she pulled back, her mother's cheeks were wet. "Promise me you'll both come back to me."

Swallowing the lump in her throat, Fina nodded. She wished her mother would not ask such things. She reached out and grabbed one of Lucrezia's hands, squeezing tightly. Her fingers were chilled despite the warm evening. "We'll see you at dawn."

Lucrezia heaved in a ragged breath. "I'll be waiting."

Stepping out of her mother's tent, Fina scrubbed at an errant tear trickling down her cheek. The desperation in her mother's eyes was like a blade to the heart. She could not stand to see such pain.

"Ready?" Talor asked. He and Muin were waiting for her. Clad in dark plaid breeches and leather vests, knives strapped to their waists and thighs, they both wore forbidding expressions.

Fina knew why.

Wordlessly, she nodded, her attention shifting to where a tall, leather-clad figure with short dark hair strode toward them.

"Why is he coming with us?" Talor growled.

"He insists we need him," Fina replied.

"Well ... he's the only one of us who's actually faced the Cruthini," Muin pointed out.

Fina cast Muin a hard look. Trust him to be the voice of reason.

"Sensible words," Varar answered, stopping before them. "Scouts have just returned with word on the Cruthini camp. They're in the hills north of Loch Coruisk, around fifty furlongs south-east of here."

Talor's gaze narrowed as he considered this information. "Good ... the terrain is rocky; there will be plenty of places for us to leave the ponies and sneak into the camp."

"Aye, it'll be harder for them to chase after us too," Muin added.

"And slower for us as well," Fina pointed out.

Varar smiled then. "There's a full-moon out tonight ... and we know the land. I'd say we have an advantage."

"Just as well," Talor grumbled. "We need one."

They left the camp without fanfare, and without saying goodbye to anyone, save Fina's hurried farewell to her mother. It was better that way, better no one realized they were gone. Only the sentries guarding the camp watched them go.

Their ponies trotted in single file under the silvery light of a full moon. Talor led the way, with Varar close behind him. Fina followed The Boar chief while Muin brought up the rear. They did not speak, save for necessities; it was a still night, the sort of eve when noise traveled.

The first stretch of the journey south was easy, over undulating hills. However, once they reached the mighty shadow of Bruach na Frithe, their pace slowed. It was here that the far edge of The Black Cuillins reached their highest eastern point: a jagged series of dark-grey rocks that thrust skyward like the carnassial teeth of some great predator. Bathed in moonlight, the mountain ridge looked otherworldly.

Fina's gelding, Ceò, was in a lively mood this evening. He jogged along, impatient to lengthen his stride. Fina had to rein him in tightly, her gaze scanning their surroundings as she rode.

The scouts had warned them that the Cruthini had sent out sentries of their own north of their camp. To avoid being spotted, the party cut east, hard against the pebbly foothills of Bruach na Frithe, before looping back toward Loch Coruisk.

Around ten furlongs from their destination, the riders drew up their ponies and tethered them in a narrow vale studded with chalky grey rock. From here they would travel on foot, for there would definitely be sentries about this close to the enemy camp.

The moon shone down, but Fina noted that a pink-hued halo surrounded it. A moonbow: a warning of coming bad weather.

Fina followed the others, her gaze sweeping over her surroundings. She had good night vision, better than most, and with the aid of the moonlight could pick out her surroundings easily. Even so, the stillness of the night put her on edge. There was no whine of the wind to mask their passing. Every scuff of their feet on rock, the crunch of loose shale, seemed obscenely loud.

They spoke in whispers and only when necessary.

They soon encountered their first Cruthini sentry. The warrior stood with his back to them, his head and shoulders silhouetted against the sky. Talor crept up behind him and took the man down with a knife to the throat. Leaving the dead sentry where he lay, they crept on.

A short while later they entered a wide, rock-strewn valley with a creek.

The babble of the water over smooth rocks was a welcome distraction after the eerie silence. It also muffled their footsteps. Crouching low, so that their silhouettes would not easily be spotted from afar, the party of four inched west.

They encountered three more sentries, each dealt with swiftly before they could cry out and sound the alarm.

Then, in the distance, Fina spotted a glow of light. A row of torches blocked their way into the camp. Just inside, she could make out the outlines of warriors guarding the perimeter.

The four of them stopped, gathering in a huddle.

"What now?" Talor whispered. His gaze was on Varar. "Any idea on how to get us inside?"

Varar grinned back, his teeth gleaming in the moonlight. Fina marveled at his arrogance, his unshakable self-confidence. Unlike Fina's companions, whose faces were tense, their brows furrowed, The Boar chieftain looked as if he was enjoying himself. "Aye," he whispered back. "But you're not going to like it."

Talor's mouth thinned, making it clear he did not like much about Varar mac Urcal in general. "Out with it then."

"Two of us need to provide a decoy and distract the perimeter guards while the other two slip into the camp."

"Have you lost your wits?" Muin whispered. "Why would we deliberately alert them to our presence?"

"Because unless we do, none of us is going to get inside that camp."

"And who is going to be the bait?" Talor asked.

"You and Muin," Varar replied. "Fina and I are going into the camp."

Chapter Twenty

Resolve

"YOU DON'T GIVE the orders here, Boar," Talor growled. "Why don't you let them hunt *you*? Let's see how fast you can run."

"Enough," Fina cut in, careful to keep her voice to a whisper. "Varar's right. We won't get inside without a distraction. You and Muin are both faster than me. Take them into the hills before you lose them, then circle back to the ponies. If we don't join you before the moon sets, ride for camp."

Silence drew out between them.

"I don't like this plan," Muin grumbled. "Two isn't enough to go in and free them."

Fina smiled. "As soon as we free my father and the others there will be five of us," she reminded him. "Just focus on drawing the guards away from the camp and not getting caught. We'll take care of the rest."

She made it sound easy, even though they all knew it was not.

Yet the truth was that now she was here, her blood was suddenly up. Every nerve in her body, every muscle, felt alive, coiled for action like it did when she went into battle.

There was no fear, just resolve.

Her cousins both bestowed her with looks of disbelief. However, they did not argue with Fina this time. Time was short. They needed to act now.

They split up—Fina and Varar creeping down the northern bank of the creek. The waterway entered the camp between a gap in the torches.

Meanwhile, Muin and Talor rose to their full height and moved south. Fina could not see them, but she knew they had only moments before the guards spotted her cousins.

She and Varar sank into crouches, crawling forward to the far edge of the torchlight. They could not go any farther without being seen.

Now, they had to wait.

"Hey, you!" A man's bellow rang out across the valley. "Halt!"

Fina held her breath. Muin and Talor had been spotted.

An instant later warriors emerged from the perimeter. Men and women brandishing pikes, axes, and long knives, their gazes trained south where they had spotted the intruders.

"Enemy scouts!" someone shouted. "Get them!"

Just ten yards from where Fina and Varar crouched in the shadows, a tall female warrior with wild hair that glinted red in the torchlight halted, swung a bow off her back, and slotted an arrow.

Fina tensed. She had not expected them to use bows, not at night. The bow sang as the woman loosed three arrows in quick succession. But no cry or sound of impact followed.

It was too dark for the archer to sight her prey properly.

A moment later Fina felt a tap on her shoulder. "Now," Varar whispered, his breath feathering against her ear. "Go."

Tearing her gaze from the shapes that hurtled south after her cousins, Fina sucked in a breath, pushed herself up off the ground, and sprang forward. She sprinted along the creek bank, leading the way.

Moments later she was past the perimeter of torches. She just had time to dive into the shadow of the nearest tent, Varar at her heels, when another knot of warriors marched in from the center of the camp.

"What's up?" One of them called to the sentries left behind.

Distracted, the men had been watching the chase and had not noticed the shadows slip into the camp behind them.

"Intruders ... two of them. They won't get far," came the gruff reply.

Fina twisted her head round, her gaze alighting upon Varar. He pointed west. She nodded back, and together they began their journey, moving from shadow to shadow toward the heart of the camp.

Somewhere in this sea of hide tents was Tarl mac Muin.

Fina had to find him, and fast.

Tarl was dozing by the fire, unable to sleep, when the sound of a nearby scuffle roused him. Wincing as fire lanced across his back, he sat up.

His body ached, and his back burned. Cathal mac Calum was brutal with a whip. He had wanted to know how many Eagle warriors followed Galan, where they would be heading now, and the state of their relationship with The Wolf and The Stag. Still, he had not gotten much information from Tarl. What little he had given to Cathal was false.

Cathal was no fool though, he had known Tarl was feeding him lies. Eventually, he had kicked Tarl to the ground in a rage and spat on him. He then warned him that they would speak again in the morning. And next time there would be no mercy.

Tarl did not doubt the Cruthini leader. He had a sinking feeling that the coming dawn would be the last he would ever see.

Despite exhaustion pulling down at him, the throbbing in Tarl's back had made it near impossible to sleep. As such, he had heard the sharp intake of breath, followed by a grunt. Then he heard the scuff of feet.

Tarl swept his gaze around him. The hair on the back of his neck prickled; something was most definitely up.

Stretching out his leg, he nudged Namet awake. The warrior sat up, blinking. Tarl held a finger to his mouth and motioned to where Lutrin still slept. All three of them needed to be awake.

Namet had just roused Lutrin when two shapes detached themselves from the shadows and crept toward them. When Tarl had lain down earlier before the hearth, there had been three sentries standing guard in that direction. There was no sign of them now.

The space around the fire was deserted, but a few yards away hunched the chieftain's tent. Cathal slept within earshot if any of them made the slightest noise.

Tarl tensed as the two silhouettes drew nearer.

Joy flooded through him at the sight of his daughter's face.

Fina wore an expression that reminded him of Lucrezia, a look of grim determination. However, Tarl's joy faded when he recognized the man with her.

Tarl had not seen Varar mac Urcal in years, but he knew him instantly nonetheless. He had the same look about him as his uncle Loxa: dark, brooding, and arrogant.

Tarl met his daughter's gaze, his own eyes questioning. Fina gave him a look that told him she would explain everything later, before kneeling in front of him. She cut through the ropes that bound his ankles and wrists.

Varar pressed a knife into his hand.

Tarl's fingers closed around the hilt and the pain in his back ceased to matter. Nor did he care that The Boar chieftain was helping free him.

This was their chance—they would not waste it.

With both Lutrin and Namet freed, and armed—for their saviors had brought an armory of knives—Fina motioned for them to follow her.

Tarl hesitated. He was tempted to go to Cathal mac Calum's tent and kill him, yet such a move would be risky. If he wanted them all to get out of the camp alive, they had to go now.

Fina led the way east, through the sea of tents and smoking fire pits. As he followed her, Tarl glanced up at the sky. The moon was sinking toward the horizon; they did not have much time left before it set. They needed to be far from this camp before dawn broke, or the Cruthini would catch them easily.

They passed a number of dead warriors on their way toward the perimeter. Fina and Varar had killed their way across the camp in order to get to them. However, Tarl could now hear shouting behind them.

Ahead, Fina increased her speed, darting like a brownie from shadow to shadow. They had lost their element of surprise, of stealth. The only way they were going to get out of this camp was to fight their way out.

A group of warriors met them as they approached the eastern perimeter. Tarl spied the glow of pitch torches up ahead, where a wall of flesh and muscle stood between them and freedom.

Fina and Varar launched themselves at their attackers, blades glinting dark with blood.

A moment later Tarl, Lutrin, and Namet followed suit.

All three men were weakened from lack of food, beatings, and days of journeying barefoot behind the Cruthini army. But now battle fury ignited in Tarl's veins.

Pandemonium reigned around them: shouting and the thunder of running feet. Many here thought the camp was under attack.

They needed to make the most of the confusion.

Tarl saw the fury with which The Boar chieftain cut down his assailants. He wielded two blades, dispatching the enemy with chilling efficiency. Tarl too unleashed his own fury, one that burned as high and bright as a Gateway fire.

They would get out of this nightmarish place. He would return to his people and help bring these invaders to their knees.

However, for each Cruthini warrior they cut down, three more appeared to replace them. The perimeter seemed to draw farther away, mocking them.

Sweat gleamed upon Fina's arms as she stabbed and slashed. She cut down one man before drawing her blade across the throat of the next one to attack her. She was relentless, magnificent, and yet she would eventually tire.

They all would.

All of a sudden, cries split the night. The barrier of bodies between them and the perimeter of torches drew back.

Tarl spied two figures, hacking and slashing their way through the fray toward them.

Muin and Talor.

Muin wielded a long blade, while Talor swung his axe with deadly precision.

The distraction was all they needed.

"Run!" Varar grunted.

The five of them bolted for the gap between two torches where a creek flowed through the valley.

Tarl's feet slid on mossy stones, but he barely noticed. He was flying, close at Fina and Varar's heels as they followed Muin and Talor into the darkness.

Chapter Twenty-one

Collecting Stones

FINA'S HEART WAS pounding so hard it felt as if it might burst out of her chest. Her breathing now came in ragged pants, and nausea clawed at her throat. Exhaustion was nearing—she had never run so far or so fast.

Glancing over her shoulder, she spied three figures pounding along at her heels. Her father, Lutrin, and Namet had kept up with them.

"Not far now," she rasped, daring to speak for the first time since they had fled the camp. "The ponies are up ahead."

And just as well, for the moon had set and the sky to the east was starting to lighten. They were nearly out of time.

Behind them angry shouts and cries echoed through the stillness. The Cruthini were out there searching for them with torches. Fortunately, they did not have dogs with them, or they would have tracked them by now.

Ahead, the large rock they had tethered the ponies behind loomed against the lightening sky.

Fina's vision swam in relief. She was not sure how much longer she could run. Her step faltered, and she stumbled. She would have sprawled headlong, if a strong hand had not fastened around her upper arm and hauled her upright.

"I've got you," Varar grunted. She could hear the same exhaustion she felt in his voice.

Fina was too tired to fight him off, or to snarl at him not to touch her. She hoped the ponies were still there—without them they would never get away.

Fortunately, their mounts were exactly where they left them. Swiftly, they loosed the tethers and vaulted onto their backs. Tarl rode behind Fina, Lutrin behind Muin, and Namet behind Talor. Only Varar rode alone. The extra weight would slow them, but these ponies were hardy and used to carrying burdens.

"I thought I told you to meet us back at the ponies," Fina told Talor as they reined their mounts north.

Her cousin snorted. "We knew you'd need our help."

"We lost those sentries easier than we thought," Muin added.

"It's just as well you arrived," Tarl croaked from behind Fina. She could hear the exhaustion in her father's voice. "We'd never have made it out otherwise."

"Let's save this conversation till later," Varar interrupted. "We're not out of danger yet."

Fina felt her father's body stiffen behind her. "One of your people has betrayed us, Boar," he rasped. "He's Cathal mac Calum's right hand ... told him exactly where to find An Teanga and Dun Ringill."

Fina glanced right at Varar; his face was cast in shadow, but his eyes gleamed. "What?" The question came out in a growl.

"Surprised, eh?" Tarl sneered. "*I'm* not."

Fina shifted in the saddle. She could hear the voices of their pursuers, see the glow of torchlight to the west. The Cruthini were getting nearer.

"Come on," she cut her father off, for she felt him draw breath to say more to Varar. This was not the time for a confrontation. "Let's ride."

Urging their ponies on, they trotted out of the valley. The land was rocky, the earth unstable underfoot. They could not risk traveling any faster until the dawn light showed them the way.

Leaving the feet of the mighty Bruach na Frithe at their backs, the party rode out onto rolling hills that stretched north. The craggy spine of the Black Cuillins marched alongside as they pushed their ponies into a gallop. Ahead, the mountains curved west, forming a cradle where the camp of the united tribes would be stirring. The morning sky blazed red. A Blood Dawn. Like the halo around the moon the night before, it promised bad weather was on the way.

It also promised death and destruction.

Varar reined in his stallion, allowing Fina and Tarl to draw up alongside as they rode into the camp. It looked like everyone had been up since the first blush of dawn. The tents had already been taken down, and folk were readying the ponies and wagons to move out.

Varar glanced over at Fina, hoping to meet her eye. However, her gaze remained fixed ahead, at where Galan walked out to meet them.

Tarl swung down from the pony's back and strode toward his brother. They hugged, and when they drew back, The Eagle chieftain's cheeks were wet with tears.

Varar watched the brothers' reunion with interest. He had heard of the bond between the mac Muins, although since he did not have a brother of his own, he had never understood it. He was close to Morag, yet the bond was not the same.

His father had been the eldest of three brothers. But Wurgest and Loxa had not been the men Tarl and

Donnel were. His father had never spoken kindly about them after their deaths. Loxa especially had shamed their people.

"Tarl!"

A raven-haired beauty with golden skin sprinted toward them. Her hair flew out behind her like a flag. Lucrezia. Varar had spotted her a couple of times since his arrival at the Lochans of the Fair folk. Then, she had hung back from the crowd, her face pale and strained. Now she appeared a different woman as she reached her husband and flung herself into his arms. It was as if years had suddenly erased from her face.

Tarl picked Lucrezia up and swung her round, his wife's plaid skirts billowing around her legs.

"I thought you were lost," she gasped.

"Not while our daughter still lives," he replied. His voice shone with pride. "Fina would have faced The Reaper herself to find me."

Varar glanced over at Fina once more. Unlike her parents, she did not weep. Yet there was a softness to her face as she watched her parents hug each other.

A cheer went up around them, and when Varar glanced back at the reunited couple once more, Tarl had swept Lucrezia up into a passionate embrace. Arms looped around his neck, his wife kissed him back with the same enthusiasm.

Varar's mouth twitched. His own parents had been happily wedded, but he had never seen them kiss like that. There was something life-affirming about seeing a couple who had been wed for years display so much passion.

Eventually, the kiss ended, and husband and wife drew apart. Donnel and Eithni approached, and Tarl went to greet them. Lutrin and Namet joined the throng too, their families rushing forward to hug them. More tears, more joy.

Looking on, Varar suddenly felt odd, detached.

This reunion, this happiness, was not his. He needed to leave them to it.

Reining Guail right, he rode into the sea of ponies, people, and wagons. A large, makeshift village had sprung up here. A rooster crowed from inside its cage perched atop a wagon as Varar passed. Nearby, a woman milked a goat she had tethered to the back of a wagon.

Varar yawned, his jaw cracking. Fatigue pressed down on him. A night without sleep was not ideal before battle. It dulled a warrior's senses, slowed his reflexes. But it could not be helped.

He found The Boar warriors on the eastern edge of the army. Morag was directing folk in his absence. Tall and proud, she stood amidst the jostling crowd, calling out instructions to the women who were packing away the last of the tents into the wagons.

Varar rode up behind her. "Coping without me, I see."

Morag turned around, her face lighting up. "You're back!"

Varar swung down from Guail. "You sound surprised?"

"I am," Morag replied, pursing her lips. "I thought we'd seen the last of you."

Varar snorted. "No such luck."

Morag stepped forward, as if to embrace him, before her step faltered. Her expression turned uncertain. "Did you find the captives?"

"Aye ... all three have returned safe."

Morag gave him a penetrating look he knew well. "Does this mean the other tribes are going to thaw toward us now?"

Varar huffed out a breath. "Who knows ... it'll probably take more than that."

"Who cares if they thaw toward us or not." Frang stepped up at Morag's side. He pushed her out of the way as he reached out and slapped his chief on the shoulder. "The Boar don't need anyone else. The Reaper can take them all."

Morag's expression darkened, the warmth that had softened her gaze disappearing. "There's only a handful of us left, husband. I'd say our survival depends on learning to trust our neighbors."

Frang cast his wife a hard look, his mouth twisting. His large hands fisted at his sides. For a moment it seemed as though he might lash out at her. Varar tensed. He had never seen the warrior lift a hand to Morag. Yet watching them interact, he sometimes wondered at how he treated her when they were alone.

Morag stared back at Frang, defiant. Her response pleased Varar—Frang would never succeed in breaking his sister.

A tense silence drew out, and then Frang turned back to Varar with a sneer. "Women ... what do they know?"

"Much it seems," Varar replied, his tone lowering as he held the warrior's gaze. "My sister is both cleverer and wiser than you, Frang ... you'd do well to listen to her."

Before they rode out to meet the enemy, the warriors of the united tribes gathered in the center of the encampment. Fina joined them, taking her place between Muin and Talor amongst the crowd.

In front of them rose a pile of stones. They were riverstones, collected from a nearby creek bed. Each stone was small and smooth, big enough to fill a man's palm. The number of stones had been counted: three hundred and eighty, one for each warrior.

One by one, the warriors stepped forward and retrieved a stone from the pile.

Fina followed Muin up and collected her stone. She knew of this ritual, yet she had never taken part in it before.

Before great battles warriors would collect a stone to take with them. Then, once the fighting was over, they would return the stone to the pile. After the stones were counted, they would know exactly how many had fallen. They would then hold a ceremony for the dead and light torches for them.

This ritual was only needed for struggles that would last many days, battles where the dead would have to be left where they fell.

Fina's mood was solemn as she slid the stone into the hem of her skirt. She sewed the hem closed with a bone needle, working deftly. The weight of the stone would knock against her thigh when she walked, a reminder of what was at stake.

Finishing her task, Fina glanced up.

Varar had just retrieved his stone, one of the last to do so. She watched him slide it into his leather vest. Like everyone, his gaze was shadowed. The act brought everything into focus.

Much blood would be spilled in the coming days, and many of their own would fall. Was Varar thinking about all those warriors he had lost already? He had so few of them left now.

Feeling her gaze upon him, Varar glanced up. For a moment the pair of them stared at each. Time stalled, and Fina's surroundings faded. She was vaguely aware of Talor saying something to her, yet his words sounded like senseless chatter.

It was as if the rest of the world ceased to exist for a moment—except for her and Varar.

A heartbeat later Varar blinked and the connection between them shattered.

Fina tore her gaze away, and turned from him, her senses reeling.

What's wrong with me?

The army of the united tribes rode south. A cool wind gusted in, buffeting against Fina's back. She was relieved that she had plaited her hair into thin braids before setting off from camp; she did not want her hair blinding her during battle.

Her eyes burned with fatigue this morning, and she felt a little light-headed. She needed to rest, but that would have to wait till tonight. She had to make it through today's battle first.

The army traveled in a wide column. Ponies led the way, followed by ranks of warriors on foot, while the folk of An Teanga and Dun Ringill, who had fled their homes but would not be fighting, brought up the rear with the supply wagons.

Fina followed Galan and Tea, her parents, and Donnel. Muin and Talor rode alongside her. The Eagle riders led the column south, with The Wolf close behind.

Twisting in the saddle, Fina's gaze traveled over the sea of riders behind her. Ever since locking gazes with Varar earlier that morning, she had felt on edge.

"Looking for someone?" Talor's voice made her tense.

"No," she replied, her tone sharper than she had intended. "Just reassuring myself that all the tribes are following."

Talor huffed. "What ... still don't trust our Boar friends?"

His tone told her that, despite Varar's assistance the night before, Talor himself did not trust The Boar chief. She also saw the suspicion in his eyes, the accusation, that *she* did.

Fina inhaled deeply. Talor could be far too perceptive at times. It irritated her, but after last night she felt as if she owed Varar a debt. They would not have made it out of that encampment without his help. She had been in awe of him, something which now vexed her in the aftermath. Even so, having the others hate The Boar would not help any of them in the coming battles.

"Galan," she called out. "I've something to tell you."

The Eagle chieftain glanced over his shoulder. "What is it?"

Fina met his eye, her own gaze steady. "Gurth was responsible for that attack in The Valley of the Tors ... not Varar."

Galan's face hardened. "Did The Boar chief tell you this?"

Fina nodded. The memory of that humiliating encounter in his tent still made her cringe inwardly. "Under duress ... aye."

Talor snorted. "Sounds like more Boar treachery to me."

"I thought so too," Fina admitted. "But there was no lie in his eyes." She did not add that she'd had a knife pressed to his throat at the time. Best her family remained ignorant of that.

Galan watched her. However, his expression did not soften. "Gurth had no love of us ... this tale doesn't surprise me."

"How long has Varar known the truth?" Tea asked, suspicion in her voice.

"Not long. Gurth told him after they battled the Cruthini ... before he died."

"I don't see how this changes anything," Talor spoke up once more. "They still attacked and butchered our people. If Varar didn't know about it that makes him a fool ... and a weak leader."

"I agree," Tarl spoke up for the first time. He had been listening to the conversation with interest, his brow furrowed. "The sight of that bastard makes me want to knock his teeth down his throat. We need The Boar's help against the Cruthini, but our alliance ends there. As soon as this fight is over, I'm having my reckoning with him."

Silence fell between them, charged with Tarl's fury. When Galan replied, his expression was no softer than his brother's. "Aye ... as will we all."

Chapter Twenty-two

Battle Fury

THEY MET THE enemy late morning.

The army of the united tribes had pushed south-east, positioning themselves near to the mountainous interior of the isle. The southern edge of the Black Cuillins approached. The dark craggy silhouette of Sgurr nan Gillean, the last peak of the great ridge, loomed directly east now.

The wind had picked up as the morning drew out, and it now raced across the bare hills. The sky had turned ominous. Dark clouds covered the sun and cast the world into shadow.

It was almost as if the Gods knew what was about to happen.

Fina angled her head away from the gusting wind, ignoring the spots of rain that now accompanied it. Instead, her gaze remained fixed upon the line of bristling spears on the crest of the hill to the west.

The fine hair on the backs of her arms prickled. Finally. The enemy was before them.

"They call themselves The People of The Serpent," Tarl spoke up from next to her. His pony danced, its nostrils flaring as it sensed the tension rippling through the valley.

"And the name of The Boar warrior that follows him?" Varar asked. He sat atop his coal-black stallion a few yards away.

Tarl shifted his attention to the chieftain. His gaze narrowed. "Tormud."

"I don't recognize the name ... what does he look like?"

"He has around forty-five winters—a stocky man with dark eyes and hair."

Varar held his gaze, his own expression hard. "That's not much help."

Tarl's face twisted, his lips parting to reply. However, Donnel cut him off. "Here's their leader." Donnel stretched out an arm and pointed to where a tall figure with wild auburn hair stepped out of the line.

"Be careful with him," Varar warned quietly. "He's as slippery as an eel."

Tarl snorted. Galan cast his younger brother a quelling look before glancing over at Varar. "I'll remember that ... come on, let's go and see what he has to say."

"I'm sure it's nothing worth hearing," Tadhg mac Fortrenn grumbled, urging his pony forward. "But we shall listen all the same."

Fina watched the four chiefs break away from the front line and ride down the gentle slope to meet The Serpent chieftain. Cathal mac Calum faced them on foot, yet he did not seem intimidated.

A huge man, clad in leather and fur, he stalked toward them with a killer's grace. Watching him, Fina was glad they had not faced the chief during the rescue. He would have made escape difficult, if not impossible.

Irritated that this warrior actually impressed her, Fina clenched her jaw. She glanced over at Muin who had drawn his gelding up next to her. He was scrutinizing the approaching enemy chief.

"He looks like he's never lost a battle in his life," Muin muttered.

"Or that's what he wants you to think," she replied, forcing a lightness into her voice. "Just because he struts like a rooster doesn't mean he won't die like the rest of them."

"Aye," Talor added with a smirk. "Surely the fact that we have many riders and their entire army is on foot, should count as an advantage?"

"It should," Muin agreed, his slate-grey gaze fixed upon the bristling bulk on the western horizon. "But a warrior on foot is just as dangerous as one on a pony ... never forget that."

Talor snorted. Yet when he answered his voice had lost some of its arrogance. "Gods ... I swear sometimes you sound as if you're a hundred years old. Thanks for the reminder."

Muin tore his gaze from the enemy and swept it round to his cousin. His mouth quirked. "You're welcome."

"Is everything in place for when the battle starts?" Fina cut in. Her cousins could finish their banter later.

Muin's face grew serious once more. "Aye ... as soon as fighting starts, the rear-guard is to pull back and take the people and supplies east into the hills, where they'll make camp and wait for the battle to end. When the horn blows three times, we are to retreat."

Fina scowled. "I hate the idea of retreating ... it's a coward's plan."

"Aye," Talor chorused. "It's no wonder Varar mac Urcal came up with it."

"It's a good idea," Muin countered. He was frowning now. "The Boar's strategy might save us all."

Talor's gaze narrowed. "You don't actually agree with him?"

"Even with our joined forces—and with ponies—they outnumber us," Muin replied. "We need to be cleverer than The Serpent if we are to beat them."

Talor muttered something under his breath to this, but did not argue the point. Fina remained silent. She still did not want to retreat, even if the move was feigned. But at the same time, she knew in her gut that Muin was right.

Varar's plan was the best weapon they had.

"What's this? All four of you have come to meet me. I should be honored."

Cathal mac Calum stopped a few yards back and faced his adversaries, legs akimbo. He grinned at them, showing his teeth.

Varar itched to reach for the knife strapped to his thigh, launch himself off Guail, and slash that smirk off The Serpent chief's face.

Sensing his animosity, Cathal's attention swiveled to Varar. "So, The Boar is back for more, eh?" He mocked. "We didn't beat you bloody enough last time?"

Varar favored him with a cold smile but did not reply. Instead, his gaze shifted from Cathal to the front ranks of the Cruthini force behind him. He was looking for The Boar warrior, the traitor. He spotted him easily. A broad, swarthy man with greying dark hair stood out from the tall, rangy, auburn and brown-haired warriors surrounding him. The man was watching Varar intently, his gaze intense. Varar did not recognize his face and wondered which part of The Boar territory he hailed from.

"Spotted Tormud, have you?" Cathal gave a soft laugh. "He's been very helpful to me."

Anger coiled in the base of Varar's belly, although concern flickered beneath it. He hoped this traitor did know this area of The Winged Isle well.

"We're not here to bandy words with you, Serpent," Galan cut in. "State your terms."

Cathal shifted his attention from Varar and viewed The Eagle chief with a look of disdain. "Galan mac Muin ... at last. Dun Ringill is a fine broch, thank you for giving it up to us so easily."

Varar watched something lethal move in Galan's eyes. It was the same expression he had glimpsed at the Lochans of the Fair Folk, before Galan attacked him. The

Eagle chief leaned forward in the saddle, his skin pulling tight over his cheekbones. "Leave this isle. Turn your warriors around and take them home. Do this, and we will spare your lives."

Cathal stared at him a moment. Then he threw back his head and roared with laughter. It was a genuine belly-laugh, and the sound echoed across the hillside despite the howling wind.

"We *are* home," he said when he had recovered from his mirth. "I find I like this isle very much. It suits my people well."

"Then you choose death," Wid mac Manus growled from Galan's left. "For we will never give it up."

Cathal favored The Wolf chief with an insolent shrug, before his gaze shifted to the fourth man in front of him. Tadhg mac Fortrenn wore the skin of a red stag, its mighty antlers crowning his head. He was easily the tallest and broadest of the chieftains here; the cloak made him look even more formidable. Cathal smiled at him. "I'll enjoy hanging those fine antlers on my wall. Soon, all your brochs will belong to me."

Tadhg grinned back at him. It was a feral smile that promised violence. "And I will enjoy feeding you to my dogs."

The battle began with a suddenness that made the wind still for a heartbeat.

Horns echoed across the hills, and heavy feathered hooves thundered. The front ranks, all warriors on foot, clashed first in a boom of colliding wood and iron. A curtain of rain swept over the valley then, and thunder rumbled overhead.

The Warrior was beating his battle drum.

Fina's tiredness vanished the moment the fighting started. Fury caught alight in her veins as she urged Ceò down the hill. She steered the pony with her knees, drew her sword, and unslung her shield.

Then, as the first Cruthini warrior ran screaming at her—a big man with long dark hair, his naked body painted in woad—she swung her blade.

Fina meted out death in that valley. Warrior after warrior fell as Ceò plowed on. She was unaware of her surroundings, had long lost sight of her cousins, or the chieftains. Somewhere in that melee Tea and Fina's mother were also fighting. But she could not think about them.

She had to focus.

The screams, the bellows, the squeals of injured ponies, all bounced off Fina. The iron tang of blood, the stench of gore surrounded her. It would have sickened her had battle lust not taken hold.

She had just cut down a woman who had tried to stab her in the leg, when the three long wails of the horn intruded. Fina glanced up, suddenly aware of the rain sluicing down her face. She did not want to fall back, but orders were orders. Gritting her teeth, she whirled Ceò around.

"Fina!" A man's bellow reached her. "Duck!"

She obeyed, throwing herself down on her pony's neck. An instant later an enemy pike brushed past her shoulder. Close. Too close.

Ceò bucked, squealing in panic. Fina clamped her thighs against his sides, her gaze swiveling to see Varar cut down the warrior who had just thrown his pike at her.

Blood coated The Boar chief. He wore a savage expression, his sword blade dark with gore.

A Cruthini warrior tried to haul him down off his stallion as he passed, but Varar kicked him in the head and continued on.

"Ride!" he rasped as he reached Fina's side.

Digging her heels into Ceò's flanks, Fina urged the gelding east. Varar followed, and the pair of them galloped through the rapidly closing enemy ranks. The ponies leaped over the fallen, swerved around axes and pikes, and thundered up the hill, following the retreating warriors.

The Cruthini followed.

Chapter Twenty-three

Owing Favors

"WE'RE GOING NOW." Talor rose to his feet, brushing the oatcake crumbs off his breeches.

Beside him Muin also stood up and reached for an oilskin cape. "Aye, best not put this off."

Fina glanced up from her seat next to the hearth. A lump of peat burned, doing its best to dry out their damp clothing. "You're both going to Bodach's Throat?"

Talor gave a terse nod. His face was haggard this eve, although he looked no worse than any of them in this tent. It had been a hard day. "A night hiding behind a boulder in the pouring rain," Talor grumbled. "I can hardly wait."

Fina favored him with a sympathetic smile. She had attended the chieftains' war council earlier. They had taken losses during the battle, but everything was going to plan. The chiefs had agreed to send half the army, Talor and Muin included, on foot to Bodach's Throat tonight. There, they would ready themselves for the ambush. The rest of them—Fina included—would provide the bait in the morning. A swift retreat would follow a violent skirmish.

"Take some more oatcakes with you." Tea handed a leather package to Muin. "Neither of you ate enough tonight."

"Battle seems to kill the appetite, Ma," Muin replied, his mouth curving. Nonetheless he took the food from his mother.

Talor tossed Muin a harsh smile. "Except for blood, eh?"

Fina watched her cousins leave; no one bid them good-bye or wished them luck. The former felt too final, the latter pointless. Skill and the will of the Gods would keep Muin and Talor alive, nothing else.

Even so, after they departed, a brooding silence settled over the chieftain's tent.

Galan and Tea sat together, while their youngest son, Aaron, perched upon a pack behind them. He was sharpening his sword with a whetstone.

Donnel sat a few feet away, his expression inward; Eithni was at work in the healer's tent tonight. His daughters, Bonnie and Eara, picked at their suppers. Bonnie wore a fierce expression, her hazel eyes fixed upon the glowing hearth. Eara—a girl of ten winters with her father's grey eyes and raven hair—pressed up against her father for comfort. Donnel murmured something to her and slung a protective arm over her shoulders.

Tarl and Lucrezia huddled together with their arms wrapped around each other. The pair had been virtually inseparable since Tarl's return.

As always Fina sat slightly apart from her parents. She sometimes felt as if she intruded, and tonight was one of those times. She heard her father murmur something to her mother, soft words meant only for her ears.

A pang of loneliness, unbidden and painful, assailed Fina. She felt on edge after seeing her cousins leave. No one had any tender words for her—and on an evening like this one she could have done with them.

Fina ducked out of the tent and pulled up the hood of her leather cloak. The rain fell steadily. It pattered against the hide tents and turned the ground to mud. Squelching through the camp, Fina glanced up at the dark sky. The rain clouds had descended in a milky veil, obscuring the outlines of the surrounding mountains.

They had traveled east into the heartland of The Winged Isle, an isolated area where few folk lived. According to their scouts, the Cruthini army had camped around twenty furlongs west. Despite the foul weather, the united tribes would attack with the dawn, if not before.

This night would pass swiftly.

On her journey across the camp, Fina passed by the large healing tent in its center. The doorway was open, and she paused there a moment, looking inside. The light of a line of braziers illuminated the long space where two figures, Eithni and Eachann, worked tirelessly over the injured.

Fina smiled at the sight of An Teanga's healer. She had not had the time to thank him properly during her escape, but she did not want to bother him now. The man's long face was taut with concentration as he sewed up a gaping wound on a warrior's thigh. The man he was tending let out a hiss as Eachann pushed a bone needle through his flesh. The healer favored him with an apologetic look but did not hesitate.

Fina bowed her head and continued on her way. The rain was driving almost horizontally now. Exhaustion had dug its claws in and was dragging her down. Each step felt heavy, and her eyelids sagged. She needed to sink into her furs and get some much-needed rest before tomorrow.

But first, there was something she needed to do.

She did not want to visit Varar mac Urcal, in fact she had avoided him ever since they had arrived at camp. However, her own cowardice when it came to looking the man in the eye vexed her.

She would not let this beat her.

Marching up to The Boar chieftain's tent, she ripped open the flap and ducked inside.

Varar stood in the center of the space, speaking to two of his warriors. They were the same ones that joined him at every council: a heavyset woman with frizzy dark hair and Frang. Blinking as her eyes adjusted to the light of the brazier in the center of the space, Fina pushed back her hood.

"Good eve."

Frang snarled at her. "Get out, Eagle bitch!"

Fina ignored him, her gaze focused only on Varar. "I need to speak to you," she said tightly.

Varar raised an eyebrow—an expression that still managed to infuriate her. "What … now?"

"Aye."

"I'll get rid of her." Frang took a menacing step toward Fina and drew a knife from his belt. "I've been looking forward to this."

"That's enough, Frang." Varar's order was spoken quietly, but its tone stopped the warrior short. "Leave us." His gaze flicked to the female warrior, who was looking on with a furrowed brow. "You too, Gara."

Fina stepped aside to let them pass. The look Frang gave her was sour enough to curdle milk, but he held his tongue. Fina resisted the urge to smirk at him.

When they were alone, Varar faced her, folding his arms across his chest. Still dressed in his blood-coated leathers from battle, he looked tired, ill-tempered—and dangerous.

Fina's belly fluttered. This was why she avoided him. The man knocked her off-guard, made it difficult to gather her thoughts. She had never felt flustered around men—but she did with him.

"To what do I owe the pleasure?" he drawled finally.

"That's twice you've helped me in as many days, Boar," she growled. "I don't like owing favors."

His gaze fused with hers, dark in the golden glow of the brazier next to him. "You don't owe me anything, Fina," he replied.

The way he said her name made Fina's breathing quicken. No one ever spoke it like that, as if her name was something precious. It made her nervous.

"Yes, I do."

He stepped closer, and Fina resisted the urge to move back. "Consider my good deeds a way of healing the rift between our people," he continued. "You don't owe me anything for that ... except ..." His voice trailed off there.

Fina frowned. "Except?"

He took another step nearer. "Except that if you wish to grant me a kiss, I won't say no."

Damn him, but she could feel her cheeks warming. Varar knew it too, the dog. He was smiling at her now.

"You mock me," she growled.

His smile faded. "No, I'd never do that."

An instant later Varar stepped so close that they were almost touching. Then, without warning, he bent his head and kissed her.

The shock of his lips touching hers momentarily turned Fina to stone. She did not move, did not breathe.

The kiss was not what she had expected from a man like Varar mac Urcal. She had imagined him to be rough. Instead, he was achingly gentle. Perhaps it was his injured lip that made him careful. Fina did not care what the reason was; it was impossible to think. The feel of his mouth tenderly moving against hers completely disarmed her, made her knees tremble beneath her.

Varar raised his hands, cupping her face and angling it up toward him as he deepened the kiss. His tongue gently parted her lips, and Fina sighed. Her eyelashes fluttered against her cheeks. She swayed against him, responding to his kiss with the same languorous, sensual movement. She drank in the taste of him. Reaching up, her fingers traced the stubbled line of his jaw. Her head spun from a sudden need that made her chest ache.

The pattering of the rain against the sides of the tent became a roar in her ears. She had never been kissed like this, had never lost herself like this.

Varar was the one to end it.

With what sounded like a stifled groan, he stepped back, letting go of her.

Fina's eyes snapped open. The spell he had cast over her the moment his lips touched hers slipped away.

Reality rushed back in. The ache of fatigue in her limbs, the uncomfortable feel of damp leather against her skin, and the exhaustion that had previously fogged her mind returned.

Their gazes met, before Varar took another step back from her. His lips were parted; his chest rose and fell sharply. Fina drew in a deep, steadying breath and dropped her gaze a moment. She instantly regretted it, for her attention slid down his torso to the prominent bulge in his leggings.

The Mother save her, she was staring again.

Fina tore her gaze away from his groin and took a rapid step backward. When she met his eye once more, his mouth had curved into a half-smile, yet his expression was hungry, his gaze searing.

I must leave.

"Goodnight," Fina said, hating that her voice came out as a croak.

Varar's mouth curved. He knew the effect he was having on her, and he was enjoying it.

He did not move, although his gaze tracked her to the tent's door. "Goodnight, Fina." His voice was a caress over her suddenly heated skin. She felt exposed, naked, as she hesitated in the doorway. "See you at dawn."

They watched each other for an instant longer, before Fina turned and ducked outside into the rain.

Varar stared at the leather flap as it swung closed behind Fina. He waited a few moments until he was sure she was out of earshot, before he let out a curse and raked a hand through his damp hair.

He did not know he had possessed such self-control.

It had taken everything he had to end that kiss when he did. The taste of her, the softness of her lips, the heat of her mouth, had nearly unraveled him. Somehow he had found the presence of mind to step back from Fina—

when in reality what he really wanted was to rip off her clothes, throw her down on the furs, and plow her senseless.

Just the thought made his groin throb.

Snarling another curse, Varar clenched his hands by his sides.

It had been a bold move, to kiss her. Fina was dangerous and unpredictable. She could gut a man as easily as look at him; he had played a risky game. That was why the kiss had been gentle. He had intended it to be a mere brush of the lips, yet the moment their mouths joined all thought fled his mind. The sensuality of their embrace, the way she had traced her fingertips along his jaw, had made him forget the injuries of battle and the weight of fatigue that made his body cry out for rest.

He wanted her so much that he felt sick with it.

Despite the glow of the brazier, the tent felt cold, empty, and dark without her presence.

The rain hammered down on Fina's head, plastering her hair against her skull. However, she did not pull up her hood to shield herself from it. Instead, she welcomed the icy needles pummeling her skin.

They cooled her down, yanked her back into reality.

Anger churned through her, turning her belly into a hard knot.

Why had she let him kiss her? She should have grabbed him by the throat the moment he bent toward her.

She should have done something to stop him—yet her will had dissolved, and her body had betrayed her. She had wanted that kiss like she wanted air. A chasm of emptiness yawned within her the farther she walked from Varar's tent.

Stop it.

Fina clenched her jaw and strode on, away from The Boar tents to the edge of The Eagle camp. Many of the folk of Dun Ringill shared large tents, while others sheltered under lean-tos that barely protected them against the elements.

Men, women, and children clustered around a smoking fire under one of the large shelters. Despite that it was high summer, the air was chill and damp tonight. It was as if The Warrior, God of the warm months, was in a foul mood as he watched over them all.

Violence, bloodshed, and death—there was still more of it to come. Fina could feel it in her bones. She had deliberately avoided Ailene after the battle, for whenever she had glimpsed the seer over the past two days she had looked haunted, her gaze troubled.

Ailene's chilling foretelling back at Dun Ringill still lingered in the back of Fina's mind.

These battles with The Serpent, these marauding Cruthini folk from the mainland, were just beginning. They still had a long fight ahead.

Among the crowd she spotted Ethan mac Brennan. The man who had once shared her furs sat with his young wife by the fireside, one arm slung protectively about her shoulders.

Fina paused, ignoring the rain that battered against her, and watched them.

Ethan's wife was heavily pregnant, her belly thrust out before her. Despite that she had been torn from her home, the girl wore a content expression as she snuggled up to her husband.

Ethan glanced down at his wife then, and their gazes met for a moment. The tenderness Fina saw there made her throat constrict.

Loneliness swept over her. She could have had that; Ethan had wanted to wed her. He would have treated her well, would have loved her—but Fina had been wedded to her freedom, to the life of a warrior.

Her decision seemed hollow now. She suddenly envied her parents' happiness, the strength they gave each other at times like this. Her independence had been hard-won, but it had come at a price.

On a night like this, on the eve of battle, she wished she had not made such a choice.

Chapter Twenty-four

Not Anymore

VARAR WAS AWAKE well before dawn. Throwing a leather mantle around his shoulders, he ducked out of his tent. The wind had died overnight, and the rain had softened to a thick drizzle. The air felt heavy with moisture.

Around him Boar warriors were readying themselves for the coming battle. Some were taking down the tents, while others saddled the ponies. There was little conversation, and their faces were grim as they chewed on pieces of stale bread and hard cheese while they worked.

Varar was about to cross to where he had tethered Guail overnight, when raised voices made his step falter. Two tents along from his, a man and woman were arguing.

The male voice was loud. Belligerent with a cruel edge.

The man let out a string of crude insults that made the warriors around Varar pause, their heads swiveling.

A moment later a woman replied in a low, firm voice that Varar would recognize anywhere.

Morag.

The dull thud of a fist striking flesh followed.

An instant later Varar was striding toward the tent.

Reaching the entrance, he tore open the flap and ducked inside.

Frang loomed over Morag, a fist clenched as he readied himself to deliver another punch. Sensing movement, Frang's head turned. His gaze widened when he spied The Boar chieftain.

Varar rose to his full height inside the tent. "What are you doing?"

"Your sister's a fat, mouthy bitch," the warrior growled. "If she will not still her fish-wife's tongue, I will make her."

"I only told you to get that wound seen to before battle," Morag snarled back. She clutched her left cheek where he had struck her. Her eyes glittered.

Varar's gaze shifted for an instant to the oozing wound on Frang's left forearm. A blade had sliced through the leather bracer. It was a deep cut. Morag was right; it needed attending.

"I warned you." Frang took another step toward Morag, his right arm drawing back to strike her once more.

"Touch my sister again, and you die." Varar issued the threat quietly, yet it fell heavily in the sudden hush inside the tent.

Frang lowered his fist, his gaze narrowing now. "You shouldn't interfere between a man and wife."

Varar raised an eyebrow. "Am I going to have to repeat myself?"

Frang stared at him for a long moment. Then his throat bobbed, and he stepped back from Morag. However, his face had turned puce. A vein throbbed in his temple. He was holding onto his temper by a thread.

"Go find Eachann and get that arm seen to before we ride out," Varar ordered.

Frang spat on the ground. "You need to have a word with your sister. The shrew should learn her place."

The words were barely out of Frang's mouth when Varar's fist smashed into it. The warrior reeled back and collapsed upon the pile of furs behind him. Blood streaming from his top lip, he struggled to stand. Varar was faster. He kicked Frang hard in the ribs and sent him back down.

Gasping, Frang curled up on the furs.

Varar stood over him, ready for the warrior to rise and retaliate. Yet this time, Frang did not.

"Get out of my sight," Varar growled. "I'll deal with you properly after the battle."

Frang glared up at him, his eyes full of hate. However, he said nothing, only heaved himself off the furs and stumbled from the tent.

When he had gone, Varar turned to Morag. "Has he done that before?"

She nodded, dropping her gaze.

Varar stepped close to his sister. "Why didn't you say anything?"

Morag glanced up. Her eyes gleamed, and he realized he had hardly ever seen her cry. "I didn't think you'd listen."

Varar stared back at her. Morag's words were a slug to the gut. "Morag," he murmured. "Is that what you believe of me?"

She raised her chin and brushed away a tear that escaped, trickling down her cheek. "Not anymore," she whispered back.

"Retreat!" Tadhg mac Fortrenn's bellow cut through the rumble of the storm and the din of battle. "Fall back!"

Thunder crashed overhead.

The hunting horn wailed.

Ceò tossed his head and danced sideways as thunder rolled across the sky once more, but Fina barely noticed. Instead, her gaze swept around her, taking in what looked like a panicked retreat.

They had to make it look convincing.

Cathal mac Calum could not suspect this was a trap, or he would never follow them east.

"Cowards!" A huge man with braided brown hair and wild eyes raced toward the fleeing warriors. He brandished a double-headed war-axe. "Come back here and face us!"

Fina snarled at his insult. She longed to face him, to make him eat his words. But any delay now would leave her cut off from the others. She could not bear to have Varar ride to her rescue again.

She turned Ceò and urged him into a canter, following the other warriors east. As she rode, she spied three faces she recognized among the dead.

The first was Frang. He lay upon his back, face contorted, glaring sightlessly up at the heavens. She would not mourn his passing, but the sight of the next two faces made her insides twist.

Lutrin and Namet lay just a few feet from each other.

The two warriors, who had been as close as brothers, had fought side by side until The Reaper came for them.

Fina's vision blurred. She loved those men. Lutrin had taught her how to ride. Namet had knocked her on her arse more times than she cared to remember in sword training. Their deaths had been violent but swift. Lutrin still grasped his sword while Namet lay on his front, his face twisted toward Fina, a pike sticking between his shoulder-blades.

Ice-cold rage splintered within Fina. She would make every last one of those bastards pay for this.

They rode hard, the enemy howling behind them. The rugged terrain slowed the ponies' progress and made it easier for those on foot to follow.

Bodach's Throat was nearing. Not long now till they would make their stand.

The ground grew higher and rockier still. In usual circumstances, Fina would have dismounted from her pony, for Ceò now stumbled on the loose shale. But she needed to keep going. Some of the riders would dismount once they were deep inside Bodach's Throat—but Fina was one of a group who would continue to fight from their ponies' backs.

A short while later she entered the gorge, splashing through a swollen creek. Wreathed in mist and rain, it was an eerie, bleak place. She had journeyed near this gorge many times when out hunting but had always avoided traveling through Bodach's Throat. She was not as superstitious as some, but the tales attached to this valley had always made the hair on the back of her neck rise.

Her instincts sharpened now in response to the watchful, oddly still air inside the gorge.

It was the perfect place for an ambush, yet she felt ill at ease here.

The valley grew narrower as she rode deeper into it. Great boulders, dark with rain, studded its sides. Sharp crags rose into the mist. Rain thundered in waterfalls down the rocks.

Fina's breathing quickened when she spied Galan, up ahead, turn his stallion on its haunches.

She watched her uncle sweep his gaze behind him, before he raised a hand high. Stillness fell for a heartbeat in the valley, like a sharp intake of breath. Even the storm seemed to dim for an instant.

And then a roar split the air.

Warriors erupted from behind the boulders. They ran in a howling tide down the valley, flowing past the Eagle, Stag, Wolf, and Boar warriors who had halted there.

They broke upon the enemy in a great wave.

Things moved quickly after that. Thunder rumbled overhead, and another storm swept in, drenching the valley. The battle beneath the misty skies raged on, oblivious to the weather.

As soon as the ambush began, Fina reined Ceò right, urging him up the southern slopes of the valley. Galan had organized for forty riders to split in half and take the left and right flanks. They were to circle around the fighting and attack from the rear.

Finally, time for these Serpents to die!

Fina led the right flank: Eagle and Boar riders upon nimble-footed ponies. Bonnie and Aaron were with her, as was Varar and his best riders. They scrambled up the steep bank, their hooves digging into the loose shale. Fina kept her reins slack, letting Ceò have his head and pick his way.

Just yards beneath them the battle boiled, an angry sea of blue woad and scarlet blood.

Reaching the western end of the valley, Fina turned Ceò back into the fray, guiding him with her knees. She was aware of Varar drawing level with her as they plunged toward the ranks of Cruthini, but she dared not take her gaze off her destination. On the opposite side of the valley, shrieks split the air as Stag and Wolf riders broke through the enemy ranks.

Fina channeled her fury. The rage at seeing Lutrin and Namet slain, turned her savage. Many more of her own people would fall today. Senseless, all of it. This isle was their home. These people had no right to be here, to seize land that did not belong to them.

She would fight till her last breath to defend this isle. If she died, she would bring ten Serpent warriors down with her.

Fina lost all sense of her surroundings. Her blood sang. The metallic tang of iron filled her mouth. She slashed and cut her way into the midst of the enemy.

Inch by inch they gained ground. The battle fury in Fina's blood burned brighter with each step that Ceò took into their midst. She lost sight of the Eagle and Boar riders around her—a mistake, for she needed them to watch her back. But such was her fury, her need for vengeance, that she forgot everything else.

The enemy surrounded her, yet she fought on. Sweat poured down her back, and her sword blade dripped with gore.

And then, across the valley, something caught Fina's eye.

Upon the northern slope, high above the fighting, stood an old man.

Wrapped in filthy grey rags, white hair whipping around a cadaverous face, he stared down at her. Despite the rain and mist, he seemed to shimmer.

Dark eyes—a demon's gaze—met hers for a heartbeat. And then he smiled at her.

Ice washed over Fina, dousing her battle fury in an instant.

The bodach had appeared. He had come for her.

Chapter Twenty-five

Despair and Determination

VARAR SAW FINA go down.

She had pushed deep into the enemy lines, farther than was safe. The ambush was working. There was a slaughter going on behind him, while toward the entrance of the valley, many of the enemy had turned tail and were fleeing. However, the Cruthini had Fina surrounded.

Varar had fought with one eye on Fina the entire time. He had seen her slash her way into the fray, perched upon her grey pony; the gelding was as courageous as his rider, plowing into the enemy lines without flinching.

But then she had frozen, her gaze seemingly seizing upon something in the distance.

It was only for an instant, yet it was all the enemy needed.

An axe clove into her pony's chest. The beast went down screaming, taking Fina with him. The crowd swallowed her whole.

Varar urged Guail forward bellowing her name.

Fina did not reappear.

Varar cut his way toward her. Cruthini warriors scattered before him, some already turning to run for cover as they realized the tide had turned against them. By the time Varar reached the spot where he had seen Fina fall, she was no longer there.

Her valiant pony lay groaning, its eyes wild.

Varar pulled Guail up, his gaze sweeping the valley. Where had she gone? He looked to the west and saw that the Cruthini had taken three ponies from their fallen enemies. They all had riders, and one had an unconscious figure slumped in front of the saddle.

Fina.

Cursing, Varar kicked Guail into a canter. They had gotten a head start; it would be hard to catch them up. Not only that, but his stallion was weary from two days of battle.

As if sensing his rider's concerns and eager to prove him wrong, Guail charged down the valley in pursuit. Rain swept down Bodach's Throat, the storm still raging. Water sluiced into Varar's eyes, half-blinding him as he rode.

As soon as Bodach's Throat ended, opening into rocky hills, the retreating Cruthini army fanned out. Varar ignored them all, except for the warrior who was carrying Fina away.

Glancing over his shoulder, the man saw that Varar was chasing him. He had broken away from his companions, slowed slightly by carrying a captive. The others thundered on ahead, oblivious to Varar's pursuit.

Varar's quarry kicked his pony into a gallop, ignoring the rough terrain. The pony plunged through a torrent of water that cascaded down the hillside—and Varar followed. Guail's body tensed underneath him, before the stallion leaped, clearing most of the water.

As Varar gained on him, the warrior—a sinewy man covered in tattoos—drew his sword with a snarl, readying himself for an attack.

Varar's mouth twisted. Reaching down, he unsheathed the knife strapped to his thigh. Drawing closer still, he let go of the reins, drew his right arm back, and threw.

Thud.

The knife embedded to the hilt between the fleeing warrior's shoulder blades. The man gasped, dropped the reins, and toppled off the pony. Varar urged Guail alongside the now riderless pony and pulled it up. Fina lay there, braids trailing toward the earth, senseless.

Varar had to check on her—but there was something else he needed to do first.

He swung down off Guail's back and strode over to where the fallen warrior lay struggling in the mud. Around them the entire hillside was awash. The heavy rains had turned the creek that usually bubbled through Bodach's Throat into a raging torrent. There would be no way back now until the waters receded.

A few yards away, the man cursed. Even close to death, The Serpent warrior was defiant. He snarled curses at Varar as he approached, fumbling for his own knife even as blood bubbled onto his lips. Varar drew a knife, stepped around the man's slashing blade, and cut the warrior's throat in one swift move.

The warrior's curses abruptly stopped.

Varar let him fall before stalking back to where Fina hung, lifeless, off the pony's back. Fearing the worst, he gently lifted her to the ground.

Her breast rose and fell.

She's still breathing. Varar's breath rushed out of him; he had not realized he had been holding it. As he watched her, Fina let out a soft groan and stirred.

Thank the Gods.

Varar sat back on his heels, his gaze tracking his surroundings. They were alone, cut off by the surging river. But with so many of the enemy upon the hillside, he had to get Fina to safety. They could not remain out here, exposed to the enemies and their arrows.

He retrieved the pony the Cruthini had been riding and tied it to his stallion. Lifting Fina in his arms, Varar looped Guail's reins over his shoulder and led the ponies up the hillside in search of shelter.

Fina opened her eyes to see Varar mac Urcal's face.

Eyelids flickering, she stretched, and winced as the side of her head gave a dull throb. The roar of rushing water filled her ears. She realized then that she was lying with her head propped upon Varar thighs.

Fina struggled into a sitting position, shrugging off the hand he placed under her shoulders to help her rise.

Muttering an oath, she reached up and massaged the back of her neck. "Where are we?"

His mouth curved. "I have no idea ... around ten furlongs south of Bodach's Throat. The river cut us off. We can't get back to the others yet."

Fina frowned. Her head felt as if it was filled with wool, her thoughts scattered. "What happened?"

His own brow furrowed. "You don't remember?"

Fina ran a hand over her face before shaking her head.

"What's the last thing you recall?" he pressed.

Fina heaved in a deep breath and closed her eyes. "I remember the battle," she murmured. "I rode with you all into the back of the Cruthini army ... we fought them." Fina hesitated here as the fog started to recede, and her memories returned. Insubstantial at first, like wreathing smoke, but then clearer. A chill swept over her.

"Varar," she rasped. "I saw the bodach."

Silence stretched between them, and she opened her eyes to see that he was watching her, his gaze narrowed. "The bodach is just a folk tale," he scoffed, yet his tone was uncertain.

"It isn't. I saw him ... an old man with black eyes. He was clad in rags. He looked at me and smiled."

"I saw you hesitate in battle," Varar replied, his voice soft now. "Is that when you saw him?"

"Aye." She replied hesitantly, swallowing as more memories washed over her. "Ceò fell." Her vision blurred. "My brave pony ... they brought him down."

"I know," Varar murmured. "I saw him fall. I saw them carry you off."

Fina drew in a shaky breath. She balanced on a knife-edge; grief gathered within her like a rising tide. She had raised Ceò from a foal. The pony was a part of her family. She felt responsible for his death. "The last thing I remember was something clubbing me over the side of the head," she whispered.

"You're lucky they didn't skewer you."

Fina squeezed her eyes shut, fighting tears. "I was rash. Ceò is dead because of me."

Silence fell, and the sound of rushing water intruded once more. When Varar spoke again, there was an edge to his voice. "It wasn't your fault."

Fina clenched her jaw. She did not want him to be kind; she could not bear it.

As hard as she tried to stem them, tears escaped, trickling down her cheeks. "I wanted to kill them all," she finally managed, each word an effort. "I didn't think about anything else."

"You were magnificent," Varar replied.

Fina's eyes snapped open. She glared at Varar, but he merely stared back at her. There was no trace of arrogance or humor there. He was not mocking her as she had feared.

For the first time since waking, Fina allowed her gaze to shift, taking in their surroundings. They sat under a rocky ledge, high up on a mountainside. She could see the smoky silhouettes of jagged peaks behind them. The rain poured down in a steady tempo. Somewhere in the distance thunder continued to rumble. A small waterfall poured down from the edge of the ledge, forming a wall of water along one side of their shelter.

Fina heaved a deep sigh and leaned back against the wall of the overhang. She stretched her legs in front of her, wincing as she reached up to massage her neck once more. Her attention shifted back to Varar then, and she gave him a rueful look. "You saved my hide ... again."

He gave her a slow smile. "You're making a habit of this ... I'm beginning to think you want saving."

Fina snorted, instantly regretting it as pain arrowed down the side of her skull. "I'm not usually so reckless. These Cruthini have gotten under my skin."

His smile faded. "They have my people's lands, my broch. I want them gone."

Fina did not answer. She shared the sentiment, for the enemy had taken Dun Ringill too.

"So much death," she murmured after a pause, staring out at the rain. "Our bandruí foresaw it. She said dark times were coming for The Eagle."

"We were winning when I left that valley to go after you," Varar reminded her. "The Cruthini trapped inside will all die—the rest ran."

"But there are still so many more."

"And we will face each one." The flint in Varar's voice made her glance back at him. Even tired, rain-soaked, and blood-splattered the man looked invincible. Did he ever let despair touch him?

Varar reached out and took her hand, entwining his fingers with hers.

Fina did not pull back, even if his touch made her heart race. He was not looking at her with lust in his eyes, but with a determination that took her breath away. "Even if it takes a lifetime, we will beat them back," he vowed. "We will reclaim our land and take back our homes. I promise you."

Chapter Twenty-six

Deny It

THE DAY DREW out, and the rain continued. Its steady rhythm had a lulling effect on Fina. They would have to remain here until the rain stopped and the water subsided. Despite managing to sleep a short while the night before, she was exhausted. It was not long before her eyelids drooped, and she fell asleep slumped against the rock wall.

When Fina awoke some time later, she found herself resting against the wall of Varar's chest. She had fallen asleep sitting up, but they both now lay upon the stony ground. Fina felt surprisingly comfortable, although Varar had positioned himself so that he bore the worst of it.

Opening her eyes, Fina listened to the gentle rise and fall of his breathing. He was still asleep. The warmth of his body and the steady thud of his heart relaxed her, as did the weight of his arm curved around her hip.

We fit perfectly.

The realization made Fina's pulse quicken. Gently, she disentangled herself from him, raising herself up on an elbow. His face was beautiful in sleep. She admired the sculpted curves of his mouth and the straight line of his nose. He had the longest eyelashes she had ever seen on a man. A dark shadow of stubble covered his chiseled jaw, and she resisted the urge to reach out and trace a finger down it.

Fina swallowed. His nearness exerted an invisible pull on her. She needed to put some distance between them, before she forgot herself and did something she later regretted.

Pulling away, she shifted back toward the wall. She pulled her knees up to her chest, wrapping her arms around them. The light was starting to fade; a grey, wet day was merging into an equally gloomy dusk. It was not cold, yet the absence of Varar's warmth and the lingering damp of Fina's clothing made goose-bumps rise on her skin.

As if realizing she was gone, Varar groaned and rolled onto his side. His eyes opened. He yawned and stretched, before his gaze settled upon her. "Fina … is something wrong?" he asked. His voice was husky with sleep.

She shook her head.

"Did you manage to rest?"

She nodded. "This rain," she growled finally, deliberately avoiding his gaze. "When will it end?"

"When it wants to." The amusement in his voice vexed her.

Fina cast him a dark look. "That's helpful."

His mouth twitched. "Someone appears to have awoken in a vile mood."

She frowned. "We have to get back to the others."

"Not until that water subsides … it's still raining."

"But they'll need us."

"Not tonight, they won't … the battle will have long ended by now."

Fina huffed. "I hate waiting around."

He smiled at her. "You don't sit still often, do you?"

Her frown deepened. "Only when I was your captive … chained up in your broch."

That wiped the smile off his face. She needed to remind him what their relationship really was. He had helped her recover her father and saved her life twice now. But the truth was she would still be his captive if the Cruthini had not invaded. They both knew it.

Silence stretched out, and a shadow moved in Varar's eyes. "I've made mistakes since becoming chief," he said finally. "My father once warned me that my arrogance would be my undoing."

Fina raised an eyebrow. "What did you say to that?"

Varar glanced away. "I laughed in his face. It was just days before his death. I'll go to my cairn regretting that conversation."

Fina's anger subsided and a vague sense of unease settled over her. She was not used to seeing this side of The Boar chief. She preferred it when he was aloof, arrogant. It was easier to hate him. Easier to summon the rage that felt like an old friend these days.

"Did you not get on?" she asked.

Varar made a face. "We clashed more than we should have … I didn't like taking orders."

Fina favored him with a wry smile. "None of us do."

His gaze swung back to her, the pain in his eyes causing her to still. "He was a good man. I didn't fully realize that until recently, didn't value it … until it was too late."

"It's not," Fina replied, her smile fading. "You can still do his memory justice." She paused here, hesitating, before she added. "You already have."

He watched her a moment and then shook his head. "Not in your eyes, I haven't."

Fina went quiet. She could find no answer to that. He spoke the truth.

Varar pushed himself up off the ground, rising onto his knees before her. "My father is gone—nothing I do now matters to him. But you're here."

Fina tensed, her pulse now racing like a startled deer's. "So, what of it?"

She knew she was being rude, yet she had to warn him off. She had to keep him at arm's length. When he looked at her like that, she felt as if she would catch fire.

His gaze fused with hers. "I want your good opinion, Fina. I want you to believe I'm worthy of leading my people."

"Why?"

He gave her a long look, one that made her limbs melt. Suddenly, the air felt heated under the rock overhang. Her belly curled in on itself.

"Do you not know?" he asked gently.

Fina stared at him. She had no idea that words held so much power. She had been congratulating herself on her ability to distance herself from him, and yet with just a few words he had completely stripped away her defenses.

Fina realized she was shaking. "Varar," she whispered his name in a plea. "Please don't ..."

"Deny it." He shifted closer to her, his hands fastening over hers. "Tell me you don't feel this too."

"I ... don't."

"Liar." Varar pulled Fina into his arms, his mouth slanting over hers.

Fina gasped. Her hands rose to his chest with the intention of shoving him away.

Only, she could not.

The moment his mouth crushed against hers a frantic yearning exploded within her. The kiss was desperate, full of unanswered questions, of things neither of them could articulate.

Of course she was a liar. They both knew it.

Fina groaned and melted against him. Her fingertips bit into the leather of his vest as her lips parted. He kissed her hungrily, his hands cupping the back of her head. Their tongues tangled, danced, explored.

Without even realizing she was doing so, Fina unlaced his vest, ripping it off him so she could touch the smooth skin underneath. Varar's musky male scent overwhelmed her. The taste of him made Fina groan once more. Her body now acted with a will of its own.

Sliding her hands up over the broad planes of his chest, Fina raised her arms and linked them around his neck. She pressed herself hard against him. Her breasts chafed against their leather binding. They felt swollen, ached to be freed.

Varar let out a growl that rumbled deep in his chest and hauled her onto his lap. She shifted to sit astride him, her skirt riding up around her waist. He slid his hands up her thighs, exploring the nakedness underneath. Fina gasped once more, her lower belly turned molten at his touch.

He set her skin alight. Her core pulsed with want.

His mouth never leaving hers, Varar reached up and untied Fina's breast binding. The damp leather fell away.

Varar fell back, pulling her with him, and then rolled over so Fina was underneath. Then he bowed down to feast upon her breasts.

Fina cried out as he suckled her. His dominance excited her beyond measure. She was used to being in control with men. Even in the heat of passion she never forgot herself. But she did so now. She was vaguely aware of the stony ground digging into her back, and the dull ache in her skull from the injury she had sustained. But she did not care.

She let go of it all: the anger, the grief, and the fear. She had leaped off the cliff with him and was tumbling into an abyss.

Varar's big body trembled when he reared back off her and began to unlace his leggings. Eyes half closed, Fina stared up at him, her body languid and aching. She had seen him naked before, but never aroused. The length and size of his shaft made her breathing catch. It strained toward her, the swollen head glistening.

Fina muttered an oath.

Varar leaned over her. He pushed Fina's thighs farther apart, exposing her to him. He then lowered his hips to her, positioned himself, and thrust deep.

Fina's cry echoed against the stone walls of their shelter, muffled by the roar of the cascade behind them. The sensation of being filled by him, the delicious ache of it, made the last of her self-control snap. She arched toward him, her body quivering as she sobbed his name.

Varar loomed over her. His eyes were dark pools. His lips, swollen from her kisses, parted. Taking hold of her left knee, he bent it back.

He took her hard. There was nothing gentle about it. Each plunge was brutal. The force of it pushed Fina along the ground until they were beyond the overhang.

The rain thundered down on them, sluicing across Fina's breasts and Varar's back. They barely noticed. Fina hooked her free leg around his hips and clung on as he rode her. Her fingernails dug into his skin and raked his back.

His hoarse cries joined hers, echoing down the mountainside. They both lost themselves in each other, lost themselves to the aching pleasure and the driving need that had steadily been building between them.

Fina knew, as she arched up to meet each thrust, that this coupling would change everything. Her life pivoted on this moment, this man. And she gave herself wholeheartedly to it.

Chapter Twenty-seven

After the Rain

LANGUID AND EXHAUSTED, they lay together under the shelter of the overhang, bodies entwined. Around them the long twilight drew out. Night was almost upon them.

Varar stretched out on his back while Fina curled against him, her head resting in the hollow between his shoulder and chest.

A sense of wellbeing, unlike any he had previously known, suffused Varar. The feel of Fina's warm, supple body curled against his. The softness of her full breasts pressed against him, felt so natural, so right that he never wanted their time here to end.

The world outside waited, a world where they were at odds. One that had been splintered by the invaders.

But here none of that mattered.

Varar was not an emotional man; he had been brought up in an environment where others saw such displays as weakness. He had never seen his father weep, not even when Varar's mother died.

But Varar's vision blurred now, and his chest ached with the force of emotion he was struggling to understand. Fina did this to him. Somehow in the past days, she had managed to access a part of him no one else ever had, a part he had not even thought existed.

It had begun back in An Teanga he realized. The link between them had been forged during those days, although she had hated him then.

Fina stirred against him, and she trailed a hand over his chest. Her fingertips traced the lines of the markings etched into his skin.

He liked the feel of her hands on him, the gentleness of her caress.

"I could lie like this forever," he murmured.

She gave a soft laugh, but her fingers still continued their exploration. "You'd get cold and hungry eventually," she teased, her voice husky.

"Or someone would come looking for us and shatter our peace," he added. "Nothing good ever lasts, does it?"

Silence fell between them. After a spell, Fina broke it. "You remember earlier, when I spoke about our bandruí?"

"Aye."

"Ailene didn't just predict dark times for our people ... when she cast the bones she saw something else."

Varar tensed. "What?"

Fina raised her head, her storm-grey eyes serious. "She said that The Boar and The Eagle would be united ... in marriage."

"Really?" He gave her an incredulous look. "How did everyone react to that news?"

"None of us believed it. I said that no one in their right mind would wed a Boar."

He gave a soft laugh before reaching out and caressing Fina's cheek with the back of his hand. "And now?"

"Now ... I don't know what to think."

A beat of silence passed.

"Would it really be that bad?" he asked. "To wed to a Boar?"

"I once thought so."

He smiled. "And now?"

She frowned at him, although her gaze was soft. "Now you're trawling for compliments."

"I'm not so bad then?"

She punched him on the arm.

Varar laughed once more, hauling her close so that she lay atop him. When their gazes met, his mirth faded. "You caught my eye all those years ago at the An Teanga Gathering, you know? So much spirit: furious, brave, and beautiful. I never forgot you. I couldn't believe it when we found you alive in that valley. That angry girl from years ago, the only survivor of a bloodbath."

Her mouth twisted. "I've always been angry ... I can't remember a time when I wasn't."

He traced the outline of her full lower lip with the pad of his thumb. "Why?"

Fina's gaze dropped. "I'm my parents' only surviving child. My three younger brothers all died as bairns. I hated that I was strong and healthy, that I lived when they died."

"You weren't to blame."

She huffed a breath. "I kept telling myself that ... but my heart told me differently." She glanced back up at him. Her eyes gleamed then. "I've spent my life raging at the world. Most men find me too aggressive—I scare them off."

He smiled. "Not this one."

Her mouth quirked. "I never understood why not."

"I like a challenge."

"Strutting cockerel." She nipped his caressing thumb with her teeth. "I don't think I've ever met such an arrogant man."

He grinned. "You like it."

He could see from the way her eyes dilated, how her breathing changed, that she did. Varar's pulse accelerated, and he became acutely aware of her strong, lush body spread out across his. His groin hardened in response, aching for her again.

A sensual smile curved Fina's lips. The sadness that their conversation had dredged up slipped away, and he saw his own desire mirrored in her features. Reaching down, she curled her fingers around the length of his shaft.

Varar let out a low groan, his head rolling back as she caressed him.

"I like this," she teased. "You, at my mercy."

His eyes snapped open. He twisted his body and suddenly she was under him, her legs slung over his shoulders. "We'll see about that," he growled back.

Fina reined in the pony, her gaze sweeping over the mountainside beneath them. "You weren't exaggerating." She glanced at where Varar sat upon Guail beside her. "The rain has changed the landscape."

The storm had ceased overnight. It was now mid-morning and the water had subsided as quickly as it had risen, leaving deep gouges in the earth. Yet a torrent still snaked down the mountainside, a frothing column of turbid water.

Varar's expression was grim as he surveyed the river. "I was hoping the water would have fallen more than this."

Fina leaned forward, stroking the pony's sleek neck. She recognized it; the mare belonged to Murdina, an Eagle warrior. Varar had tethered both beasts under a neighboring overhang overnight so they too had sheltered from the rain. A weight settled in Fina's breast as she remembered Murdina. If a Cruthini had taken her pony, it was likely the warrior was dead.

"We can cross it," she replied. "If we ride down to where the water spreads out a bit."

"Aye," he replied tersely, "although we'll need to be careful."

Fina cast him an arch look. "Always."

They urged their ponies down the washed out slope. It was slow going, for the rain had scoured it down to the clay in places. The ponies' hooves slipped as they picked their way down.

During their descent, Fina spared Varar the odd glance. He had been in a strange mood since they had left the overhang: subdued, introspective. A veil of well-being still hung over Fina; her limbs felt loose and her body gloriously alive. But Varar had changed.

She had seen a different side to him during that long night together. In the dim light of dusk and the glow of dawn, she had seen the real Varar mac Urcal. A man of strong passions and deep feeling. And yet now the aloof shield of earlier had risen once more.

Fina did not question him over it. Like her, he had lost many people over the past days. He was likely thinking about what would come next and wondering how the battle had ended. Fina's own thoughts gradually shifted from the passion of the past night to the violence that had preceded it.

Even before she had fallen, she had seen many others die. Eagles, Boars, Wolves, and Stags cut down and trampled by the wave of Cruthini who had followed them into that valley.

Bodach's Throat. Fina suppressed a shudder at the memory of that cursed place. It had been the perfect choice for an ambush. The image of that spectral old man looking down on the battle still chilled her blood. The way he had smiled at her made Fina's belly cramp. She would never forget him.

Ceò had fallen in that cruel place, her loyal big-hearted pony. Her belly twisted at the memory of his scream as he fell. She remembered the rage, the helplessness, of that moment.

Fina squeezed her eyes shut, shoving her jagged-edged memories aside. Torturing herself wasn't going to bring her beloved Ceò back.

Reaching the foothills of the mountains, Varar and Fina forged the muddy water. It swirled around their ponies' bellies, the strong current pulling at them. Fina's mare tossed her head, nostrils flaring.

"Go on, girl." Fina reached forward and stroked the pony's neck, letting it have its head as the mare followed doggedly behind Guail. It seemed to take forever to get to the other side of the torrent, where the pony lunged for the bank, scrambling up the loose shale to safety.

"Well done." Fina leaned down and hugged the mare's neck. The pony's sides heaved from the effort, but they had managed to cross.

Fina glanced over at Varar. Gaze narrowed, he was sitting tall upon Guail, surveying their surroundings.

"Where will the others have made camp?" she asked. "The same place as the night before Bodach's Throat?"

"We'll try there first," he replied. "It's not far ... come on." With that, he urged his stallion into a canter and headed north-west.

Fina hesitated, still wondering at his aloofness this morning, before she gathered the reins and followed.

When they reached the campsite, they found it empty. No tents, no ponies, only sodden firepits and muddy ground.

"They didn't come back here," Fina observed, watching Varar kneel next to one of the firepits to inspect it. "Do you think they pulled back farther east?"

He shook his head. "They'd only do that if they lost the battle."

Unease feathered down Fina's spine. "What if they did?"

Varar rose to his feet. "We were winning. I saw the enemy fleeing."

Fina held his gaze. "Well, in that case our people must have followed them. They'll have made camp farther west.

He nodded. "Let's hope so."

Varar crossed to Guail, swung up onto his back, and they continued north-west. The rain had made tracking hoof and footprints almost impossible, but a few furlongs on they found deep grooves in the mud.

"Wagons," Fina said, relief gusting out of her. "They traveled this way."

They followed the tracks north, toward the shadowed outlines of the Black Cuillins. The grey clouds had lifted, and the sky was a pale blue. A soft breeze blew in from the south, bringing with it the scent of heather and rich, damp earth. Fina inhaled the smell and felt the nerves in her belly slowly uncoil. Their people had returned to their original camp just south of the Cuillins—a position that protected the north of the isle.

Finally, they spied them: a carpet of tents covering a gentle slope in the foothills of the northern ridge. It was not far from the path that led up to the Lochans of the Fair Folk.

Fina reined in her pony and glanced over at Varar. He still wore that inscrutable expression. His gaze was shuttered.

"What is it?" she asked. Soon they would be surrounded by others; this was the last chance they would have to speak openly before scouts spotted them.

He glanced at her. "Nothing."

She gave him a level look. "You've been surly ever since we set out."

"Have I?"

Fina huffed a frustrated breath. "Aye … and now you're starting to vex me."

His mouth quirked, a little warmth returning to his gaze. "That's not hard to achieve."

Silence fell between them for a moment, before Varar urged Guail up next to her. They were riding so close that their thighs nearly touched.

"Things … will be different back at camp," he said finally.

Something deep in Fina's belly knotted. Truthfully, she had not given their return to the tribes any thought beyond being reunited with her people. "What do you mean?"

His mouth tightened. "Us … your kin aren't going to like it."

Fina frowned. "Since when do you care about what others like?"

He loosed a sigh. "I don't."

"So why the concern?"

"The Eagle and The Boar are allies for the moment, Fina—but we *aren't* friends. Our tribes are at war ... we need to focus on what lies ahead. Best we keep this quiet."

Fina drew herself up in the saddle, her irritation rising. "Did you think I was going to ride into camp and start weeping and wailing ... and beg Galan and my father to give us their blessing?" He drew back slightly at her venom, but riled now, Fina continued. "Clearly you think me a dull-wit. I know we're at war. I had no intention of telling *anyone* about us."

That was a lie, but now that he had angered her, Fina's shields rose.

His expression shadowed. "Fina ... I didn't—"

"Spare me," she snapped. "I'm not a fool. You don't need to explain yourself further." With that she kicked her pony into a canter and rode toward the camp.

Chapter Twenty-eight

The Ceremony for the Dead

TARL HUGGED HIS daughter in a bone-crushing embrace. "Thank The Warrior." His voice had an edge to it she had never heard before. "I thought we'd lost you again."

He let go of her then, and Fina stepped back from him, blinking away tears. "So did I," she murmured.

Beside Tarl, Lucrezia was weeping. She had been the first to embrace Fina upon her arrival at the camp. Lucrezia took hold of Fina's hand now and squeezed tightly. There was a desperation to her mother's grip.

Tarl's gaze shifted from Fina, moving to the man standing three feet behind her. Varar had not spoken since they had entered the camp.

"Thank you." Tarl's voice caught; the words choked him. A nerve flickered under his left eye. Even though he was grateful to have Fina back, Tarl did not want to give his thanks to The Boar chieftain.

Fina glanced over her shoulder at Varar. He was not looking at her but at Tarl. The two men's gazes locked, before Varar gave a tight smile. A beat of silence passed, and then Varar turned and walked away. He headed in the direction of The Boar tents.

Fina watched him go. Despite her joy at seeing her parents, she felt as if there was a boulder sitting on her chest. This was not how she had envisaged returning to camp. Last night had been magical: a union not just of the body but the soul. But with just a few badly chosen words, they had both ruined it.

He had not meant to, but he had offended her. She had responded in the only way she knew how. To attack.

Part of her wanted to go after him. Another part wanted to lash out.

Confusion churned through her. Why did she feel so conflicted?

"Fina?" Lucrezia asked. "What's wrong?"

Curse her mother, she *would* notice. Schooling her features into a neutral expression Fina shrugged. "Nothing ... I'm tired, that's all."

Lucrezia's dark gaze narrowed as she studied her daughter. "Go and rest for a bit ... you can use our tent."

"The ceremony for the dead isn't far off," Tarl warned them. "We're holding it mid-afternoon."

Fina swallowed, turning to her father. Resting was the last thing she felt like doing. "I saw Lutrin and Namet," she said softly.

Tarl's features tightened, his grey eyes guttering. "We found them afterward," he rasped. "There are others too, Murdina, Diarmid, Fingal, and Muir ... all of them fell."

Fina inhaled sharply. The news was a punch to the gut.

Tarl's mouth twisted then into a bitter smile. "But their deaths weren't in vain. Far more Cruthini died in that valley than us. And those who didn't die ran like whipped dogs."

"Where are they now?" Fina asked.

Her father's smile faded. "They've fallen back to Dun Ringill."

"How many are left?"

"Still too many," Lucrezia answered. She stepped closer to her daughter then. "Talor took a bad injury. We think he'll live, but he had us worried when we carried him into camp."

Fina went cold. She could not believe her parents had waited this long to tell her. She turned to her mother. "Where is he?"

"In The Eagle healing tent with Eithni."

Talor was propped up on furs, his face ashen, when Fina stormed into the tent. Injured warriors, some of them stretched out on the ground, filled the interior. Eithni was nowhere in sight.

"Fina!" Despite his weakened state, Talor managed a smile at the sight of her. "Back from the dead again, cousin?"

Fina snorted. "Aye ... and I owe Varar mac Urcal my life."

Talor's smile faded. "You do?"

Fina nodded. She went over to where her cousin lay and knelt down next to him. "Ma said you were in a bad way. What happened?"

Talor pulled down the edge of the furs to reveal a blood-stained bandage around his ribs. "Serpent bastard stuck me with a pike."

Fina muttered a curse. "I can't believe you survived that."

Talor waved her away. "Enough about me. How did that Boar save your life?"

"The Cruthini brought Ceò down and clubbed me over the back of the head. One of them rode off with me, and Varar chased him down," Fina broke off here. Talor's penetrating look was making her uneasy. "We would have made it back last night but flooding prevented us."

Talor leaned back against the furs and regarded her coolly. "So does this mean I've got to be civil to him in future?"

Fina huffed. "That's up to you."

His gaze shadowed then. "Muin found Ceò after the battle. He made sure the pony didn't suffer."

Fina swallowed. "I will thank him," she replied huskily.

"Talor mac Donnel ... why aren't you resting?" A woman's voice interrupted them. Fina turned to see Eithni enter the tent, a pile of clean linen in her arms.

"Sorry, aunt ... it's my fault," Fina replied.

Eithni favored Fina with a warm, if tired, smile. "You're a welcome sight, lass. I've just seen your mother—she told me what happened."

Fina felt her face heat up. Gods knew what her mother had said to Eithni. Those two could gossip like crones. She had not liked the knowing look in her mother's eyes earlier. It made her feel as if Lucrezia could read her mind. However, there was no such speculation in her aunt's gaze. Just gentle concern.

Rising to her feet, Fina cast Talor an apologetic look. "The Ceremony's starting soon. I should go."

"Wait." Talor winced as he reached down and retrieved something from beside him. "Take this for me." He handed her a small smooth river stone. "The injured are giving their stones to kin to take to the ceremony ... here's mine. I'm alive, after all."

Fina took the stone and slid it into her belt. "I'll add yours to the pile," she assured him.

On the way to the Ceremony, Fina ran into Ailene. The bandruí squealed at the sight of her, threw her arms around Fina, and squeezed her tight.

Ailene's blue eyes were gleaming when she drew back. "Gods, I was so worried ... we all thought the worst."

Fina gave her an arch look. "You should know by now that I'm not easy to kill." She looped her arm through her friend's, and the two women continued on their way toward the northern edge of the camp, where the ceremony would take place.

"I heard Varar saved you?" Ailene said, meeting Fina's eye. "Is it true?"

Fina stifled a groan. Was there anyone in the camp who had not heard? "Aye ... he did," she admitted, glancing away.

"Your cheeks have gone red," Ailene noted. "I don't think I've ever seen you blush before."

"I'm not blushing."

"Yes you are ... it's spreading down your neck now."

Fina tore her arm away and turned on her friend. "Enough!"

"Very well," Ailene replied, her mouth twitching as she fought a smile. "I think I just hit a nerve."

"No you didn't. You're just annoying."

Ailene huffed a sigh, looped her arm through Fina's once more, and propelled her forward. "And you're pig-headed." She paused here, waiting while they passed through a group of women plucking grouse for supper. When they were out of earshot, she resumed speaking. "He's very attractive ... if insufferably arrogant. But I can understand why you might like him."

Fina clenched her jaw. "Just leave it."

Ailene gave a soft laugh. "I'm sorry, Fina ... I didn't mean to torment you. It's only ... I've never seen you this way."

Fina glowered at her. "What are you talking about?"

Her friend favored her with a level look. "You're different. I knew the moment I saw you. Others might not notice but I do. Even if you haven't yet admitted it to yourself, it's as clear as the sun in the sky to me."

"Talk plainly," Fina replied between gritted teeth. "You know I hate it when you speak in riddles."

Ailene met her eye. "Very well ... although you might not want to hear this." She paused, no humor on her face now. "That man has your heart."

The Ceremony for the Dead started with each surviving warrior placing a stone in the center of the clearing.

Using her knife, Fina slit open the hem of her skirt and removed the stone she had carried over the past days. Then she followed Muin and his brother Aaron up to the rapidly growing pile before placing hers and Talor's stones on the stack. Talor's sister, Bonnie, appeared at Fina's shoulder, her young face stern beyond her years. This had been the girl's first battle. She had done well, but Fina could see from the haunted look in Bonnie's eyes that the days had taken their toll.

Fina returned to the crowd that had formed a crescent around the clearing, and waited for the others to do the same.

Both her parents had fought in the battles, and so they too went up and left their stones. Her uncle Donnel went next, his cheeks wet with tears as he placed his stone with the others. Then Galan and Tea took their turn.

The Boar warriors went next.

Varar strode up. Fina's gaze devoured him, willing him to look her way. Yet he did not. His face was the most severe she had seen it, far from the lover of the night before. Only twenty Boar warriors followed him.

Fina's breathing caught. *So few have returned.*

Of all of them, The Boar had suffered the worst of this invasion.

After The Boar, went The Wolf. Wid mac Manus wept openly as he stumbled up to the stones.

"He lost one of his sons," Ailene whispered to Fina. "Bred ... the youngest."

Fina's throat ached as she watched the proud Wolf chieftain kneel before the stones and bow his head. She could feel Wid's agony from here. Her hands clenched by her sides as she fought to keep her roiling emotions under control.

The Stag went last, led by Tadhg mac Fortrenn. The Stag chieftain's bearded face was thunderous as he placed his stone upon the small hillock. His warriors followed behind him, completing the stack.

Once they had finished, a deep hush fell upon the waiting crowd. Fina's gaze remained focused on the pile of stones; it was much smaller than the one at the Lochans of the Fair folk.

"Ailene," Galan broke the silence. His voice held a deep rasp. "It's time."

The bandruí stepped past Fina and walked into the clearing. She then turned to face the crowd. Her eyes appeared huge and dark on her pale face. "Three hundred and eighty rode out to meet the Cruthini." Her voice rang out in the silence. "Two hundred and forty eight have returned."

Fina swallowed the lump in her throat. *Well over one hundred dead.* The number seemed unthinkable. That was almost the entire population of Dun Ringill.

Galan stepped forward into the clearing, before the remaining three chieftains did the same.

"We will honor our dead tonight," Galan spoke up once more. His face was haggard with grief. "A torch will burn for each lost warrior." Galan's voice caught here, and his throat bobbed.

"We will remember them," Varar added, taking over from Galan. His gaze glittered as he spoke. "They will light up the darkness. They will give us strength in the days to come."

Chapter Twenty-nine

Consumed

ONE HUNDRED AND thirty-two pitch torches ringed the perimeter of the camp after dusk, throwing their fiery glow into the night. Fina stood on the edge of the Eagle encampment, arms folded before her as she watched the torches burn.

Unlike many in the camp, she could not weep. Her eyes were dry, burning. Instead, the grief just churned inside. It sought release, but she could give it none.

Fina ran a hand over her face. She was beyond tired tonight. Her weariness felt timeless, ageless. She felt as if she had lived a hundred long winters, and every one of them pressed down on her now. For the first time ever, she did not thirst for battle, for vengeance.

She just wanted all of this to be over.

They had won this battle against the Cruthini, but there would be others if they wanted to regain Dun Ringill and An Teanga. She felt drained at the thought.

"There you are," a low male voice interrupted her brooding.

Fina tensed. She glanced over her shoulder, her gaze settling upon Varar. Torchlight gilded his face, and the sight of him made her belly dive.

Pushing aside the sensation, she frowned. "How did you find me?"

"I spoke to your parents ... they said you'd be here."

Fina's gaze widened, anxiety fluttering under her ribcage. "You asked *them*? I thought you wanted to keep things quiet?"

She heard the brittleness in her voice, and it annoyed her. Today had taken down her defenses. She did not have the strength to argue with him now, or to be angry.

Varar took a step closer. "I changed my mind."

Her gaze narrowed further. "What did you say to my parents?"

His mouth curved. "Nothing, don't worry. I'd say your mother knows though ... although your father is suspicious. The look he gave me could have slain."

"I'm surprised he was civil," Fina replied. "He can be more hotheaded than me at times."

"Today has softened him a little I think ... it has us all."

Fina drew in a sharp breath. "I saw how few of The Boar are left. I'm sorry, Varar. Your people ... they're nearly gone."

He moved closer, towering over her. "We will rally," he said quietly. "The Boar are survivors."

Fina looked up at him. She had to crane her neck to meet his eye when he stood this close. Her mouth curved. The man's self-confidence had to be admired, especially in grim times such as these. "Does anything bother you?" she asked. "Sometimes I think you could walk through fire and it wouldn't touch you."

Their gazes fused. "Not much," he admitted, smiling back. "My father brought me up tough." He reached out then, brushing one of her thin braids off her cheek. "There is something that would break me though ... knowing you hated me."

His nearness was making her head spin.

"It never bothered you before," she replied, attempting to lighten the conversation. He was steering her into deep, dangerous waters. "I remember you laughing in my face back in An Teanga when I spat venom at you."

His thumb traced her jaw line. "That was then. Things are very different now."

The Maiden save her, his touch was turning her limbs to porridge. "How?" she whispered.

"You've ... I ..." His mouth twisted, and with a sharp exhale he pulled away. Varar brought up a hand, raking it through his short hair. "Sorry ... I'm not good at this."

Fina inclined her head. She liked seeing him like this, unbalanced, unsure of himself.

He let out a growl of frustration and moved close to her once more. "What I'm trying to say, woman ... is that I love you. I can't concentrate when you're near. And when we're apart you consume my thoughts. There ... is that better."

Fina stared at him. Long moments drew out, before a slow smile spread across her face. The heaviness of the day sloughed away, lifting like fog. "Aye," she murmured. "Much."

In the flickering light of the brazier, Varar slowly undressed Fina.

There was not much to take off, for like most warrior women she dressed lightly. However, he still made sure he took his time over it. He unbound her breasts, admiring them in the brazier's golden glow. Full and proud, they arched toward him as he trailed kisses down from her collar bone. He captured a nipple and started to suck, a thrill arrowing through him when she gasped.

Lazily, he unfastened her skirt and let it fall to her feet. His hands slid down the smooth skin of her back, cupping her bottom. Then, moving from her breasts, his lips trailed down to the plane of her belly. Her fingers tangled in his hair and dug into his scalp when he slid lower still.

Her gasps and soft groans inflamed him, made him reconsider his intention to take his time. This woman filled his senses like strong mead and tested his usually iron-clad self-control. He wanted to lose himself in her, forget everything but her. Fina's groans filled the tent as she arched against him.

He rose to his feet before Fina, his mouth claiming hers for a long and sensual kiss. She responded with a wildness that made hunger claw its way up from his belly. When her deft fingers unlaced his leggings and stroked the length of his rod, he muttered a curse.

Fina breathed a soft laugh and sank to her knees before him. Then she took him in her mouth and his breathing stopped. It was his turn to tangle his fingers in her hair, to arch toward her. The heat of her mouth, the wicked workings of her tongue, nearly unleashed him.

With a growl, he drew back from Fina, pulling her to her feet. Any more of that and he would lose control.

The sensual smile on her face, the delight in those beautiful eyes, made him ache to take her.

Not yet. He wanted this night to last. Who knew what the next day would bring. He had a council with the other chiefs at dawn. Things would move swiftly. He and Fina had to make the most of the time they had together.

Varar moved behind Fina, pushing aside the curtain of thin braids so that he could kiss her neck and shoulders. She leaned back against him, her bottom nestling against the hard length of his shaft. His hands slid over the long supple length of her body, before they cupped the fullness of her breasts once more.

Fina's soft groan as she ground herself back against him, her body writhing, was his undoing. Varar clenched his jaw and pushed her down on all fours upon the deerskin that covered the floor of his tent. Then, unable to wait a moment longer, he entered her in one deep thrust.

She cried out and pushed herself back up against him, so that she took him in even deeper with the next thrust. The tight heat of her made sweat bead upon his skin.

Varar heard a low groan that could only be his own. It was an effort for him not to go into a frenzy. The first time he had taken her under that overhang, he had been rougher than he had intended. Fina had matched him, but she was much smaller than he was. He did not want to hurt her. This time, he paced himself. He gripped her hips and moved in slow thrusts while she trembled and moaned under him.

"Varar," she whispered, her voice hoarse. She writhed back against him. "Please ... more ... I need more."

Gasping now, he leaned forward, reaching under to where their bodies joined. He stroked Fina there, and moments later her body shuddered in response. She arched her back, bucking against him, urging him deeper.

Varar's self-control shattered. With a curse, he plowed her hard, as both their cries now filled the tent. And when he finally found his release, the world spun out of control around him. This woman, this moment, was branded upon his soul.

Fina lay upon the furs, her body curled around Varar's. The night was silent save the whistling of the wind.

They had both made enough noise to wake the entire camp.

Fina smiled at the memory. She reached up, her hand sliding across the muscular planes of his stomach and chest. This man was beyond delicious. She wished they had days to feast on each other. But time was against them at the moment; they would grasp the moments they could.

Varar stirred, his eyelashes fluttering against his cheeks, as her caresses slowly drew him from sleep. His eyes opened, his gaze snaring hers. "Lusty wench," he murmured, a smile curving his mouth. "Don't you need to sleep?"

She smiled back. "I'll have plenty of time for that when I'm dead, Boar."

He huffed. "I can see you're going to wear me out."

Fina laughed. "I think not." Her hand continued its lazy progress to his groin. "You're only just getting started."

His blue eyed gaze darkened at that, the rise and fall of his chest quickening as she stroked him. Fina's own breathing changed at the feel of him growing hard in her hand. "Is that a challenge?" he growled.

She grinned. "It's a promise." With that, she pushed herself upright and climbed on top of Varar. Then, she lowered herself slowly down on him, watching his face as she did so. The passion and tenderness on his face, the hunger in his eyes, made a wild need rear up within her. She wanted to consume him, to burn like a bonfire together, till nothing else remained, till the rest of the world was reduced to ash. Tomorrow, their focus would be on other matters.

But tonight, they were all that mattered.

Fina emerged from Varar's tent at dawn to find Morag cooking oatcakes over the firepit outside.

The woman's face was drawn and tired in the glow of the embers. Behind her the eastern sky was starting to lighten. Morag had tied her long dark hair back as she flattened small discs of dough and placed them upon a griddle.

At the sound of footsteps, Morag glanced up. Her lips pursed when her gaze settled upon Fina. "I should have known," she greeted her. There was no hostility in Morag's voice, just weary resignation.

Fina smiled in answer. "Good morning, Morag." She noted a bruise on the woman's left cheekbone then. The firelight softened it, but in broad daylight the mottled yellow and blue bruise would be impossible to miss.

Since Morag was not a warrior, Fina could guess who was responsible.

Seeing Fina's expression alter, Morag favored her with a rueful expression. "My man's parting gift. After Varar threw him out of our tent, I never saw Frang again."

Fina frowned, glancing back at the tent behind her, where her lover was getting dressed. "Varar intervened?"

"Aye," Morag replied softly. "I suppose I should take back what I once said about the men in my family … they're not all the same." Her face twisted, and Fina saw that Morag's eyes glittered with tears.

She stepped closer to Morag, reaching out a hand to comfort her. However, Morag shook her head and stepped back. She scrubbed away her tears with the back of her hand before bending to tend the oatcakes. "I'm not going to pretend to grieve for Frang," she said. "But I'm sad our bairn will grow up without a father."

Fina wanted to say that such a man would have made as bad a father as he had a husband, but she held her tongue. Morag knew who Frang was; there was no point in rubbing her nose in it. She was a proud woman, as Fina herself was. She did not want anyone's pity.

"You will make up for the lack," Fina replied after a moment. "And you have Varar."

Morag nodded and gave her a watery smile before sniffing. "I don't know what's wrong with me these days … must be the bairn. I'm not usually weepy."

Fina smiled back. She liked Morag, she decided.

"Here." Morag scooped the oatcakes up onto a wooden platter and held it out to Fina. "You'd better start on these before my brother finishes the lot."

Chapter Thirty

Making a Stand

"THE SERPENT HAS fallen back," Galan massaged a muscle in his shoulder. A deep, permanent groove had formed between his brows. From where she stood to Galan's left, Fina could see the lines of tension and fatigue on his face. She wondered if she would ever see her uncle smile again. "We should press our advantage."

"I agree," Varar spoke up. The four chieftains stood around a smoking firepit in the center of the camp. Dawn had broken; the sun had lifted over the edge of the hills to the east. "We need a proper base, somewhere with a forge, stables, pastures, and gardens ... somewhere to rally before we take back Dun Ringill and An Teanga."

Tadhg mac Fortrenn loosed a deep breath. He stood next to his wife, Erea, an arm looped around her slender shoulders. "Do you have a location in mind?"

All gazes swiveled to Galan. They stood in The Eagle territory; Galan would decide which settlement they chose.

"Balintur," Galan said after a brief pause.

"The Serpents will have the village by now," Wid reminded him. The Wolf chieftain appeared to have aged ten years since his son's death. Wid's surviving son stood to his right and his wife, Alana, to his left. Alana's eyes were red-rimmed, her face drawn with grief.

"Aye," Galan replied, his expression turning steely. "It lies no more than forty furlongs north-west of Dun Ringill. It's valuable as it has arable fields and stores. They will have left warriors to defend it … but far fewer than at Dun Ringill."

"Then we take the village back before they have a chance to fortify it," Varar replied. "We hit them hard … today."

Silence fell. Tea, who stood at Galan's side, spoke up first. "He's right. The longer we wait, the greater chance they have to reorganize themselves and call for reinforcements."

"Once we have Balintur, we will be able to gain our strength and prepare ourselves to take back Dun Ringill," Galan agreed. "But we will need more warriors for that."

Varar nodded, turning his attention to The Stag and Wolf chieftains. "Can you send any more warriors from your forts?"

"We left a defense at Dun Grianan," Tadhg answered, "but I will send a rider back today to see if any warriors can be spared."

"I will do the same," Wid added.

Galan raked a hand through his long, grey-streaked dark hair. "Then we ride out with one hundred warriors this morning," he announced. "The rest will stay behind to defend the camp. Once we take Balintur, we will send word for them to follow."

Fina saddled Murdina's bay mare and prepared to ride out. Next to her Guail tossed his head as Varar attempted to slip the bridle over his ears. The stallion could sense the excitement, the grim purpose that rippled through the camp. A few yards behind, Gara and two other warriors were mounting their ponies, swords at their sides, shields slung across their backs.

Varar finished putting on Guail's bridle and glanced across at Fina. "Will you ride with us today?"

She held his gaze for a long moment, before she shook her head. "I can't." She saw disappointment flare in his eyes. Fina left the pony's side and approached him. Till now she had been wary of showing affection toward Varar in daylight with others looking on. Yet she cast her concerns aside now. She reached up and pulled his head down for a kiss.

Varar responded with breathless swiftness, pulling her hard against him. Fina heard Gara mutter something behind them, but they both ignored the warrior as they became lost in each other.

"My kin will think I've deserted them," she gasped when they broke apart. "It's important I stay with The Eagles today. Galan needs me."

Varar nodded before favoring her with a half-smile. "I'll still be looking out for you during the attack," he promised her.

Fina grinned back. "And I you."

He snorted. "Don't worry about me. I'm not the one who's needed rescuing of late."

Fina cast him an arch look and returned to her pony. "I swear, your self-confidence will get you into trouble one day, Boar."

Fina reined in her pony next to Muin as they rode south. Her cousin looked ill-tempered this morning, unusually so.

"What's wrong?" she asked. "You remind me of your father when you glower like that."

Muin glanced her way. He obviously had not realized she had ridden up next to him. "It's nothing," he replied, his tone brusque.

"Is it Talor? I thought he was on the mend?"

Muin shook his head. "He'll live. I'm not worried about him."

"Why the stern face then?"

Muin huffed a breath, clearly irritated by her persistence, and glanced away. "Can't a man keep his own counsel?"

Fina inclined her head, observing him. There was a brittleness to Muin this morning she had not seen before. Compared to Talor, who wore his emotions for the whole world to see, Muin could be an enigma. He had inherited his father's quieter, more introspective character. She adored Muin. He was strong, big-hearted, and loyal—but he was also intensely private.

She knew if she pushed him too hard, he would raise a shield she would never be able to get past.

Feeling her gaze upon him, Muin swung his attention round. He had the same storm-grey eyes as Fina—mac Muin eyes—startling in their intensity. The cousins looked at each other for a moment before Muin's mouth curved, revealing a dimple in his left cheek. He did not smile often, and the expression transformed his face. "The whole camp is talking about you and Varar, you know?"

Fina laughed in an attempt to cover up her embarrassment and glanced away. "Well, you know how folk love to gossip."

"So, it's not true then?"

Fina did not answer, she only glanced back at him, her gaze veiled.

Muin's smile widened. "No need to say a word. Your eyes tell it all."

She snorted. "If you say so."

He gave a soft laugh. "I do."

Silence fell between them then. They rode near the head of the column, behind Galan, Donnel, and Tarl. Tea and Lucrezia had stayed behind to help guard the camp. Aaron and Bonnie rode at their heels.

"Mind he treats you well," Muin said after a pause. "He'll have me and Talor to face if he doesn't."

"I can look after myself, thank you," Fina replied, her brow furrowing. However, in truth she was touched by Muin's show of protectiveness. She had no older brothers: Talor and Muin had always watched her back until she was old enough to watch theirs.

Not remotely cowed by her frown, Muin shrugged. "I'd say you've met your match in Varar mac Urcal, cousin. The man doesn't back down for anyone either."

Fina merely smiled.

Balintur sat in a shallow valley, on the edge of a creek that flowed west toward the sea. A high wooden palisade ringed the village and a patchwork of fields covered the surrounding hillsides.

From afar it appeared a peaceful, bucolic scene. Smoke rose from the tops of the sod-roof huts inside the palisade, and the bleating of goats could be heard. Yet appearances were deceptive.

Fina knew that all her people had left this village and joined the retreat north. Those were not Eagle hearths lit below, but those of The Serpent. It was early afternoon, and the fields beyond the walls were usually filled with folk working the land. But there was not a soul in sight.

They were all inside the palisade. The wooden gates were bolted.

"They'll know we're here by now," Muin said from next to her. "They'll be ready for us."

"That won't help them." Aaron, who had ridden up beside Muin, drew his sword and favored his brother with a vicious smile.

"No, but it won't help us either," Muin reminded him with a cautionary look. "Folk are most dangerous when cornered."

Aaron rolled his eyes at his elder brother's words but did not disagree with him.

Meanwhile, Bonnie urged her pony—a shaggy dun with huge feathered feet— up alongside Fina. The girl gave her a sidelong glance. "Ready for battle?"

Fina nodded, her gaze sweeping the terrain before her. "Aye," she murmured.

A heartbeat later the wail of Tadhg mac Fortrenn's hunting horn echoed across the valley. Fina dug her heels into her pony's sides, and the bay mare responded, leaping forward alongside the others. Together, they charged down the hill, the thundering of hooves shattering the afternoon's stillness

As she neared the walls, Fina spied the outlines of figures, silhouetted against the green hills beyond.

"Archers!" Fina shouted. "Raise your shields!"

She swung her square pine shield off her back, holding it aloft before her as the arrows rained down. The arrows hit, pounding against the wood, iron, and leather of the shields like hail. They needed to get closer, right under the palisade where it would be difficult for the archers to hit them.

Around her she heard the cries of warriors and squeals of ponies as some of the arrows found their mark. But she did not let her gaze waver. She had learned that lesson at Bodach's Throat. A moment of distraction was all the enemy needed.

Instead, she urged her pony toward the gates where a group of men, Varar and Muin among them, where attacking the wood with axes. It was slow work, as the warriors had to hold their shields up to protect themselves—but there were no archers atop the gates to prevent them.

The splintering sound of oak splitting rent the air, and then the warriors charged. With a final groan of timber and iron giving way, the gates flew inward.

The way into the village had been breached. Death had come to Balintur.

Chapter Thirty-one

Blood at Balintur

A HOST OF SERPENT warriors awaited them inside the gates. They surged in a great wave toward the charge led by the chieftains of the united tribes, sunlight glinting on the whetted iron of their weapons.

The crunch of the two groups colliding made Fina's teeth clench; she could almost hear bones breaking. The Cruthini howled, faces savage. Muin had been right: desperation had turned them into mad dogs.

As soon as they were inside, Varar and the other chiefs swung down from their ponies and launched forward on foot, forming a protective wall that allowed the warriors behind them to ride into the village.

Fina steered her pony sharply right, the moment she entered, charging through the group of Cruthini who tried to block her path. Blood sprayed as she hacked her way in. Her pony's viciousness came as a welcome surprise; the mare kicked and bit at anyone who drew near, her long neck snaking left and right.

They were through in moments, thundering in-between two squat, circular huts with sod roofs. Screams and yells rose into the air behind Fina as others followed her. Fina guided the mare with her thighs, shield looped over her left arm, sword swinging from her right, as she led them in a semi-circle.

They would attack from behind.

The battle for Balintur seemed to go on for an age.

Trapped within the walls of the village, the fight was bloody, brutal.

The Serpent warriors were formidable fighters. Having already faced them twice before, Fina knew not to underestimate them. Their women were nearly as tall as the men, but lighter on their feet and faster. One of the women managed to get under Fina's guard, a knife slashing across her thigh.

Ignoring the fiery pain, Fina kicked out, catching the woman in the belly. The warrior stumbled back, and straight onto Bonnie's sword.

Bonnie pulled her blade free, her face twisting. The warrior crumpled to the ground, clutching her chest.

Bonnie reined her pony in close to Fina. "Your leg—"

"I'm fine for now," Fina replied between gritted teeth. She deliberately avoided looking at the wound, but she could feel warm blood trickling down her knee. "Come on."

They charged back into the fray, and slowly, inch by inch, the tide began to turn against The Serpent. The fighting had spread out, taking place in clusters throughout the village.

Fina cut down yet another Serpent warrior and yanked out the axe he had just embedded in her shield. Her thigh was throbbing now. She chanced a look down at it, wincing at the sight of the deep gash. The bleeding had slowed, but she would not be able to fight much longer without binding the wound.

Glancing around, Fina realized that there were no more Cruthini left alive on this side of the village.

However, she could hear shouting coming from the far side. She turned her mare in that direction.

On the way she passed The Stag chieftain. Tadhg mac Fortrenn had just taken down two warriors. Galan and Tarl fought back-to-back nearby. They both looked unharmed although their bodies and faces were splattered with blood.

Fina pressed on. She had not seen Varar since the fighting had begun. Until now her attention had been entirely focused on staying alive and bringing down as many of the enemy as possible. But as the red haze of battle fury drew back, she felt unease squirm in her gut.

Where has he got to?

She rode by Donnel. He had just gutted a warrior who had run at him with a pike. Blood slicked one side of her uncle's face, trickling down from a wound to his temple. Donnel barely seemed to notice.

Fina rode on, her gaze scanning the scattered crowd for Varar.

She found him on the southern edge of the village— surrounded by a knot of Serpent warriors who were slowly closing in on him.

Varar had been cut off from the others. Dead and injured warriors from both sides lay around him. He fought savagely, his twin swords gleaming dark with blood, but for every warrior he cut down another took their place.

Fina sheathed her sword, drew her hand-axe from her belt, and threw it. The axe embedded between the shoulder-blades of the woman nearest. The warrior went down with a shriek. Next Fina drew the knife from her right thigh and threw that. It slammed into the neck of another warrior. Choking on blood, he grappled with the hilt and fell to his knees.

Violence swept over Fina.

She drew her sword once more and leaped down from her pony's back. Pain tore around her right thigh as she landed, and she stumbled.

Gods, it hurt.

Meanwhile, Varar was contending with another warrior who bore down on him. The man was huge with wild auburn hair. He wielded a magnificent sword, with a blade that gleamed bright. It was not iron but a harder, sharper material—a sword that had once belonged to the Caesars. Fina had seen one before, a spoil of war from the campaign to the Great Wall.

This warrior was someone important, Fina realized.

Fina fought her way toward where Varar and the red-haired warrior were still fighting. Their faces were twisted as they slashed and stabbed at each other. Both men were starting to tire, Fina noted. She could see the strain on Varar's face.

Gritting her teeth against the constant throb in her thigh, she ducked and rolled as the last female warrior lunged for her. She swept her sword low and cut into the woman's legs, bringing her down. The warrior's scream echoed high into the air, and she fell back, crashing into the man flanking her.

Fina bounced to her feet and attacked him before he had a chance to recover his balance. He collapsed, blood gushing from his neck.

Panting, her head spinning from pain and exertion, Fina straightened up. She staggered, shifting her weight to her uninjured leg. The wound on her right thigh had opened up again. A sickly sensation swept over her, and the world tilted. She needed to rest.

Fina looked around. Where was Varar now?

The sound of crashing, followed by grunts, filtered out from a nearby doorway. The entrance to the hut was partially stoved-in; the two men had crashed through it during their fight.

Fina sheathed her sword and retrieved a knife from one of the fallen warriors. She then entered the hut.

Blinking, as her eyesight adjusted to the dimness, Fina straightened up to see Varar and his opponent locked in a death grip. In the light filtering in from the doorway, she could see they were grappling on the floor. They had cast aside their swords and were fighting with fists. One moment Varar was on top of his opponent, the next they rolled, and he was pinned under him.

Fina hesitated, her fingers flexing on the hilt of her knife. She wanted to intervene, yet it was difficult to get close. They were moving so fast, fists flying, she risked injuring Varar.

Over they went again. A crunch sounded when Varar smashed his fist into his opponent's nose. Blood flowed, but the man did not lessen his grip. If anything, the pain made him frenzied.

With a snarl, he reached out, his fingers grasping.

Too late, Fina realized what the man was trying to do. He was reaching for one of the stones that lined the hearth next to where they fought. Fina moved, intending to stamp on his fingers, but he was faster. His fingers fastened around a stone, and he swung his arm up, slamming the rock into Varar's temple.

Varar's body sagged, and he collapsed. In an instant the warrior twisted so that he was ontop of him once more.

"Die, Boar," he snarled, lifting the stone high.

In his frenzy he had not even noticed that Fina was present.

She stepped up behind him, reached forward, and in one deft movement slit his throat. The stone fell from the warrior's nerveless fingers, thudding onto the dirt floor of the hut.

Breathing hard, Fina shoved the dying man off Varar. He collapsed, hands clasping his ruined throat. Blood flowed through his fingers, and he slumped to the ground. His green eyes fixed upon Fina, glaring, as the life drained from him.

Fina turned from him, her attention focusing upon Varar. He lay on his back, his face ashen. A purple welt had already formed on his temple, and his breathing was shallow.

Fina knelt beside him, stifling a gasp as she did so. Her thigh hurt badly.

Clenching her teeth against the pain, she cradled Varar's head. Her gaze slid down the length of his body, checking for other injuries. He was covered in blood, but none of it appeared to belong to him.

"Varar," she whispered, stroking his face. "Wake up."

He groaned, his eyelids fluttering. Varar opened his eyes. "Fina," he rasped. "What happened?"

Her mouth twisted. She tried to smile and failed. "You nearly got your skull smashed in."

Varar groaned again. He then reached up to gingerly touch his temple, wincing. "Bastard got me."

"Aye." Fina helped him up. "You think you're invincible ... but it turns out you're not."

He managed a wry smile, yet his gaze was still shadowed with pain. "I like a challenge."

Fina huffed out a breath, trying to ignore the tightness in her chest. She had come close to losing him. "Dolt," she murmured, although the insult lacked bite.

His gaze met hers, and he raised a hand to touch her blood-splattered cheek. "Are you hurt?"

She nodded. "Aye ... my thigh."

Varar glanced down, his mouth thinning when he saw the wound. He muttered a low curse. "We need to get you to a healer."

"Don't worry about me," she brushed him off. "I'll be fine."

"Not if we don't stop that bleeding." He heaved himself up off the ground, shook his head to clear it, and scooped her up.

"Varar, you're injured ... put me down."

"No."

Fina opened her mouth to argue with him, but something stopped her. In truth, the feel of his strong arms around her, cradling her against the hard wall of his chest, felt wonderful. It was life affirming after all this fighting and bloodshed. The strength ebbed from her limbs, and she sank into him. His grip tightened in response.

He ducked his head and left the hut, stepping out into eerie quiet.

The fighting had ended. The hush after battle was an unnerving thing. It was as if nature itself was silenced.

There was not a breath of a wind; even the sun had dimmed. Broken, bloodied bodies lay around them, and the stench of carrion hung in the air.

They had won this battle too, but like all the others it came at a cost. A young Wolf warrior lay on his back just a yard from them. The light fuzz of his first beard marked his cheeks. He had died clutching the pike that had stabbed him through the chest.

Fina's breathing constricted. She too had taken many lives today. Would there be reckoning in the afterlife for all the blood she had shed? The Bodach's leering face returned to her then, the coldness of those dead eyes. Was he waiting for her on the other side?

Fina's mouth thinned at the thought.

It seemed that Varar was struck by the scene as well, for he stood there awhile, gazing upon the carnage around them. When he spoke, there was a rasp to his voice. "This was my hardest fight," he admitted. "The Reaper was breathing down my neck the whole time."

He tore his gaze from the dead and looked down at her. His eyes were gleaming, and a muscle feathered in his jaw. "Will you wed me, Fina?"

She stared back at him, taken aback. "What?" she breathed. "Now?"

His mouth curved although his gaze still seared hers. "As soon as we can manage it, aye."

Fina inclined her head. "Afraid I'll run off?"

He shook his head. "No ... afraid our time will run out. Life is fleeting. I'll not waste another moment. I want you with me, at my side, till I take my last breath."

Fina's eyes misted, and a lump rose in her throat. "When you put it that way, how could a woman refuse?"

"So you will be my wife?"

"Aye," she whispered. Tears now trickled down her cheeks, but she did not move to wipe them away. "Gladly."

Chapter Thirty-two

Your Blessing

"YOU WANT TO wed my daughter?"

Tarl mac Muin folded his arms across his chest and favored Varar with a hard stare, the kind Fina knew only too well. Her father was about to dig his heels in.

"Aye," Varar replied. "I love her."

The words were quietly spoken, bald in their simplicity—and they pulled Tarl up short. His features tightened, and he cast a glance at his wife. Lucrezia met his eye, a soft smile curving her lips. "You can't argue with that, Tarl," she replied.

They stood outside a hut in the heart of Balintur. Around them the light was fading, the sky a bloody blaze. They had spent the rest of the afternoon carrying the dead out of the village. At dawn the following day they would build mounds for them, including The Serpent warriors, upon the hillside.

The remainder of the camp had just arrived at the village, traveling south as soon as they heard about the victory. Men, women, and children trickled into Balintur, their voices rising into the still gloaming.

"I *can* argue it," Tarl growled, his gaze swinging back to Varar. "The man's a Boar. He's Wurgest's nephew. Surely you don't want your daughter wedding him?"

"Varar isn't Wurgest," Fina cut in, "or Loxa."

Tarl's attention shifted to her, and she saw the hurt, the confusion, in her father's eyes. He thought she was betraying him. "You really want this, Fina?"

"I do." To make her words carry more weight, she stepped closer to Varar, wrapping an arm around his waist.

"But I thought you hated him?" Tarl persisted.

Fina favored him with a rueful smile. "I did."

Tarl huffed a breath. "I don't understand." He glanced once more back at his wife. "Do you?"

Lucrezia sighed, before she reached out and placed a hand on her husband's arm. "I once hated you too, remember?"

Tarl tensed. "It was different between us."

Lucrezia gave him an arch look. "Was it? You attacked my home and took me as your slave. I loathed you for it."

Silence fell. Fina saw high spots of color appear on her father's cheeks. She hoped her mother had not angered him. That would not help her and Varar.

Beside Fina, Varar remained silent. That was wise.

Tarl inhaled sharply, a sure sign he was struggling with his temper, and fixed The Boar chieftain with another hard stare. "So does this mean there will be peace between our tribes?"

"It does," Varar replied. "The Boar will never raise weapons against The Eagle again."

"I'm glad to hear it." A rough voice sounded behind them. Varar and Fina twisted to see Galan limp up. The Eagle chieftain bore a bandage around his left calf and a thin cut across one cheek. His iron-grey gaze settled upon Varar as he stopped a few feet from him. "I once wed to forge peace ... it didn't go exactly as I'd planned."

"Aye, but it worked out in the end," Fina reminded him.

"We're wedding for love." Varar's arm lifted, looping protectively over Fina's shoulders. "I'd already decided there would be peace between our people ... if you will agree to it?"

The two men stared at each other a long moment. Fina watched her uncle's face. Galan was a good man, one who had fought his whole life for peace. Yet life had fought him every step of the way. She wondered if he was tired of the fight, if he would let bitterness and a need for reckoning worm its way into his heart as it had once done to hers.

"There's enough hatred in this world already without me adding to it," Galan said finally, a smile softening his features. "I'd gladly make peace with your people."

Varar smiled back, and deep inside Fina something unknotted.

Varar shifted his attention back to Tarl. "Will you give us your blessing, Tarl mac Muin?"

"Do you really need it?" Tarl grumbled. The hostility had gone from his eyes although his expression was still disgruntled.

"I do." Fina left Varar's side and approached her father. "I want you to be happy for me." She met his eye. "You know I wouldn't give my heart away easily ... there is, and there will be, no one but Varar for me."

Did she imagine it, or did her father's eyes suddenly gleam. His throat bobbed. "I only want you to be happy, lass."

"And I am ... happier than I've ever been."

His arms dropped to his sides, and he stepped forward, pulling her into a hard embrace. Fina hugged him back, her eyes tearing for the second time that afternoon.

"Then I give you my blessing," he murmured.

"Balintur has fallen ... Dunchadh is dead."

Cathal mac Calum lowered his cup of mead, setting it upon the chieftain's table with a thud. Around him the feasting hall of Dun Ringill went deathly silent.

Cathal paid none of them any mind. Instead, his gaze remained fixed upon his daughter. Mor stood at the foot of the raised platform. Drenched in sweat, her auburn hair pulled back from her face, she stared back at him. Her eyes were red-rimmed, the only sign of her grief.

"How?" His question fell like a hammer, reverberating across the hall.

She lifted her chin, inhaling deeply, before replying. "The united tribes launched a surprise attack this morning. Dunchadh had no time to send for reinforcements. We sent for provisions from Balintur this afternoon ... the men have just returned. The village has been taken." Mor broke off here. "All our warriors there are dead."

A beat of silence passed, before Cathal slammed his fist down upon the table. Folk started around him, gazes widening as they watched him.

He then let out a string of curses that echoed off the rafters.

No one moved, no one spoke; even Mor remained still and silent. Cathal turned then to his surviving son, Tamhas. "It should have been *you*, not Dunchadh."

The young man blanched, a nerve flickering in his cheek. "Father, I—."

"Silence," Cathal roared. He lunged up from his seat, grabbed the table and upturned it. Wooden cups and plates, and their supper of bread and cheese, flew everywhere.

To his credit, Tamhas did not flinch, did not jump back. He merely remained seated, watching Cathal. The expression on his son's face made Cathal want to slam his fist into it.

"Say one more word to me," he growled, "and I'll rip your face off."

Cathal stepped down from the platform, his gaze shifting to his brother. Artair had been standing by the firepit when Mor entered the broch.

Sensing the danger that crackled through the air like an approaching thunderstorm, Artair held his tongue. His brother had told Cathal to leave a bigger force at Balintur, and he had planned to. No one had thought the tribes would launch another attack so soon.

Tormud stood behind Artair, his dark eyes watchful.

Cathal felt The Boar's gaze track him as he stormed across the floor.

Air. He needed to breathe.

Cathal stormed out of the broch, crossed the yard beyond, and climbed up onto the walls that circled the tower. It was windy up here; a salty breeze gusted in off Loch Slapin. It whispered over the bare flesh on Cathal's arms and shoulders like a lover's touch. But he was in no mood for tenderness.

Fury coiled itself in the pit of his belly, warring with the bone-deep ache of loss.

Dunchadh, his first born, was gone.

It hardly seemed real. The young man was built like an ox and fought like a god.

He should have outlived me.

Bitterness filled Cathal's mouth. The world was full of 'shoulds'. His wife should still be alive. They should still be farming their fields upon the mainland. They should never have had to leave their homes, but feuding had finally driven them out.

They should have won their last battle.

Cathal's guts twisted. He had made a mistake following that retreating army into the mountains. Tormud had warned him not to but he had cast the advice aside. His blood had been up. He had been looking for reasons to push on not draw back.

Cathal stared out at the rippling loch, at the blush that stained the darkening sky. He loved this wild isle, its lonely brochs, wide skies, and dramatic mountains that made a man feel tiny in comparison. He wanted his people to grow roots here.

He would ensure they did.

He realized now that he had tried to push too far, too fast. His people had already gained a lot of ground. It would be folly to try and take The Wolf and Stag territories while trying to hold Dun Ringill and An Teanga. It was time to settle in, build his defenses at the two strongholds—and ensure The Boar and The Eagle never regained them.

The ambush in that gorge had been a setback, a large one. However, it was not a trick the united tribes could use twice. He would never let them lead his army into dangerous ground again. He would fight them out in the open. Each of those proud chieftains would kneel before him before he took their heads.

Varar mac Urcal would be the first he would kill. The Boar had been a bur up his arse since the moment he had landed upon The Winged Isle. Along with Galan mac Muin, he had united the people of this island.

Cathal clenched his hands by his sides so hard his bones creaked. Vengeance. He would have it. He would stain the earth red with it. And like a Mid-Winter Fire feast, he would savior every last bite.

Chapter Thirty-three

Reflection

FINA GRITTED HER teeth, her fingers digging into the
furs. "How much longer is this going to take?"

"A while if you don't sit still."

Eachann's voice was not without sympathy. However,
Fina caught the edge of exasperation in it.

"I'm sorry," she muttered. She deliberately kept her
gaze averted as she spoke. The sight of the gaping wound
on her thigh earlier while he cleaned it had made her
gorge rise. "I'm not patient by nature."

"You never were," Eithni spoke up behind her. "Even
as a child. Lucrezia and Tarl could never send you to the
furs early ... you'd always get up to mischief."

Fina glanced over her shoulder, catching her aunt's
eye. They sat inside a large hut near the southern
perimeter. The two healers tended to the wounded here.
Eithni's face looked drawn in the light of the braziers
illuminating the space. It had been a hard day for her
and Eachann. The wounded had outnumbered the dead,
and some of the injuries had been serious.

Eithni held her gaze a moment before inclining her head. "I hear there's a handfasting taking place later."

Fina smiled. "Aye … and you're invited." She swung her attention back to Eachann, meeting the healer's surprised gaze. "Both of you."

Behind her Eithni cleared her throat. "It's sudden … isn't it?"

Fina huffed, wincing as a stabbing pain lanced through her thigh. "I suppose it is."

Eithni moved round so that Fina did not have to crane her neck to meet her eye. Her aunt held a clay pestle and mortar, where she was mashing woundwort to spread on Fina's thigh after Eachann had finished stitching.

Eithni's hazel eyes were filled with gentle concern. "Are you certain about this?"

Fina smiled at her. "Haven't you just 'known' something was right?"

Her aunt nodded, but her gaze shadowed further. "But how well do you know him?"

"Well enough … life has been intense of late. I feel as if I've lived a decade in the past days. Varar and I have been through a lot. I know that this all seems rushed … but with war upon us, we can't afford to wait."

Eithni glanced away, continuing to mash the woundwort with more force than was strictly necessary. "When I look at him … all I see is Loxa."

Fina tensed. Varar's uncle—the youngest of the mac Wrad brothers—had died before she was born. He had abducted Eithni at a Gathering and would have raped her if Donnel had not killed him.

"He has the same swagger, the same unshakable confidence," Eithni continued. "I'm sorry, but I worry he has the same cruelty."

"He doesn't," Eachann spoke up then.

Both women turned their heads to him. The healer had put down his bone needle for a moment and was sitting back on his heels observing them.

"I only had seventeen winters when Loxa died, but I remember him well." He paused, his gaze guttering.

"Loxa cornered my older sister at Harvest Fire one year. She told us he had forced himself on her. We believed her, but no one else in the fort did. He was the chieftain's son after all. A few months later … she died giving birth to his bairn." Eachann's words were spoken softly, yet they caused Fina's breathing to still. "Loxa was vain and selfish—rotten on the inside," Eachann continued. "But Varar is not. I watched him grow up. Aye, he has the arrogance of ten men, but he also has the bravery of the same number. He also has his father's big heart."

Silence fell in the healing hut. When Fina glanced back at Eithni, she saw that her aunt's gaze was no longer shadowed.

"He's not without his flaws," Fina said gently. "But then neither am I." She smiled then. "Somehow, we bring the best out in each other."

Eithni smiled back, her expression softening. "Then, I'm glad … for you both."

Fina limped away from the healer's hut. A pensive mood settled over her, a strange melancholy that was at odds with her happiness. Her conversation with Eithni and Eachann made her reflect—there had been little time for that of late.

Around her the twilight was fading into night. Not long now till the handfasting. A smile stretched across Fina's face, excitement fluttering under her ribcage. She had not lied to her aunt, nothing had ever felt so right.

Entering her parents' hut, she found her mother digging through a wooden chest.

Fina walked over to the hearth and gingerly lowered herself onto a stool. Eachann had bound the wound on her thigh after stitching and dressing it. However, she would need to be careful with it in the coming days. Her gaze remained on Lucrezia. "What are you doing?"

"It's lucky I insisted we bring this chest from Dun Ringill," her mother replied. "Or you'd have nothing to wear for your handfasting."

"I don't care about that. I'll just go as I am."

Lucrezia's head snapped up. She twisted, fixing her daughter with a fiery look. "You're filthy, and your hair looks like a rat's nest."

Fina laughed. "Varar won't care."

Lucrezia's gaze narrowed. "But, I do. This is a special eve, and you can make an effort for once."

Fina knew that tone; her mother was not in the mood to be argued with. She pulled a long green garment out of the chest. "Here it is ... I knew I packed it."

Lucrezia turned, holding up a sleeveless tunic made out of fine wool. It had a detailed hem, embroidered in gold.

Fina's breath caught. "It's beautiful."

Her mother's mouth curved. "It took me a summer to make this dress. I'd like you to wear it tonight."

Mother and daughter's gazes met and held. Despite her earlier dismissal, Fina did want this evening to be special. The pride on her mother's face, the love in her eyes, made refusal impossible. "Then, I will," Fina replied softly.

Lucrezia left Fina alone to bathe and prepare for the handfasting.

Standing before a clay bowl of steaming water, Fina stripped off and washed herself down. Her mother had added a few drops of rose-scented oil to the water. Fina inhaled the sweet scent and felt the weight of the day fall away.

The world might be harsh and cruel, but the smell of roses reminded her that there was beauty to be found in the smallest of things.

Fina unbraided her hair and washed it. Then, seated by the fire and dressed in her mother's gown, she slowly combed her long hair out. It occurred to her then that she rarely spent time over things like this. She was always in a rush, always tense. She had looked upon such activities as silly female frivolity. But she did not tonight.

A knock sounded upon the door then, interrupting her thoughts.

A moment later Ailene appeared. She carried a posy of heather and wild daisies. "I gathered these for you before it got dark," Ailene said with a smile. "I thought you might not have time."

Fina smiled back. "Thanks, I'd forgotten about flowers ... come in."

Ailene did as bid. She placed the posy upon a table by the door, before she lowered herself upon a stool opposite Fina. "You look beautiful," she murmured. "Varar's going to get a surprise."

Fina arched an eyebrow. "You're as bad as my mother ... anyone would think I looked a mess most of the time."

Ailene chuckled. "You know that's not true. It's just nice to see you dressed like this. It makes you look ... softer."

"Well, Ma said I should make an effort for my handfasting."

Silence fell between the two women then, broken only by the gentle crackle of the burning peat in the hearth. Fina was happy to sit quietly, combing her hair as it dried in heavy waves over her shoulders.

It was a while before Ailene spoke, and when she did her voice carried a wistful edge. "What's it like, Fina ... to be in love?"

Surprised, Fina glanced up. "What do you mean?"

Ailene's face was solemn as she watched her. "You seem so different. It's as if a weight has lifted off you."

Fina considered the question. "It's so new, it's difficult to put into words," she answered finally. "I never noticed I was lonely until Varar. When I'm with him it's as if I don't need to fight anymore. I can just *be* ... I don't know if that makes sense?"

Ailene's blue eyes darkened, her expression growing sad. "You are lucky. I don't think I'll ever feel that way."

Fina tensed. "You don't know that ... I certainly didn't expect this."

Ailene shook her head and looked away. "I'm not like other women. A bandruí's life is a solitary one."

"It doesn't have to be. Ruith could have wed ... she just chose not to."

"Our gift comes at a price," Ailene replied with a shake of her head. "Ruith knew that."

Fina watched her friend for a long moment. Ailene was nearly four years older than her. She had never really questioned why the seer had remained alone. In truth, despite her warm and sociable nature, there was a part of Ailene that had always remained aloof. A part of her no one could touch.

Fina wondered if losing her parents young had left too deep a scar. Or maybe Ailene was right. The role of bandruí was not one Fina would have wanted for herself. Seers were respected, but they were also feared.

Noting Fina's furrowed brow, her concern, Ailene huffed out a breath. "Enough of such talk. Don't listen to me, weariness has turned me maudlin that's all. Handfastings always make me emotional."

"Careful with that blade."

"Don't you trust me, brother?"

"I don't want to go to my handfasting with a lacerated throat."

Morag snorted. "Stop talking, or my hand might slip."

Varar did as bid. He sat before the fire in Morag's hut while his sister shaved his jaw. Outside, he could hear the murmur of voices, the clatter of iron pots as folk prepared supper.

Not long now, and he and Fina would be making their vows to each other.

He was surprised to discover he was nervous.

Morag drew the blade along his jaw one last time and pulled back, examining her work. "I wish our parents were alive to see this."

Varar met her eye. "Do you think they'd have given me their blessing?"

She nodded. "Da wanted peace between our tribes."

Varar raised his hand to his jaw, noting the smoothness of the shave. "Good job," he said with a smile.

"I got lots of practice with Frang," she replied with a wry look.

Varar snorted. "I'm surprised you didn't take the opportunity to slit his throat."

"There were times I was tempted."

Varar rose to his feet. "He didn't deserve you, Morag. When you wed again ... it should be for love."

His sister smiled, her eyes glinting. "Listen to you. I never thought I'd see the day."

He huffed. "It's our secret ... don't tell anyone."

Morag laughed. She stepped back from him, her gaze sliding over the leather breeches and vest he had donned for his handfasting. Her gaze turned critical.

Varar tensed. "What?"

"There's something missing. Wait ..." Morag turned and went to a corner of the hut, where she dug around in the large leather bag she had brought from An Teanga. She withdrew a golden torque. "This was Da's. Ma told me he wore it at their handfasting—you should wear it at yours."

She crossed to him and held it out. Varar took the torque. It was surprisingly heavy. Two boar heads had been carved onto the ends; the workmanship was exquisite. Varar's throat constricted as he looked at it. He realized then, just how much he missed his father.

Glancing up, he saw Morag watching him. He handed the torque to her. "Put it on me then."

Morag nodded, reached up and wrapped the torque around his neck. She adjusted it so that the boar heads sat at the hollow of his throat. Then, she stepped back, a slow smile creeping across her face. "It suits you."

Epilogue

Breathe For You

FINA AND VARAR wed under a moonless sky. A carpet of twinkling stars looked down upon the lovers as they stood barefoot on the banks of the stream that ran outside the walls of Balintur.

Fina wore her long sleeveless dress, belted at the waist, and her hair, unbound, tumbled down her back. Before her she carried her posy of heather and daisies. Varar stood in front of her. The golden torque that encircled his neck glinted in the light of the braziers that formed a semi-circle around the ceremony.

Ailene wrapped a plaid ribbon around their joined hands. The bandruí's voice lilted through the soft night air. "Varar mac Urcal, Chieftain of The Boar, I join you to Fina, daughter of Tarl mac Muin."

A crowd of kin and friends surrounded them. All Fina's extended family were there, even Talor who had risen from his furs to attend the ceremony. Varar's sister, Morag, stood to the right of her brother, a group of his warriors behind her.

"May The Mother light your way. May The Warrior protect you," Ailene continued. "May The Maiden grant you healthy children. May The Hag bless you with long, healthy lives ... and keep The Reaper from your door."

Ailene turned her gaze to Varar, indicating that it was his turn to speak. He nodded and met Fina's eye. The intensity she saw there made it difficult to breathe. "I, Varar mac Urcal, pledge to protect you, Fina, daughter of Tarl mac Muin, with my body and my life."

Fina drew in a ragged breath. Emotion swamped her, and her vision suddenly swam. She was not easily moved to tears, but today was different. Suddenly it was difficult to get the words out. "I, Fina, daughter of Tarl mac Muin, pledge to honor you, Varar mac Urcal," she said huskily. "With my body and my life."

Ailene smiled at them, her eyes shining. The seer stepped forward once more and unwrapped the binding around their wrists. "You are wed ... you can kiss your bride now, Varar."

Varar arched an eyebrow at Ailene, a silent gesture that told her he needed no encouragement, nor permission. He gathered Fina up in his arms, his mouth claiming hers. The kiss was long and searing.

Finally, breathless, Fina pulled away. Even with an audience, this man's kiss completely scattered her wits. The look he gave her as they drew apart made her feel stripped naked. Her belly fluttered; she could hardly wait until they were alone.

Galan stepped up to congratulate them. The light of the braziers, and his smile this evening, softened the hawkish lines of his face. He embraced Fina, while he and Varar took hold of each other's right forearm, a symbolic gesture of friendship between warriors. Tea stepped up next to her husband, her eyes shining. "Congratulations to you both," she said, hugging them.

The rest of the family and warriors followed, each embracing the handfasted couple and offering them their best wishes.

"We're family now, eh Boar?" Talor winked at Varar as he grasped his arm.

"I'm afraid so, Eagle," Varar replied. "Try not to take it too hard."

Talor huffed a laugh before wincing as the wound on his ribs pained him.

Muin cast his cousin a censorious look as he stepped up next to him. "Congratulations to you both," he said stiffly. "I wish you happiness together."

"For the love of the Gods, Muin, relax a bit." Ailene, who had moved close, gave Muin a playful elbow in the ribs. "A smile wouldn't crack your face either."

Muin cast her a wounded look before shifting his gaze back to Fina and Varar. His mouth curved. "Sorry … I'm not good at this."

"Come here and give me a hug." Fina threw her arms around her cousin, her arms barely meeting around the breadth of his back. He squeezed her in return. His eyes shone when he pulled away.

The ceremony over, the handfasting party made their way back toward the gates of Balintur.

A number of sentries had taken position outside the walls. Their army was too large to camp entirely inside the perimeter, so many folk had pitched tents outside. A watch had been set up across the valley to guard them. If the enemy approached, they would have some warning.

The sentries hailed the group as they approached, calling out their congratulations. Fina smiled and waved back. It was an odd night to be handfasted, at the end of three days of violence and death. The bodies of today's dead still lay beyond the shadow of the walls, awaiting burial. The barrier between life and death, violence and joy, seemed stretched thin today.

And yet this handfasting had to be now, deep in her soul she had known it was the perfect night for it. What better way to hold back The Reaper than to show him that even in the face of death, life continued?

Fina walked slowly, with a slight limp.

"Are you in pain?" Varar asked. "Do you want me to carry you?"

Fina glanced up at him, her gaze narrowing. "Don't you dare."

"Why not? Your mother tells me it is a tradition of her people … for the man to carry his bride into their new home."

Fina smiled. She knew that story. Her father had told it many times, for he had carried Lucrezia into the broch after their handfasting celebration.

"My mother is one of the Caesars," she reminded him, her smile turning wicked. "I'm an Eagle woman. We aren't carried. We drag our new husbands to the furs."

Varar threw back his head and laughed, earning curious looks from Muin and Ailene who walked ahead of them. "I can hardly wait … wife."

They entered the walls of Balintur, walking in between the slumbering huts to the dwellings that would be their homes for the days to come. The village had good stores, and the fields around it were ripe with summer produce. They would regain their strength here, rest, and prepare for their next encounter with The Serpent.

Varar and Fina bid the others goodnight and walked across the large clearing in the center of the village, toward the squat, sod-roofed hut they would be sharing. Halfway across, Fina slowed her pace and angled her face up at the sea of stars above. Heaving a deep breath, she stopped and studied them.

"Looking for a sign?" Varar asked. "An omen of what is to come?"

Fina exhaled slowly and favored him with a wry look. "No … I'll leave that to Ailene. She's better at it than me."

"What then?" He inclined his head as he spoke. The starlight kissed his features and twinkled off his earring.

Fina smiled. "I was thanking the Gods," she replied softly. "I don't know what the future will bring, or what will become of us all. But I do know that I'm glad our paths crossed. You've shown me a side of myself I never knew existed." She paused there, her throat constricting from the force of emotion that now welled within her. "I breathe for you, Varar mac Urcal."

He stared down at her. His eyes gleamed, the intensity of his gaze pinning her to the spot. His throat bobbed. He then raised a hand and traced the line of her jaw with the pad of his thumb. "And I for you, mo ghràdh," he murmured back.

The End.

From the author

I hope you enjoyed the first installment of THE PICT WARS.

WARRIOR'S HEART was a high-action, high-adrenalin story to write, and it took me in a few unexpected directions. I didn't expect Fina and Varar's story to be so emotional, but I'm glad it turned out that way. Initially, it was supposed to be a story about forbidden love ... however, it evolved into an intense enemies to lovers romance, which I think suited the characters better. I really enjoyed Fina's feisty kick-ass resilience, and the way Varar never quite loses his bad-boy edge.

As this book is set back in the mists of time, there were few historical events for me to anchor my story on. However, I have woven in a few cultural details I hope you appreciated.

During the clash with the Cruthini, I use the 'Ceremony for the Dead' ritual. In my research, I uncovered a practice used by some Celtic warriors before battle. Each warrior would take a stone from a stack, and then after the fighting had ended they would replace the stones onto the pile. This way they would have an exact count of the number they had lost and would then be able to honor them.

I also incorporated a bit of Scottish folklore with the figure of the 'bodach'. A bodach is a mythical spirit or creature, rather like the bogeyman. The word is a Scottish Gaelic term for "old man". The bodach was said to slip down the chimney and steal or terrorize little children. He would prod, poke, pinch, pull and in general disturb the child until he had them reeling with nightmares. According to the stories of most parents, the bodach would only bother bad or naughty children. A good defense would be to put salt in the hearth before bedtime. The bodach will not cross salt. I took this creepy figure and gave him my own twist in this tale.

I am aware that this was quite a blood-thirsty tale … well you can't call a series 'The Pict Wars' and not have a bit of warmongering, right? The Dark Ages were brutal times for many and feuding between tribes was commonplace. I have tried to keep the gory details to a minimum though. For me, one of the most harrowing parts of the fighting (and a scene I didn't enjoy writing) was the death of Fina's pony, Ceò. If you've read my other books you will know that horses feature heavily, and I usually avoid harming them. However, in battles such as the ones in this book that just wouldn't be realistic.

See you again soon, with another tale from the Dark Ages!

Jayne x

Historical and background notes for WARRIOR'S HEART

Glossary

Aos Sí or Fair Folk: fairies
bandruí: a female druid or seer
Broch: a tall, round, stone-built, hollow-walled Iron Age tower-house
Caesars: the Ancient Romans
mo ghràdh: my love

Place names

An t-Eilean Sgitheanach: Gaelic name for the Isle of Skye
Dun Ardtreck: a broch located on the Minginish Peninsula of Skye
Dun Ringill: an Iron Age hill fort on the Strathaird Peninsula of Skye
An Teanga: an Iron age broch located on the southern coast of Skye
Dun Grianan: an Iron age broch located on the north-western coast of Skye
Balintur: village in the north of The Eagle territory
The Black Cuillins: mountain range in the Isle of Skye

The four tribes of The Winged Isle*

The People of The Eagle (south-west)
The People of The Wolf (north-west)
The People of The Boar (south-east)
The People of The Stag (north-east)

Gods and Goddesses of The Winged Isle*

The Mother: Goddess of enlightenment and feminine energy—the bringer of change
The Warrior: God of battle, life and growth, of summer
The Maiden: Young goddess of nature and fertility
The Hag: Goddess of the dark—sleep, dreams, death, winter, and the earth
The Reaper: God of death

Festivities on the Isle of Skye*

Earth Fire: Salute to new life and the first signs of spring (February 1)
Bealtunn: Spring Equinox
Mid-Summer Fire: Summer Equinox
Harvest Fire: Festival to salute the harvest (Aug 1)
Gateway: Passage from summer to winter (October 31/November 1)
Mid-Winter Fire: Winter Equinox

* Author's note: I have taken 'artistic license' when it comes to the names of the tribes, festivities, and gods and goddesses upon the Isle of Skye. The historical evidence is very scant, making it a challenge for me to get an accurate picture of what the names of the tribes living upon Skye during the 4th century would have been. Likewise I could not find any references to their gods and festivities. The Picts were an enigmatic people, and we only have their ruins and symbols to cast light on how they lived and whom they worshipped. To make my setting as authentic as possible, I have studied the rituals and religions of the Celtic peoples of Scotland, Ireland, and Wales of a similar period and have created a culture I feel could have existed.

The culture, language, and religion of the Picts is one largely shrouded in mystery. Unlike my novels set in 7th Century Anglo-Saxon England, which is a reasonably well-documented period, researching 4th Century Isle of

Skye proved to be a challenge. Pictish culture is largely an enigma to us. However, they did leave behind a number of fascinating stone ruins, standing stones, and artifacts, as well as a detailed collection of symbolic art.

I created the four tribes of The Winged Isle from Pictish animal symbols. This is not a far-fetched idea; many Iron and Bronze-age peoples identified themselves with animal symbols. The clans we identify with Scotland did not appear until a few centuries later.

Cast of characters

For those of you who have read THE WARRIOR BROTHERS OF SKYE, understanding who is who in THE PICT WARS shouldn't be too much of a stretch. However, I am aware that my cast of characters is gradually expanding (especially since I've now thrown another tribe into the mix!). So here are all the characters, and their relationships to each other, categorized by tribe:

The Eagle tribe
Galan mac Muin: Eagle chieftain wed to **Tea** with two sons, **Muin** and **Aaron**.
Tarl mac Muin: younger brother of The Eagle chieftain, wed to **Lucrezia** with one daughter, **Fina** (they had three sons who died in childhood: **Bradhg, Fionn**, and **Ciaran**)
Donnel mac Muin: youngest brother of The Eagle chieftain, wed to **Eithni** (healer) with one son and two daughters: **Talor** (son from his first marriage), **Bonnie,** and **Eara**
Ailene: the seer at Dun Ringill
Cal, Namet, Lutrin, and Ru: Galan's four most trusted warriors
Ethan mac Brennan: a farmer (Fina's former lover)

The Boar tribe
Varar mac Urcal: Boar chieftain

Urcal mac Wrad: previous Boar chieftain – the eldest of three sons: **Wurgest** and **Loxa** (all three deceased)
Morag: Varar's sister, wed to **Frang**
Gurth mac Bolc: Boar warrior, cousin to Varar's father
Bothan and **Gara**: Boar warriors
Eachann: healer

The Wolf tribe
Wid mac Manus: Wolf chieftain, wed to **Alana** with two sons, **Calum** and **Bred**.

The Stag tribe
Tadhg mac Fortrenn: Stag chieftain, wed to **Erea** with two daughters, **Moira** and **Ana**

The Cruthini (The Serpent tribe)
Cathal mac Calum: Serpent chieftain
Artair: Cathal's brother
Mor: Cathal's daughter
Dunchadh and **Tamhas**: Cathal's sons
Tormud mac Alec: Boar warrior, now a member of The Serpent tribe

Acknowledgements

This book would never have been written, if you, dear reader, had not loved my first series, THE WARRIOR BROTHERS OF SKYE, set in this world—and asked for more! I'd especially like to thank the members of my Dark Ages Inner Circle Facebook group who have given me lots of support and encouragement. I regularly posted juicy snippets during the writing of the first draft and received a great response.

Also, I'd like to thank my husband, Tim. He works tirelessly on the edits for every book—and was especially looking forward to reading this one!

About the Author

Award-winning author Jayne Castel writes Historical Romance set in Dark Ages Britain and Scotland, and Epic Fantasy Romance. Her vibrant characters, richly researched historical settings and action-packed adventure romance transport readers to forgotten times and imaginary worlds.

Jayne lives in New Zealand's South Island, although you can frequently find her in Europe and the UK researching her books! When she's not writing, Jayne is reading (and re-reading) her favorite authors, learning French, cooking Italian, and taking her dog, Juno, for walks.

Jayne won the 2017 RWNZ Koru Award (Short, Sexy Category) for her novel, ITALIAN UNDERCOVER AFFAIR.

Get Jayne's FREE prequel novella to her first series, THE KINGDOM OF THE EAST ANGLES:
http://www.jaynecastel.com/home/sign-up

Connect with Jayne online:
www.jaynecastel.com
Email: contact@jaynecastel.com

Made in the USA
Middletown, DE
20 January 2022